Praise for Katie

THE COMPANIONS

"The timing couldn't be more surreal."

—*The San Francisco Chronicle*

"Beautifully atmospheric and emotionally intense, *The Companions* is an unnerving and engrossing story. The radiant, somber voice of this near-future speculative novel ratchets the suspense while also illuminating what makes us human and how we endure beyond death. This is a spellbinding novel that will linger with you."

—Kassandra Montag, author of *After the Flood*

"Flynn's dystopian story explores the idea of a pandemic-ravaged world, coincidentally published amid the coronavirus."

—*The Hollywood Reporter*

"With deft narration and unforgettable characters, Katie M. Flynn weaves a tale of high-tech dystopian reincarnation. Each detail is beautifully sketched and thrilling to discover, creating a near-future world of endless fascination. *The Companions* is a compelling, gripping, whip-smart piece of speculative fiction."

—Jennie Melamed, author of *Gather the Daughters*

"[S]urreal . . . wrestles with the question of what separates humans from intelligent machines."

—*The New York Times*

"A suspenseful, introspective debut."

—*Kirkus Reviews*

"This sweeping novel of near-future dystopia has an ensemble cast and covers continents and years of time, but it never loses its intimacy and immediacy. There's a deeply moving humanity to each of these characters—even the ones who aren't quite human. I loved this book so much I didn't want it to end."

—Dan Chaon, author of *Ill Will*

"Flynn's vibrant characters movingly answer the oft-asked question, 'What does it mean to be human?' This will satisfy fans of literary and science fiction alike."

—*Publishers Weekly*

"If you wished the *Black Mirror* episode 'Be Right Back' had explored the greater ramifications of uploading the dead into artificial bodies, Katie M. Flynn has you covered. She has explored every facet of the idea from every perspective, and the result is gripping."

—Ariel S. Winter, author of
The Twenty-Year Death and *Barren Cove*

"Flynn tells an emotive, mesmerizing speculative story in her excellent debut."

—*Booklist*

"*The Companions* is one of those rare novels that leave you feeling euphoric and hollow, filled with questions about the loss and loneliness that shape life after a loved one is gone . . . and comes back. A stunning debut novel. We can't wait to read Katie M. Flynn's next book."

—Kathleen O'Neal Gear and W. Michael Gear,
New York Times bestselling authors of *People of the Canyons*

THE
COMPANIONS

A NOVEL

KATIE M. FLYNN

SCOUT PRESS

NEW YORK LONDON TORONTO SYDNEY NEW DELHI

Scout Press
An Imprint of Simon & Schuster, Inc.
1230 Avenue of the Americas
New York, NY 10020

First Scout Press trade paperback edition October 2020

SCOUT PRESS and colophon are registered trademarks of Simon & Schuster, Inc.

For information about special discounts for bulk purchases, please contact Simon & Schuster Special Sales at 1-866-506-1949 or business@simonandschuster.com

The Simon & Schuster Speakers Bureau can bring authors to your live event. For more information or to book an event, contact the Simon & Schuster Speakers Bureau at 1-866-248-3049 or visit our website at www.simonspeakers.com.

Interior design by Jaime Putorti

Manufactured in the United States of America

10 9 8 7 6 5 4 3 2 1

Library of Congress Cataloging-in-Publication Data is available for the hardcover edition.

ISBN 978-1-9821-2215-7
ISBN 978-1-9821-2216-4 (pbk)
ISBN 978-1-9821-2217-1 (ebook)

For Thea and Ren

1

TWO YEARS SINCE QUARANTINE BEGAN

LILAC

Dahlia reclines on her bed during her regularly scheduled break, inspecting her hair for split ends. She finds one, her lips tucked in concentration as she tears the hair in two. She lets the long string of cells loose, glowing like fool's gold as it bobs and arcs its way to the carpeting. Behind her is a parting in the clouds, just the right angle, a rare dose of sunlight amid the clustered towers of downtown San Francisco. It lights the floor-to-ceiling windows on fire, Dahlia too, her skin aglow, lips shimmering with the gloss she applies religiously. Sometimes she balances the round silver canister on my head and I stay very still. It is not hard to balance things.

Dahlia rolls to her side and gives me a wide lopsided smile. "Tell me the story again."

I inch closer to her bed, close enough that I could reach out, stroke her hair. But I do not, I will never, not without invitation. "What if Mother hears?"

"Please, Lilac. I'm so bored," Dahlia groans. I do not blame her. She has not attended group night on the 143rd floor for several months now and it has been two years and seventeen days since she went outside. And me? I may have memories of before, of outside air, but technically I have never been past this door, never gone outside Dahlia's room—it is Mother's dictum.

I call up the memories, feel them supercharge my system, and begin the telling.

Nikki and I sat cross-legged in the quad enjoying our sack lunches. We were close enough to the huddle of girls who knew everything that I could hear them or nearly so—I had to study their mouths to understand. They were talking about a boy, his penis actually, and the one with red hair had her hands out like bookends demonstrating its length. She had pink skin, a mole like a lost button peeking out from her oxford, open to her bra line, a uniform infraction worthy of detention.

The girls used words I knew in other contexts like cock *and* rod, *coloring them with new meaning, and I sank my teeth into my turkey sandwich, storing away the information.*

Dahlia laughs, clutching her pillow, rolling side to side. It is funny to her, this talk of penises. She is an adolescent, so it is perfectly natural. But I do not find it funny. I can laugh. It is not hard to let out a barking sound. I do this now, bark with Dahlia until she is ready for me to continue.

Red explained an encounter with a senior, so tall he was too tall, deceptively heavy, the girls debating the benefits and disadvantages of being on top. I listened, not daring to chew, until the blonde with the orange rub-on tan locked eyes with me.

"We've got an audience," she said, and Red glared at me, running her finger around that mole, an unpleasing habit.

*I swallowed, cough-choking a bite down, as the girls who knew
everything walked away flipping hair and huffing.*

"Mother's coming," Dahlia hisses, but already I am zipping into my
closet. Dahlia pretends to sleep as Mother stands on the other side
of the door, the twin shadows of her feet darkening the cream carpeting. I turn my gaze to the window decorated with purple butterflies, the metal and glass glare of the towers beyond. Hovering in
the clouds is a lone hawk, red-tail if my feed is accurate.

Mother stalks back down the hallway and Dahlia whispers,
"Go on."

Nikki slouched across from me, cringing down a sip from her thermos.

"What are you drinking?"

"Herbal tea. DeSoto's the only teacher who'll let me sleep."

*Mr. DeSoto was our clueless social sciences teacher with alarming
chest hair sprouting out over the collar of his shirt. We all—students and
teacher alike—silently agreed to operate in separate worlds: him at the
board writing and writing and us with our notes and romances and
power moves.*

"Sleep?" *I said.* "Why do you need to sleep?" *Nikki and I did not have
separate lives. If one of us was up late, the other one was on the phone
hearing about it.*

"I've been having these dreams. Like I'm someone else. An old woman
with wrinkles and a husband." *She dropped her voice to a whisper.* "We
have sex together. I do things in my dreams I never knew existed."

"That's disgusting."

Nikki bit the tip off a baby carrot. "It doesn't feel disgusting. It feels
real. That's why I believe in reincarnation. I'm certain I lived that life.
That woman is me."

"Well, you can't do that in class," I said too loudly.

Her eyes darted about, her voice hushed. "No one will know."

"I'll know."

"So?"

"So, I don't need that mental picture."

"You couldn't picture it if you tried." She gagged down the rest of her tea and gathered her things. I wanted to stop her, to tell her I was sorry—she was my best friend, my only friend—but I could not find the words. I can say them now, over and over. I am sorry. I do not know why it was so hard then.

"You should've asked for details." Dahlia pouts from her treadmill. It is time for Exercise and she must stay on routine. She huffs up a steep incline, pumping her pudgy arms, hair tied in a messy knot at the top of her head. "It would make for a better story."

"You are right," I tell her. "Should I continue?"

She is always interrupting. It is her habit, telling me how to tell my story. I do not discourage her. It is better for us both if I learn to tell it the way she wants. Only it is always changing, what she wants from me. I am not particularly advanced though I try, playing up the parts she likes, skipping over the boring details. When I should be dozing, I steal off on my feed for her, to learn new words, new ways of saying what I mean. But in my head the story never changes. They play for me, memory after memory, every word, every smell, every last itch.

Red glared at me from her desk near the back. I tried not to make eye contact as I slipped into my seat, mercifully buffered by Belinda McCormick's perky ponytail. Nikki had rested her head on the desk in front of me, though I could tell by her tense shoulders she was awake.

Mr. DeSoto was writing out our roles in the upcoming mock trial of Harry Truman. I saw my name in the list of jurors, determining whether the president had committed a war crime when he bombed Hiroshima and Nagasaki, already ancient history by the time I was studying it. But Mr. DeSoto could not be convinced to pick something more culturally relevant.

Nikki was asleep now. Her face had sagged into her forearm, a sliver of drool zigzagging her chin. I twiddled my pencil, chewed on its end in a way that suggested I was somewhere else entirely, only it was Nikki who was traveling.

The kids around her laughed when they saw her sleeping. Red zipped a paper airplane over Nikki's desk. Mr. DeSoto kept on writing. Of course Red was given a big part. She would play the defendant's attorney. She sneered at the board, her eyes meeting mine as I dared to register her reaction.

"Mr. DeSoto? Will I be able to vet my jurors?"

Mr. DeSoto paused at the board, sighed, and went back to writing.

"Sorry, you're stuck with me," I told Red.

"Excuse me?"

"You heard me. And I won't be bullied into changing my vote."

"I'm going to kick your ass."

I shrugged like it didn't matter—the idea of a public beating. "You'll have to make a good case."

She opened her mouth to insult me, but Mr. DeSoto was writing Nikki's name now: her part, Harry Truman. Red snorted. "Give me someone I can work with, Mr. DeSoto!"

He turned, squinting as if into a spotlight, breaking our silent agreement. Then he noticed Nikki asleep. He balled up his list, slammed it into the trash can, and shouted, "Wake up!"

The whole class shrank away from him like trees bending in a storm as Nikki raised her head, wiped the drool from her chin.

* * *

"I would hate that," Dahlia says from the shower, the bathroom steamy, the mirror mercifully fogged—I do not enjoy the sight of myself. My body is not so much mine as a thing I am in. "Sitting in a classroom with all those kids. How embarrassing!"

"It was embarrassing. Many times we were embarrassed."

"Mother says it builds character. Do you believe that?"

"I do not know."

"Oh, come on, Lilac. Use your imagination."

I want to tell her I am trying, but it comes out like a hiccup as it always does when she asks for instant answers to questions that require processing. "I do not know."

"Forget it. Can you go on?"

"Certainly." I omit my usual request for advancement. There is no question it would make me a better companion. But Dahlia is tired of my asking and it is not her fault. There is no convincing Mother, who does not like me, who has many voices. She is in sales, for a chemical company, some magical solvent. Sometimes I hear her making her screen pitches through the door. For the first few weeks I thought there was someone else living in the apartment, another woman, pleasant and laughing. I would hear the smiling sound of her voice as she made her sales calls and wonder who this woman was who glowered at me, who barked.

We shuffled out the school's doors into a bleak afternoon, misty with marine layer. Everyone thinks Laguna Beach is all sunshine and beaches, but I remember it as gray.

"I feel so free!" Nikki gushed, linking her arm in mine. I had never seen her like that. If she was going crazy, her paranoid parents would not be much help. They were skeptical of modern medicine and anti-

vaccination, which was why Nikki came down with the shingles in eighth grade and how she became my friend. She was pretty enough to sit higher in the high school hierarchy, but weird, with strange ideas about science and medicine. Once she even argued with me about becoming an organ donor on my driver's license.

"You're getting off track." Dahlia wipes a circle of mirror clean and examines her face from various angles, trying on various pouts. "Can you please just stick to the story?"

I apologize, ask if she would like me to brush her hair as I recount.

"No thanks." She touches the spot at the base of her head where the hair is starting to come back in. I think she meant it as a joke, asking me to braid her hair, but it got caught in my joints. Some of the hairs are still there. Dahlia cannot get them out, not even with tweezers. "Just the story," she yawns, and I know I must get to the exciting part soon.

Nikki dug her head into my neck as we broke free of the crowd, hustling down the sidewalk. "He made me paella."

"And?"

"And, what?" She wanted me to ask about the dream, to admit I was interested, but I would never and she knew it, blurting out, "We did it in the kitchen."

"Can you be more specific?"

"I cannot. What happens between a husband and wife is private."

"Ha."

"I'm not going to argue with you about my faith."

"Your faith?"

"Reincarnation is a central tenet of the Hindu religion." She stabbed a bony elbow into my side and I winced away from her. She had incred-

ible reach with a jab and a long gait that got the cross-country instructor
interested though Nikki had asthma.

"You're Truman, you know."

"What?"

"In the mock trial."

"No."

"And Red's your lawyer."

"Why do you pretend you don't know their names?" she asked.

"Who said I'm pretending?"

She threw an arm over my shoulders and I clasped her waist and we
were walking together down the uneven sidewalk, trees shaking leaves
loose, lodging in our hair, crunching underfoot, and I felt it, how free she
was, how it caught on me, carrying me with her.

"I want to meet someone," Nikki said, "I want to feel it in my own
skin."

"You mean sex?"

She gave me a savage roll of the eyes. "Why not? I'm not a virgin
anymore."

"Gross," I said like a hiccup. Most things were gross to me then—the
periods and strange coarse hairs and animal smells that no one warned
me about, the truths of the body that felt like lies.

"In my dreams I'm her and me at the same time. Here, I don't know.
I haven't figured it all out yet. But I think my husband wants me to be
happy. Who knows? Maybe I'll even find him in a hot new body."

I was not sure what to say to that. She sounded like she really believed
it, but what was even more irrational was that I believed it too. I could
feel it, the wanting. That was all I knew of faith.

"That's enough." It is Mother and she is frowning at me, arms
crossed, long nails decorated with a colorful flurry of dots tap-

tapping on her forearm. How long has she been listening and why did I not notice?

Dahlia is equally alarmed. I can tell by the lie she delivers. "We were just talking about the differences between our schools. Did you really go with all your friends? That's fascinating, Lilac."

"Sure you were," Mother says to Dahlia. "Should I turn it off or are you going to?"

"Time for bed." Dahlia pats me on the head. I do not feel it exactly, but my system registers the touch's vibrations. That is something like feeling.

"It is only seven fourteen," I offer. "According to my clock, we still have eleven minutes."

Mother stomps over to me. "You little—" She reaches around to my back and darkness falls.

I awake fully charged, Dahlia smiling into my face. "Hi," she says, munching on a brown breakfast bar that looks like excrement.

I know exactly where I left off but she does not ask me to continue. When I pause midstory, I cannot stop thinking about the moment where I left off, trapped there, on pause with Nikki. I would not mind—it is nice to be with her—but I know she is just something I have saved to memory.

I watch Dahlia at School, watch her Exercise, watch her Shop and Socialize on the screen. She has a very structured schedule. During Nap I stare at the door, half-open, listening for sounds of Mother. Often she uses nap time to smoke in the bathroom. My system registers the presence of airborne toxins though I know from past experience not to sound an alarm. But today there is no sign of smoke, no sign of Mother. I have never been past this door, yet I can see how easy it is to pass into the hallway. And Mother—she is not watching. She is not here. I do not make footsteps and my whirr—it is nearly below human hearing. And I want to see—why can I not see? I hear Nikki's voice in my head, where I left off, playing on repeat: *I want to feel it in my own skin.*

I am in the hallway! And nothing happens, no alarm sounds, no one comes to take me away. I am almost disappointed.

The living room is what you would expect of a living room. There is a mauve sectional, a few potted plants, a shelf full of break-ables, a coffee table made of plastic meant to resemble stone. A voice fills the room and I rev-bump into the table, nearly toppling the lovely arrangement of fake flowers. The whole wall is alight with a man's solemn face. He talks of vectors and safety regulation extensions and assurances that public safety is the administration's top priority during what appears to be a second outbreak, a new strain of virus, this time in Los Angeles—

"Be quiet," I tell him, and he obeys, the wall returning to an even white. I enjoy it, this power. I have the urge to call him back so I can tell him to shut up again. But I am distracted by the collection of tiny breakables on the shelf, zeroing in on a crystal egg casting a rainbow on the wall.

I reach for the egg, try to hold it, slippery, in my awful hooks, only it falls to the ground, shattering loudly. I want to shrink but I am not made to compact. Mother's door creaks open and I wheel madly in reverse, flip around and rev into Dahlia's room, make like I am in sleep mode.

Mother comes thumping in, cupping the broken base of the egg. "Look what you've done!"

I fake-startle out of sleep, see her bent over me, hand out, the clutch of crystal.

"This belonged to my grandmother! It's worth more than you, you stupid—"

"Dahlia is napping. Perhaps you should not yell."

"Get back in your closet!"

I zip away and Mother stands there, breathing heavy, pulse heightened. Then she stomps out, hurling the door shut.

I know I have made a mistake and there will be consequences. I am supposed to be command-driven. Why can I not abide by my basic programming? There is something wrong with me.

"What did you do, Lilac?" Dahlia whispers.

"It was an accident."

"You've upset Mother." She looks serious. It is unusual, this serious look. I want to make her smile.

"I recall where I left off. Would you like me to continue?"

Dahlia climbs out of bed. "I should check on her." Then she disappears down the hall.

When she returns seven minutes later she is in tears and I ask her what is wrong, but I know what is wrong. In that time I processed what the man on the wall said, the second outbreak. Three weeks ago, a masked and gloved technician administered vaccinations to Dahlia and Mother. From Dahlia's room I heard Mother say, "They should lift quarantine any day now, don't you think?" I did not hear the technician's response, which means he did not respond. That night Mother got drunk and smoked many cigarettes and passed out on the couch. Dahlia stayed up past Bed Time dancing and I whirred and scooted around on the carpeting like I was dancing too.

"The city is not going to lift quarantine," I say now to Dahlia.

She shakes her head, scrunches up her red face as sad as I have seen her.

"There, there." I pat her lightly on the arm, attempt to squeeze her bicep. She shrugs loose of me and face-plants onto her bed, and without prompting I go on with the telling.

We found Nikki's mom in the kitchen. I always liked her. She did not bother to dye her hair and she wore controversial buttons like Elect Satan: Why Pick the Lesser of Two Evils? and Affordable Healthcare Starts with Breastfeeding.

Nikki gave her mom a kiss on the lips, lifted her up in a bear hug. They had that kind of relationship—physical, adoring—nothing like the way I was with my parents. Mine were more interested in intellectual connection, seeing art films and discussing the mise-en-scène over gelato, going to the park for a free lute concert or a local production of A Midsummer Night's Dream.

Nikki borrowed clothes from her sister, Lea the rebel, who probably had an abortion, according to everyone. She walked the halls like she was ready to do battle in tight jeans and a G-string that showed when she stooped at her locker.

Her room smelled like old food and feet and I lingered near the door, mouth-breathing while Nikki dredged through the mountain of clothes on the floor. She unearthed a pair of purple jeans, shredded and filthy along the bottom, and a black mesh tank top. Then she undressed. I had seen her change before, but not like this. She cast off her uniform, straightened her underwear, as if I were not there, as if she were alone.

"I can see your bra," I told her once she was dressed.

"Good." She bent forward, mussed her long hair, giving it a healthy dose of Lea's hair spray.

"What did Nikki's mother say?" Dahlia asks, her voice muffled by the duvet.

"She asked us if we wanted to make brownies."

"Are you kidding? Mother would have freaked out. She says I'm ruined, you know. Circumstances ruined me. She says she can't parent under confinement. What does that even mean?"

"I do not know," I answer, but in my head I am processing. Even before quarantine, Dahlia rarely went out. She has always attended School on the screen, always had difficulty making friends and joining in. I imagine she was quite lonesome before I came along. She must have been for Mother to agree to companionship.

I think of my own parents. Dahlia never asks about them, so it is with rare focus that I call up a single memory. The rental van packed for a skiing trip, windows half-down, a cool breeze running through the cab, shaking the map in Mom's lap, Dad making us laugh with the CB. "Breaker breaker oh-niner," he said in a phony played-up accent. "This is Ham Hock on the line. I'm out here with Ms. Piggy and her little piglet." He held the CB out to me. "What's your name, little piglet?"

"Lilac here," I said into the CB. Then I collapsed into giggles. It was not really funny. I had only added a *c* to the end of my name, but somehow Lilac seemed like the perfect name for a pig. And when I woke in my companion form and Dahlia asked me what she should call me, I said it without much processing: *Lilac*. It sounded right.

Dahlia inches to the edge of the bed. "I think *she's* ruining me. If I'm being ruined at all. I don't think I'm ruined. Do you think I'm ruined?"

I wheel closer to her. "Not at all. You are a wonderful girl and I am lucky to be your companion."

"I love you, Lilac."

"I love you too."

"Someday I'm going to get you skin."

"Really?"

"I want you to have the best processor."

"I would like that very much. I think it would make me a better companion."

In moments like these, when Dahlia is feeling particularly affectionate toward me, she has told me things I cannot access on my feed, about where I come from, what I am, a low-functioning companion, the least advanced. It is all Mother would pay for. She has told me about the many models with varying processing speeds, some with the ability to extrapolate, to change like a person. The top model, the most expensive, even grows skin. It is alive, on some level anyway, though Dahlia could not explain the science to me in an intelligible way and my own searches have been fruitless. I may be a low-functioning companion, but I can tell my feed is filtered.

I ask a question I have been holding on to for some time: "How did this happen to me?" Then I realize something, a truth lodged inside me, not the telling. "My parents would never have agreed to this."

"You were an organ donor, right? I remember reading that the first to upload were organ donors. That would make sense. You're nearly first-gen. Maybe your parents didn't even know."

It is nice, this thought. I want to believe in it. But I am certain there are some things I will never know, even with advancement.

The porch was packed with kids whose glares I recognized from school. I should have changed out of my uniform. Following, I was following Nikki as she hopped up the stairs and pushed her way inside the house, where Tally Turner was doing a keg stand in the middle of the living room. This is a disaster. That is what I was thinking as I tugged at Nikki. "We have to go."

"My turn," Nikki called. Hands clasped at her ankles. A brutish football player with a gamey smell, sweat stains smiling from his pits, lifted her up over the keg and the room exploded with cheers and chanting. Nikki's mesh tank top fell to her chin and I could really see her bra, each sharp rib bone, the scar where she'd had her appendix removed. "This is a disaster," I caught myself saying as I backed toward the wall, right into a shove that sent me sprawling into the ring around the keg.

I turned to see Red glowering at me from the waist of a veritable giant. He must have been nearly seven feet.

"A disaster would be an unnecessary extension of war, don't you agree?"

"I'm not going to tell you my position before the trial."

"Do a keg stand," Red commanded.

"No."

"You will, juror. You will do a keg stand."

There was some hooting and clapping. The football player came up behind me, tossed me over his shoulder and carried me off even as I swatted at him.

I did a keg stand, the plastic nozzle stuffed into my mouth, choking down an endless spray of low-priced light beer, my skirt flopped over my face as they all laughed. What underwear was I wearing? The worst, of course, the oldest pair decorated with little bunnies munching on carrots I'd kept too long. When the football player put me down, Red was gone. I went to the bathroom to cry, staring at myself in the mirror, at my face, neither pretty nor ugly, just a face, trying to make the tears come—I wanted them out of me. I slammed the mirror with my hand and there was some blood, some fracturing of glass. It felt glorious, the pain. I almost felt new. I dug through the medicine cabinet for a Band-Aid, washed the blood from the sink, and straightened my hair. It was nice hair, light brown, red in the light, auburn, some people called it. I *liked it when they said that. When they told me about the varied shades of my hair.*

"Enough about your hair," Dahlia groans. She is losing interest, flagging items for purchase on her screen while she devours a blond snack bar, perched on the giant ball she sometimes does Exercise with.

"I am sorry. It is a detail I recall with some vigor."

"Can you skip ahead to the good part?"

"If I skip ahead, the telling will not be suspense-filled."

"You're losing your audience."

"Okay, I will skip ahead."

Nikki was knotted up with the sweaty football player in some swaying dance. I want to die. *That was the thought running through my head, the words I repeated without processing. Perhaps if I had processed them, I would have seen the real danger.*

I slunk down the hall, searching for a room where I might hide for a few songs, enough time for Nikki to enjoy herself. I should have left, *you must be thinking. I had the same thought as I opened the door and saw Red on the bed, moaning, the giant with his head buried between her thighs. He was not wearing pants. I screamed when I saw the enormous rigid thing.* Cock. Rod. *Now it made sense.*

The ball squeals underneath Dahlia as she bounces. "How long was it exactly?"

"I was too excited to determine actual length but it was at least as long as your forearm."

"My goodness."

"Yes, it was very long."

"Go on."

*   *   *

The scream I let out brought silence to the house. The music stopped, the hooting and hollering and laughing. It was just me and Red and the giant and we were all silent and still, as if we were stuck like that, on pause. Then I heard the thumping, the rumble of them coming down the hall, their breathing behind me. Out of the silence came a single bark of laughter, then a current—they were all laughing and I was in the center of the room and Red was yelling at them to get out, waving her arms violently, and I knew I was done for. I knew it.

Dahlia falls back onto her bed, staring up at the poster on her ceiling of Jakob Sonne with his floppy silver locks and goofy sideways grin, the latest focal point of her star obsession. "That's my favorite part."

"I know. You like it when I talk about the penis."

"Shut up!" she squeals.

"I am sorry. Should I continue?"

Her face falls into a pout. "What's wrong with your hand?"

I peer down at my hook, pinch my tongs. One of them hangs limply as the other two flex and release.

"You poor baby. You need a tech."

"I can still complete the telling. The part that matters most comes next."

"Maybe tomorrow. I've got to get back to school."

"Should I go to my closet?"

"Good idea."

As often as possible I announce my exit. That way there is little chance of Dahlia flipping the switch. I can journey off on the feed, learn new words, or I can stay alert, watching the session. Dahlia has recently passed my level in School. Someday she will grow tired of me. Maybe if they gave me a more advanced processor, I could extrapolate, grow, keep up.

Mother pushes the door open, not bothering to knock. Her nails are a rich cobalt blue, except for the tips which glow gold. "Good, you're studying. Where is that thing?"

"Lilac is in her closet."

"Good, that's very good. You know, I've been thinking. Perhaps it's time we got you an Outside Pass."

"Really?"

"Sure, but as you know, they cost a lot of credit. You'll have to give up some of your expenses if we are to afford it."

"Like what?"

"Like the insurance and service fees on your companion."

"Mother, we've talked about this. I'm not giving Lilac up."

"Not even for an Outside Pass?"

"Not even for an Outside Pass."

"You need real friends."

"Where am I going to find those?"

"You could go to group night on the 143rd floor. You used to love group night."

"I don't like those kids."

"Why?"

"They call me Doll Head. They tell me my head is oversize. They say I'm strange to look at."

From my closet, I measure her head. "Your head is only slightly above the average size."

"What? Has it been listening?"

"She's in her closet. Isn't that enough?"

"No, that is not enough. I don't like it. I wish I never got it for you. Always listening, telling that terrible story. It's not right!"

Mother stalks over to my closet and gives me a hateful look. Then it is darkness.

It is nearly midnight when I wake. I shift to night vision and see Dahlia staring into my face.

"I would like you to take the Outside Pass," I tell her. "I would like you to go outside."

"Oh, Lilac." She wraps her arms around me. Is she crying? "They're coming for you tomorrow. They're going to take you away."

"Take me where?"

"Back to the agency."

"Will I be serviced?"

"You'll be returned. I'll never see you again." I cannot feel the hug she gives me. "I don't want to lose you."

"I do not want to lose you either." I stroke her hair, careful not to get my hooks caught. It is nice hair, long and thick all the way to the tips. Dahlia takes excellent care of it. "Will you still get to go outside?" I ask her.

"Oh, who cares? To go out you have to get all your immus updated, and when you come back, they make you take off all your clothes, hose you down, sit in a bubble for like three days. And for what? So I can go shopping in a real store? I'd rather be here with you."

"You could go dancing." I would like that, to go dancing with Dahlia, but not like this. Not in this can.

"Tell me the rest of the story."

Nikki took my hand and we pushed past the crowd, Red still raging behind us. We were laughing as we ran out onto the porch, almost free, when Nikki's dance partner caught up with us. He told us he knew a place we could go. He had a friend for me, a smiling, brawny midget who materialized at his side at that moment.

They drove us to the cliffs, land marked for development overlooking the ocean. I could hear its crashing. There was no moon, the ground dug up and soggy with ocean mist. The football player tickle-chased Nikki into the darkness. I watched them go, felt the strange short boy come up behind me, wrap his arms around my waist. Just then the moon came out, shining across the ocean, and it felt good, being held like that. He had a broad, mus-cled chest that made a nice backrest and he did not have to slouch to place his chin on my shoulder. I have to admit I was enjoying it. Until he stuck a hand up my skirt. I wriggled loose and he got the idea to tickle-chase me too. It had worked for his friend, after all. He chased me around a stack of rebar covered in plastic, a heap of tools, over the rope border between lots. I heard him grunt and go down behind me and I whirled around to see him tangled up in the rope. "Nikki!" I shouted, running on, after her. "Nikki!"

A voice carried over the crush of waves: "I'm here!" I followed it to the edge of the cliffs, so high up I could barely see the water breaking on the rocky beach below.

"Where are you?"

Then I heard it—moaning from the next lot over. Between waves came the slapping sound, the squelch of mud. "Nikki?" I saw her spindly limbs, yellow in the moonlight, the football player on top of her.

A whisper from behind me: "I'm right here." I turned in time to see Red swing the shovel. I do not remember falling—I wish I did. I would like to feel the rush of air, the weightlessness. The next thing I remember is your face. You were fourteen then, younger than me, and I was able to tell you things, about people, things you needed to know.

Dahlia plants a kiss on my head. "I have an idea. Let's look Nikki up!"

"That is a fruitless search. It was too long ago." I do not tell her that I have already searched that name 403,232 times in 403,232 different configurations. Dahlia is only allowed seventy-five minutes of companionship per day, so I must make the most of my downtime. I never found Nikki, but she had been right—I did know Red's name. I tracked her down, tracing a time line of feed items—marriage, a child's birth, a long gap of nothing, then a dead son, by suicide, leaping from a tower window, survived by his mother who resides in an elderly care facility in Del Norte County, 432 miles north of here. Something I have processed over the years: if I had lived, I would have been an old woman by now, a whole life behind me, and I would not have to worry about what they did to Nikki.

"How do you think they did it?" I ask. "Upload me, I mean. If there is such a small window, mere minutes as you told me, after death. I fell into the ocean."

"Hold on." Dahlia slides off her bed, engaging her screen. "I've been waiting for the right time to show you this." She pulls up an old police report. I scan the document. Me—they are talking about me. So focused on Nikki, on the telling, on pleasing Dahlia and not angering Mother, I missed it.

"Where did you find this?"

"I've been doing a little research while you were in sleep mode." Dahlia grins, so proud of herself. I am proud too. An act of kindness! It is hard for Dahlia to concern herself with others in this isolation. Perhaps companionship has made her more caring. Maybe I had a little to do with that.

"Look," she says, "you didn't die right away. Your back was broken and you were nearly hypothermic when a jogger found you on the beach. Really, it's a miracle you didn't drown."

I do not know how to process this, but the report, it confirms what Dahlia is telling me. "Suicide," I read aloud.

"I know. I couldn't believe it either."

I try to recall, to pull up a memory after my last memory. I have never looked before—perhaps it is there waiting for me?

But, no. There is nothing, and I slam my hook into the wall, leave a mark.

"Lilac!"

"Sorry, I am sorry about that." We both listen for Mother but she does not come, and I am peering down at myself. I do not have excellent peripheral vision, so it is a challenge to see much more than my wheel belt.

Dahlia whispers, "If something did happen to Nikki, wouldn't it be in the report?"

Often I think I know Dahlia, everything about her, but then she goes and changes and I feel blindsided. "I have no way of knowing." I do not mean to shout. She is probably right. It is possible Nikki is still out there, but I cannot find her from this tower.

"You're right. I'm sorry."

"Do not be sorry. You brought me back. I love you." I wish I had tear ducts. I want to cry. "What will happen to me?"

"I don't know." She cries for the both of us.

She cannot lift me into her bed so she sleeps on the carpeting, a blanket wrapped around my wheel track, her body. I wait until she is asleep to rev out from under it.

Mother is on the couch, the wall alight, footage of a plane burning, an explosion shaking the camera. "The terrorists who attempted to steal an airplane from the Burbank Airport are dead, along with an undisclosed number of hostages," the reporter announces to a backdrop of smoke and flames and a fire crew. I am not very advanced, but I know quarantine is not just for everyone's protection. It is also meant to keep the people in affected areas confined.

My hooks pinch at the throw pillow. It takes a few tries to get it. Mother stirs on the couch and I wait for her to settle before placing the pillow over her face.

She struggles, her arms waking, swinging and seizing, legs kicking. I have a good grip on the pillow and I am surprised at my strength, at how I can hold her down without much effort, even as she clocks me in the head. It does not hurt but it draws memory, the shudder-hit of the shovel, the terrible stretching black, and I remove the pillow.

Mother gasps, gags, rolls off the couch, crawling on all fours away from me. "You crazy beast!" She leaps up, grabs a vase from her shelf of breakables, throws it at me. It pings off my square head, the lid over my left eye caving in. The vase is in pieces, scattered on the floor. Mother clutches at her neck.

"I am sorry. I should not have done that." As I roll toward her she yelps and runs into the bedroom, slamming the door shut. I go to the door, knock with my hook. "Can you please not send me away?"

"It's gone crazy," she screeches, "it tried to kill me!"

I wheel to the front door. There is no handle. I hit it. It does not budge. I hit it again. Again. I am banging and banging. I shout, "Why will you not open?" And as if all it needed was prompting, it slides away.

I tell the elevator to take me down to street level and feel the jolt of movement, watch the numbers descend, all those floors, hurtling me earthward.

The elevator is paneled in mirror. I cannot avoid the white can of a plastic body staring back at me, its bent eyelid. It waves at me, one of its tongs hanging limply. I say out loud, "Am I myself?" Even the voice that speaks is not my own, some strange approximation of teenage girl.

I almost forget to exit the elevator, its doors caving in on my wheel belt. I stutter forward, my alignment off, a brace in my track knocked loose. They did not make me to last—that is apparent. I check my battery, 70 percent. At least Dahlia charged me recently. Dahlia. Across the street, I turn to find her window.

I had no idea how tall the towers actually are. Their tips lost in a low-lying fog, I still cannot tell. There are so many, densely clustered, blinking with the living. I find Dahlia's floor, the 112th, and zoom in, though it is a challenge with my damaged lid. There it is—the window decorated in purple butterflies, lights on, shadows darting about the room. Then she is at the window, hands to the glass. I cannot hear her, but I can see her mouth saying my name, *Lilac! Lilac!*

I rev back to the building, certain I have made a mistake—I cannot leave her. But the doors that glided open for me a moment ago will not move now. It does not matter what I say, whether I amplify, how many times I ram them, they will not part now that I am outside. When an alarm sounds, I force myself forward, speeding down the empty sidewalk, not one soul in my sights.

CAM

The day the companions came was always exciting. The residents would never admit it, but I could see their busying, their nice clothes, smell their brushed teeth, their too-strong perfume. I liked companion day because everyone made an effort, most of all me.

It was my job to build buzz around the event, posting daily reminders to the rec room's screen, arranging the reception table, making sure to have extra chargers on hand in case the ones the agency sent were bunk (that had happened before, what a disaster). Most importantly, I contacted the agency in neighboring Crescent City, made appropriate selections—age, era, sophistication. I tried to get the companions who'd died suddenly—car collisions, freak accidents. No one at the Jedediah Smith Elderly Care Facility needed to hear about the process of dying.

The best models were beyond our meager budget, but low-end would do. When the companions told their stories, the residents listened with rapt attention, hands folded, nodding along. It could be anything—a trip to the market, standing in line for a movie, getting a teeth cleaning—as long as it was from before. The residents found the past tense soothing. It was something I noticed, how they bristled when I spoke of now. We didn't show them the news and they didn't ask for it, not that I blamed them. Last time I tuned in, I'd learned that quarantine had come down statewide, borders shut, *for our safety*, they said. Not exactly comforting. If I wanted the headlines, I had to catch them on my own time, and at night I preferred the quiet—caretaking took a lot out of me. I would meet James in the redwoods past curfew. In the caretaker's handbook, breaking curfew was a fireable offense, but behind the tall perimeter fence of Jedediah Smith, nestled in twelve acres of dense redwood forest, six and a half hours north of San Francisco, we hadn't had a stray visitor in all my five years of service. And so far, well, Tina, our middle-aged supervisor, hadn't complained about the couples who congregated in the woods behind the dorms. To avoid the others, James and I met below the residents' windows, knowing they'd never hear our knocking sex, sending me to oblivion.

James grinned at me as he gave the rec room a final sweep of his push broom. I smiled back shyly, making a point not to talk to him. Professionalism—that was of the highest order to me.

Tina caught me at the refreshment table. She was wearing a new suit for the event, pinstripes and pale pink. "Have you set out enough refreshments?"

"No one's eating. They're all too excited."

"Excited, well, I can't tell you how much it pleases me to hear that. What a wonderful job you've done, kiddo." It was important to us all that the day went well, especially the children of the residents. They couldn't come in person, given travel restrictions, so they paid extra for the companionship program and expected to hear positive results when they screened their parents. If not, Tina would get an earful, and there would be a cascading effect, blame and anger making waves through the whole facility.

"You did a sweep of the rooms?" Tina asked.

"I did."

"Good. I want them to enjoy themselves, but not too much." She shifted her attention to the Hernandez couple staring glumly at the refreshment table's array of healthy beverages and snacks, mostly plucked out of our own garden by the resident doctor—Dr. Tim, he insisted we call him. He was the only one of us with a green thumb and interest in growing things. Even he was in the rec room, watching out the window for the Metis van.

In addition to arranging companion day, one of my responsibilities was to confiscate the residents' sweets and booze, their porn, anything that might overexcite them or mix unpredictably with their meds. It was a mystery to me how they got the stuff since there were rarely any visitors and all packages were inspected upon delivery. They must have had someone on the inside—a staff member, I figured—smuggling it in for them.

When I found their stashes I liked to give them one last chance, one last sip or peep or bite. They liked me. I liked being liked.

The bell sounded, and James was at my side. "You look hot," he said.

"Stop it—they're here!"

Following protocol, I slipped on my mask. The odds of the Metis drivers being carriers were low—no doubt they were tested regularly—but the precautions were not optional. I unlatched the door and stuck my head out, struggled my hands into gloves, enjoying the flood of cool breeze.

"Got your companions, ma'am."

"Wonderful." I looped in a signature on the man's tablet with my latex finger. So unsatisfying, those interactions, masked, maintaining safe distance, no touching whatsoever. Here I was with a stranger, someone who lived out there, who got to be in the world, and I could never think of anything to say.

The rec room went quiet. The residents' faces were so eager, so hopeful, as they watched the plastic wheeling procession—all low-end identical twins save the scars their stout white bodies had taken on since companionship, the perfect height for visiting with a seated person or child, their hooks not good for much besides holding hands. That's the other reason I liked companion day. I might be able to encourage a smile, but happiness, that was harder. The companions—they could do that, light the residents up from the inside. It was—I was certain—the best kind of therapy.

I did a sweep of the residents' quarters, walking the twin arms of the facility lined in windows, potted plants giving the impression of outdoor exposure. Doors were open, rooms empty, all residents accounted for, except Mrs. Crozier, whose door I found characteristically closed. She always had to be difficult. Ear to wood, I listened to her usual grumbling. Then I knocked loudly. The door was not locked; at Jedediah Smith, the residents' doors were more gestures than actual barriers. "Mrs. Crozier? Everyone is enjoying themselves so much. I wish you would give it a chance."

"Leave me alone!"

"Tina has asked me to bring all residents to the rec room."

"Come and get me," she taunted.

"Mrs. Crozier, please don't make me call them." Them, the orderlies, two brawnies in scrubs. Tony's arms were spangled with tattoos. José was mute physical force when met with an uncooperative resident.

That was when I saw it hiding in the shadow of a potted window plant. We were paying good credit for companionship and it irritated me to see the thing wasting our purchased time, not to mention listening like that, a hard drive absorbing memory. "Why aren't you with the others?"

"I want to talk to her." Sometimes it was difficult to tell the age of a companion, but not in this case. The voice that came out had the impatient pang of a teenage girl.

"There are many others for you to talk to in the rec room."

"No. I came to see her specifically."

"Mrs. Crozier? Do you know her?" A companion had never requested conversation with a resident. Certainly it was possible to have a return visit, but to develop a relationship? It didn't seem likely.

"I knew her before. Please. My battery is very low."

"I have chargers in the kitchen."

The companion wheeled forward, peeking out from the fern's enormous fronds. The plant had taken well to indoor living. "High humidity—that is the key to life," Tina always said.

As the companion came out of the shadows, I could see it was damaged. It moved shiftily, something wrong with its wheel belt. Its white plastic body was dinged and dirty, and its left eye—it looked as if it had been struck, the lid caved in, the light gone out.

"I need to see her. Then I swear I will take a charge, go talk to those old people."

"You need a tech."

"No techs. Please."

"Did they damage you in transport?"

It shook its square head vigorously. "I knew her—when we were kids. I can get her to come out. I can make her smile."

I was a sucker for that sort of scenario, the long shot, the impossible case. It was my weakness, wanting to be a hero. "Okay. Two minutes."

I opened the door, standing back far enough that Mrs. Crozier couldn't see me. She was the kind of resident who never let you see her smile. Her misery, it was part performance, I was sure of it.

"Hello, Red."

"Who's that?" Mrs. Crozier bellowed. "I can't see you."

"I am down here."

"What're you doing in here? Get out."

"I came to see you. It has been a long time, since high school, the cliffs, you remember?"

Silence. No one had ever quieted Mrs. Crozier like that, not without a sedative anyway.

"I know you remember," the companion persisted.

"You—you're a can."

"Well, you are old. Someday I will get skin. Young skin. Beautiful skin."

"What do you want? Did my son send you? The shit stain."

"Your son is dead."

I sucked back a quick breath. Not what I was expecting, not exactly therapeutic. Naturally Mrs. Crozier had been informed, but dementia was taking her as it had so many others, time morphing past into present, whole memories cleaved, lost, sometimes for the better.

"Get out," Mrs. Crozier shouted, her voice ragged. I knew I should intervene, but I wanted to hear what the companion would say next.

"You were the last person I saw with my own eyes. The shovel— you hit me—pushed me off that cliff—Nikki—what did you do to Nikki?"

I heard shattered glass and ran into the room, smack into the reek of spilled booze, the crunch of broken bottle underfoot.

"Get it out of here!" Mrs. Crozier spat at me, crying, she was crying, wiping at her face with wayward hands. The companion's square head was bent forward as if it were in sleep mode. I tried its reset button, but I could see that the bottle had split the plastic plate above its eye, the shower of booze causing it to short-circuit.

In the dorm that night, I walked in on my bunkmate, Jude, masturbating. She went still, pretending she was asleep. I grabbed my robe and raced off to the communal shower, had a good cry. I don't know why I was so affected. It was a machine, after all, but what happened when it broke? Was she gone, the girl inside? While she was carted off by the Metis drivers in their masks and gloves, all the residents were sequestered in the rec room, Tina in a tizzy. She didn't like it, those Metis people coming in, the rogue companion. It stunk, she said, unnecessary risk—she even threatened to squash the program. "No," I pleaded, "it was my fault. I let her in to see Mrs. Crozier."

I didn't notice Jude until the showerhead next to me went on. "What are you so worked up about?" she asked.

I reached for my towel and wrapped up as Jude put her head under the water, watching me from its spray.

"It was awful. Mrs. Crozier—" I stopped, not wanting to start a rumor. Jude was a terrible gossip, and Mrs. Crozier had a bad enough reputation as it was.

"I heard. A stowaway? Did you get its story?"

"It happened so fast."

Jude groaned. "Companions don't just run away—they're command-driven. It's, like, *exciting*, and you don't have a single detail for me?"

"What's going to happen to it?"

"I thought you were our companion expert." Jude had a menacing smile; I hadn't noticed before how much I didn't like her. "My cousin Trixie's a companion. Did I ever tell you that? Killed herself a few months shy of her sixteenth birthday. Did it at home, the idiot, so my aunt found her in time to upload. Used all her savings to get one of the top models, skin and all. Sometimes Trixie screens me in her new body." Jude shivered even under the steamy spray.

"The broken companion—they won't junk it, will they?"

"I don't know what happens if the hardware is damaged. Under normal circumstances, I'm sure Metis would repair, but it sounds like there was a breach of contract. My bet? It's a goner."

I felt responsible, or at least involved. "Could someone—buy it?"

"Are you serious?" Jude said. "No one owns a companion. For lease only." She wrapped a towel around her scrawny frame. She was in her late thirties, but she had the body of a girl, flat-chested, all limbs, a tiny bulge of belly. "It has no soul, Cam, only a consciousness. It's not the same."

I met James in the redwoods, where we had sex standing up, my face pressed into the moss side of a tree. After, we shared a joint shoulder to shoulder. I never asked him where he got it. Probably from the same person who smuggled in contraband for the residents. Better not to know, I reasoned, taking in a chestful of smoke. James tugged on the dirt-colored curls above his ear, fingers wishing them longer. His nose was crooked, broken in a collision on the football field and never right again, his neck stubbled with ingrown hairs, but I liked many things about him. His smell, for example, like sweet bread on his arms, strong and tangy when he sweated, the narrow spread of his chest, fragile, bony, running a finger along his rib cage, charting the territory of his precious internal organs. He had strong arms, ropy and veined, calloused hands, rough when I needed them to be.

Still, I did not love him, not the way I thought I should at my age, twenty-two, a child, though I hadn't lived with my mother for six years, not since I took a mentorship with career possibilities in the growing eldercare field.

"So I'll go to live with them?" I'd asked my mother.

"Not only that. You'll go to learn, to hone skills that can carry you through life. You're a natural caretaker, Cam. It's your calling."

"But what if I want to stay here?"

"Here" was our Outer Sunset duplex, so close to Ocean Beach I could hear the waves slamming against the seawall when Grandmother was taking her nap and the trio of cousins from Chengdu were off at their corporate jobs. They had plenty of credit, but they couldn't take up residence in one of the towers until their corporate-sponsored citizenship had been fast-tracked through approval. One by one they found housing, and then another came from Great-Grandmother's home region, and another, always three; that was the number of mattresses we kept in the back bedroom.

"Sweetheart, this is your home. You are *always* welcome. But I can't guarantee as good a future as this track offers. Are you willing to jeopardize your future?"

I'd been at Jedediah Smith ever since. I tried not to let it hurt, Mother wanting me gone. She was just being practical—she needed the room.

I was only four hundred miles north of San Francisco, but it was as if I'd been shot into space or stranded on an island. Those first years were hard. Abandoned, I felt abandoned, yet I had chosen to leave. No, I felt tricked, duped—the word, the feeling, it changed with age and time and experience. I felt many things when it came to that transaction. Even before travel restrictions, the cost of fuel made the trip home impractical, and Mother wouldn't hear of me wasting credit.

At least I could go outdoors. If I'd stayed in San Francisco with my mother and grandmother, I'd be sequestered in my home, a bubbled existence—*airborne virus number whatever letter tag we've all heard enough*. What I heard when I turned on the news was a low hum, cell death, a certain shade of dying that didn't seem to matter much in the towering redwoods.

I told James about the companion. "She knew Mrs. Crozier before, when she was alive, I mean, not a companion."

"Really. I can only imagine what that beast must have been like."

"The companion, she said something I can't shake."

"What?"

"You can't tell anyone."

"Not a soul."

"I think Mrs. Crozier killed her." And then there was this Nikki—what had happened to her?

"Holy shit." James choked out a cloud of smoke, wafting up and around the great columns of trees.

"The whole thing, no consequences." I was shaking my head, shaking all over.

"Hey, you don't know that. She could have gone to prison for all we know."

"I read her file."

"You did what?"

After the companions' procession back to the van, Tina had called me into her office to give me a good scolding. Then she left me to think about my poor choice. Through the tears and shame,

I'd slunk around to her screen and found it unlocked—she must have really trusted me! I felt a tiny guilt stab as I pulled up Mrs. Crozier's file. No criminal record. No allergies. No living relatives except a daughter-in-law who'd been placed on the do-not-call list. Under career, it said homemaker. "She didn't go to prison. She was a housewife."

"Well, according to my mom, that's a prison in itself."

"I'm serious."

"So I see." He grinned, tousled my hair. We were like that most of the time, playful, buddies. "I'm thinking of leaving." I could tell by the way he blurted it out that he'd been waiting for a chance to say it. "It's starting to make me crazy, staying here." He had only been at Jedediah Smith two years, so the itch to be in the world was still strong with him. Over time, well, it had to fade.

"Have you applied to another facility?"

"No. I'm thinking of going it alone."

"But—you can't." I was practically breathless with reasons. "If you go out there without the proper paperwork—without a job—they'll—they'll never let you back and—"

"I don't want to hear about life expectancy out there. I know." His voice changed. Frustrated, he was frustrated with me. "Forget it."

An icy silence wedged its way between us. We never fought. "Uncomplicated," that's how James described our relationship.

Maybe we weren't the best communicators, but I knew some things about him. I knew, for example, that he was from Maryland, that his father was a college football star, that James was a terrible athlete, an embarrassment, *a clod of shit,* his father called him. It wasn't the worst of scenarios—he wasn't beaten or abandoned or orphaned, just bullied, not good enough, *never gonna amount to a thing.*

James took a mentorship in South Dakota to get away. His exams had put him on the caretaking track, but he swore he'd just bubbled in "whatever." And it was obvious that it didn't come naturally. He couldn't keep the disgust from his face when one of the residents had soiled her pants, and he always overlooked the booze and porn and cigarettes. It was in those small ways I could see that he was not fit for this work, yet I did not want him to go. We sat, shoulder-pressed and still, and I did not tell him not to leave me.

Three weeks later he was gone. No note, no goodbye, just gone. I cried in the shower, in our redwood grove, in my bunk when I was certain Jude was asleep. I scripted messages to him in my head, furious messages that I would never send—how could I? I had no idea where he'd gone. I found myself getting impatient with Mrs. Crozier's antics, her awful moods, strangling the happiness right out of Jedediah Smith. She'd zoom into the rec room in her chair, bump into the couch where a resident napped, into the legs of a nurse balancing a tray full of meds or the table where the more alert residents played bridge. She liked to bump into things, people—we all knew she was doing it on purpose. She never bothered to apologize, gliding on as if nothing had happened. When I brought it up to Tina, she told me, "It's probably senility. I'll have James—sorry, José—take her chair down a notch. That'll slow her down."

Mrs. Crozier didn't appreciate her chair's adjustment. As she inched into the rec room, she shouted, "Who did this? I have rights, you know, human rights, even in this place!" She inched up to me, pinning the rubber tip of my running shoe under her wheel. "Fix it."

"I can't."

"Fix it," she pleaded. I could see it, the sorrow, the everlasting dread—she was drowning in it.

"I don't know how. José might be able to—"

Her face shifted, going wide-eyed, terrified. "Where is she? Is she here?"

She was talking about the companion—I could feel it—but I said it anyway: "I don't know who you mean."

"That fucking mock trial, I had to defend her friend! Harry Truman," she spat. "Wouldn't even look at me." Mrs. Crozier was hitting herself, smacking her head with open hands—I had never seen her do that. I shouted for the orderlies.

"Useless!" she screeched at me. "You're useless!" And I could think of nothing comforting to offer. She was right.

After that, she started soiling herself daily. It wasn't my responsibility to change her, but I felt for the ones who did. I found myself fleeing every time she came into the rec room. Afraid, I was afraid of her, repulsed. It was the first time I'd ever felt that way about a resident.

Tina called me into her office shortly after the incident. She was wearing her pearls, her strawberry jam–colored sweater. Behind her, the sky was an anemic brown, smoke traveling in from the east. The window was closed, but the white sill was filthy with new ash from the latest brownout, some adjacent forest burning. There was nearly always an adjacent forest burning, but never once had the fires come here. In that way, we were lucky. "You've been dragging around this place for weeks. What's eating you? Is it James?"

That was part of it, sure, but no way was I going to admit it to Tina—she wasn't supposed to know about that. "Have I not been fulfilling my duties?"

"Sure you have. But, how do I put this? You lack your usual warmth, the brightness you bring to the residents."

"Have there been complaints?"

"Not exactly."

"Well?"

Something passed over Tina's face, a tightening effect. "You know full well that this job is about more than meeting responsibilities. You are in the field of care. If you do not fix your attitude problem, we will find a replacement, just as we did for James."

"What?"

"I thought you knew. He was smuggling in contraband. He had to go."

I hyperventilated behind the dorms, sucking in the charred air, the redwoods circling above me. A scrub jay hopped down to the ground not a foot from me, whisked away a discarded candy bar wrapper. I couldn't go home, not with travel restrictions, not after six years. I'd have to be a San Francisco resident to join my family in the tower where they now lived—my mother so excited it was like she'd won the lottery—and I was no longer a resident. And no other facility would hire me, not once I'd been let go from Jedediah Smith.

I was deep in my despair when I heard the yelling. A shaken Mrs. Hung flung the back door open. I nearly screamed in surprise. Had I left it unlatched? So reckless!

She clutched my hand, her skin dry and paper-thin. I could feel her heightened pulse, veins throbbing on the inside of her wrist. Then I saw the blood on her cheek, the collar of her powder-blue cashmere sweater.

I ran into the rec room, followed the howling to the residents' quarters. I knew that the sound was coming from Mrs. Crozier's room. She had cut herself. I could see the gashes from the doorway, along her wrists, somewhere under her housecoat. Blood pooled at her ankles as she stood—by God, she was standing—shaking off José and Tony, howling, a terrible sound, animal frenzy, anguish.

I did not stay to watch her die, hiding in the kitchen, head planted in the fold of my arms on the crumby counter. The back door whined open, Dr. Tim, knees soaked in mud, a basket full of garden treasures.

I told him what had happened, and he dumped the basket onto the counter. "Why didn't someone get me?"

"She's dead," I said, because what was he going to do, bring her back?

He ran down the hallway toward the infirmary—I had never seen him run, a strange sight, the way he leaned into it as if he were carrying an infant or a sports ball, as if he might tip over.

No family to call, we followed protocol, incinerating the remains, burying them in the cemetery of uncollected we'd started deep in the woods. Most plots were so grown over that the nameplates marking them had disappeared entirely.

As I boxed up her things for disposal, I found an old photograph, a young girl, high school age, with long orange-yellow hair. "Red," that was what the companion had called Mrs. Crozier. I could see no signs of ill will, no ill omen; she was beautiful, glowing, smiling—she was smiling. What had happened to her? I slipped the photo into the box for disposal and taped it shut.

That night I fell asleep to some terrible movie starring that smirky Jakob Sonne, about a pirate who falls in love with the companion he's captured. Seen it a dozen times. I found myself laughing at the serious parts, breaking down during the sex scenes. I went to the kitchen and stood at the back door, daring myself to run, pulled back by my bed, by warmth, by exhaustion and the sweet bloom of dreams no matter how strange, no matter who visited.

GABE

It's the best kinda day for slinkin, streets slick and steamy, smellin like hot piss and ramen, the old doctor's parcel abouncin in my shirt. She's always sayin be careful, Gabe! Breakable, it's breakable, get it?

She tried bringin me in once. I got a bed and everything till she noticed the necklace missin. It'd been her mam's. I wasn't gonna keep it and I told her so, but that was that, out in the garage I went. Lucky, she said, you're lucky I don't kick you out entirely! She's been watchin me ever since, afrownin real stern-like, but she won't get rid of me—who'd do her most important missions?

I go run-slidin down Market Street, past ol Civic Center BART, Main Library, shuttered up and empty. Mam used to take us there to clean up in the bathroom, practice our letters. Bee caught on quick, readin by five, but I never took to letters. Sassin, that's what Mam said I was good for, but mostly it was drawin. Hours I'd spend at the long library table, shushin Bee cuz she didn't know about readin in her head, drawin my pages and staplin my books at the checkout counter, the librarians askin me what you drawin this week? I'd tell em bout the screamin boys who live on another planet and are tiny and don't talk at all. They fight and war and eat eyeball soup and the librarians'd say, well that's imaginative, and hand me a sticker I'd save for Bee cuz she was always askin for stickers.

But that was before. Now I'm best at thievin and runnin, back street sprints, fence hops, hidey spots in the dayest of light. Mam's not here to tell me not to.

Cruiser! I duck low. The squaddies stop like they seen somethin. Shit. Tuckin under the half-up gate of an old shop, in some soggy leaf and trash soup. I'm in the shadows and the smell, dead things. I can hear those cops muckin about outside, so I crawl into the darkness, liftin up and feelin with my hands, nearly knockin down a dummy I find in the black. It's still got clothes on, and boobs. I can feel em as I hold tight to her.

I watch the light comin from under the half-up gate, see their boots castin shadows, and I'm holdin my air, holdin the dummy tight, hopin they won't follow me in.

They don't. Too scared, you'll never catch me! I nearly shout it, but I hold my air, the dummy, till they're gone. The smell—I gotta get out, rollin under the gate, runnin. They're down the road and maybe they see me, maybe they don't, but I'm runnin, slippin down Sixth. I trip over a man covered in cardboard, all swipin arms and angry, and I yelp and sprint down the block.

I slink into the garage next to the soarin Metis tower on Montgomery, usin the code the man made me put to memory. He's waitin next to a delivery van, wearin his gloves and mask, all fancy and crisp. Mine are the color of dirt. I'd like to hug him up good, blacken him a bit, but the doctor's always tellin me stop and take a few deep breaths before I do somethin cuz she knows I'm wild. Hoppin and hollerin when I can. But Mam, she's the one who showed me how to control it—five dots in each palm, count em out, then big squeezies on the arms, the shoulders. I feel better after that.

The man sticks a gloved hand out. "What do you have for me?"

I pull the doctor's package out my shirt. The doctor doesn't tell me what she's smugglin. She thinks I'm not smart enough. She doesn't know I'm the smartest nine-year-old on the planet. Mam said, and Mam was a truth teller for sure.

Besides, I snuck a peek. Just some cards of credit wrapped in a rubber band. I thought about stealin em, runnin, but I like the pancakes the doctor makes most mornins, havin a place I can hide in at night, even if it is the garage.

He holds out a package, pulls it back when I grab for it. "I had her shipped all the way down from Crescent City. It's what the doctor's been looking for. Tried to kill somebody, then ran off," he says, almost laughin. "This is all that's left of her, so you'd better be careful."

I turn it over in my hands. "What do you mean, *her*?"

"I mean a consciousness." I give him spittin face like always when he talks fancy at me. "It's a person. The inside bits. You know, the thinking part, the feeling part. The brain, essentially, though some people prefer to call it the soul."

I know that word from church and Mam and stupid Sunday school. Even when we were squattin the underpass she made me go, stink and all. The kids at St. Kilian's mussed up their noses and made fun, but the nun, she wouldn't have it. Sister George, soldier of Jesus. That's what she called herself. And I saw it, her soldierin, the way she cut those kids up for sayin shitty things about me. Hellfires for those who make fun of the less fortunate, she'd scold. Soldier of God for sure.

The man hands me the package and I slip it into my shirt. "You can't get caught with it either. Stealing a consciousness is a felony offense akin to kidnapping."

Spittin face.

"They'd put you away. In prison. For a long time."

"I'll be careful. I'm awful sly."

"I know." He frowns, slips me a candy wrapped in plastic. He always brings me candy. That's the only reason I don't rip that mask off and breathe in his face, give him a good scare.

I slink out the garage, that conshushness tucked into my T-shirt, and check the sky for the buzzin 18s. They're less up there since quarantine, and sure nuff, the sky's bright and empty, the late-day sun splashin orange on everything, and I cross the street into shadows. Lots of blocks to Bernal, skip-hoppin and wonderin if I'm invisible. Mam told me once it was so. You're the slinkiest snake, Gabe, but I see you. She'd say that all the time, but she didn't see everything. If she did, she woulda known better than to take that bus with Bee, that man acoughin, just before I turned seven. Some birthday. Mam and Bee behind the see-through curtain, tubed up and sleepin, and me on the other side, a sittin stone, a watchin stone, never movin cept when those freak nurses in their head-to-toes took me to a room and needle-jabbed me. Findin out I gotta go to a home for kids with no parents. They shoulda chained me down if they were spectin me to wait, the fox, the slinkiest snake. I was out on the road runnin, long gone before they even knew.

Headlights. I go shadow deep and makin small. Just a delivery van slowin to turn. I could use a ride and they're headed my way so I jog out the shadows and hop onto the van's back step, grab hold of the door's handle. I'm spectin it locked but it comes flappin open and I nearly go off the side. I'm floatin, holdin on by that swingin door, and the driver isn't goin slow no more, like he's tryin to lose me, yup he's tryin, snakin up Market, tires slippin over old Muni tracks.

I hear awhirrin behind me, an I8 starin me right in the eye, its three blades churnin air as it calls in a cruiser. I can't jump off, not with how fast the van's goin, so I find the step with my feet and get a good hold. Then I send the door flyin, smackin the I8 in the face, smashin and smokin to the gutter. Awesome! The van is all aswervin and I fall into the back. Feet—I'm starin at feet, a woman's in some strappy sandals, her toenails pink. There's a whole row of em, ladies sittin hands on knees, all straight-like, eyes open. They all look the same, no they *are* the same cept their clothes, and I don't mean to yelp, but they don't start or jump or nothin. The van screeches to a stop and I go fallin into lady arms.

Bright shiny on my face. I scrabble under lady legs, away from the squaddies with their Tasers. *Zap.* The lady's bony limbs are herky-jerkin, a smoke smell, her yellow hair burned black at the top.

The driver shouts, "What do you think you're doing? She's fuckin fried, man! You got any idea how much a skin job costs?"

I push one of those ladies off the bench, onto the nearest squaddie, and race off down Market, cut west between buildings, hoppin a fence, another, another, huddlin small in a backyard bush and tryin to hold my breath.

An I8 passes overhead, scannin the yard in its slow-makin circles, and I'm scared, pee-in-my-pants scared, haven't gone since morning, and it's happenin, I'm peein my pants, and I can't do nothin about it.

I remember the doctor's package, check my shirt, still there. *Kidnap,* that's what the Metis man said, *prison.* I can't be in no cage.

Mam'd be so mad if she knew. She was always hissin at me, you gotta be more careful than that!

I8 gone, I bolt out the yard, for the underpass, sprintin down Bryant, skeleton towers comin up between old Victorians.

When I push open the door to the doctor's purple house, she hobbles to meet me, swishy pants swishin over bone legs, afrownin like I done somethin bad. She takes hold of my sweatshirt and drags me into the house explodin with books and papers covered thick in the doctor's scratchy writin. A smell like pancakes and hand-san.

"What'd you do?" she asks me.

"Nothin!" I peel off my mask, my gloves, tuck them into my sweatshirt. "I got your package."

The man on the couch has a cool eyebrow scar and a terrible pirate beard like Dad. Mam always said face hair was revoltin, a place for germs to grow, but she was just mad at Dad for gettin caught. He's in a cage somewhere, beard and all. Mam told me how he done somethin to help us get ahead, how the cops caught him and took him. And when I asked her what he done she said he's a thief, Gabe, like you.

I wish I liked Dad more, but he was always stompin round and tellin us no no no, don't touch, don't jump, don't be drawin when I talk to you. Bee felt the same about him, hidin in her room, buildin towers or readin out loud when he was home.

"Pretty impressive," the man on the couch says, "destroying that I8. Foolish too."

"How'd you—"

"The footage is all over the police feed."

"Nat here's a whiz with the computer. He helps out from time to time," the doctor tells me like I don't already know. I seen him here before, huddled up with the doctor.

"That I8 captured your face, clear as day," Nat says. "The cops are looking for you."

Spittin face.

"Don't you spit at me, boy."

"I'm no boy. And don't you be tellin me what to do. You're not my dad."

Goofy grin. "What's your name?"

"Gabe."

"That's a boy's name."

"It's not a boy's name. It's a nickname. Short for Gabrielle."

"Why are you pretending to be a boy?"

"I'm not pretendin nothin."

"Stop it, you two," says the doctor. "Gabe, give it here."

I pull the conshushness out my shirt and hand it over. "What's so special about it?"

"Her," the doctor says. "She left. Companions don't leave."

"Why not?"

"Something in their programming. They're command-driven."

"Command-driven?"

"You know, like, 'Fetch me that hard drive, boy,'" Nat says.

Spittin face.

"You better be careful. Somebody's liable to smack you on the back, and you'll be making that face for the rest of your life."

"Mam tried that one on me before. You're alyin."

"Your mam sounds like my kinda lady," the man says, "smart."

"The smartest."

He doesn't ask where she is. Where else? Burned to dust like the others, Bee too. Before the hospital I'd been pretendin I didn't like it when they kissed me. It was a game, kind of, they'd chase after me, smackin lips, and I'd be runnin and complainin and they'd capture me up in their arms and kiss and kiss me.

The doctor sits down at her desk, at the screen where I play games sometimes, and Nat drags a chair up next to her. They work awhile and I'm so bored and hungry, waitin and waitin till finally a girl asks, "Where am I?" and the doctor and Nat are starin at each other all asmilin.

"You're in my lab. I'm Diana. I'm a doctor. Please, can you tell me your last memory?"

It's quiet for a while. Then the girl's voice comes from inside the screen. "I found her. She was so old, stuck in a wheelchair. I did not realize the danger. She screamed and threw something at me—a bottle—over the cliffs—she sent me over—the shovel—I was flying—I—"

"Quiet," the doctor says, but the girl keeps on goin.

"I—I—I—" It's like she's stuck, skippin the way Mam's old record player did, the one we left behind when they took our Western Addition complex for condos. The doctor dims the screen.

"This is an interesting case," she says to Nat. "Not only is she not responding to commands, but from what my Metis connection said, she's undergone a second bodily trauma. She's died twice, in essence. God, I wish I could get Dorothea in on this. She's an amazing psychotherapist. What we could accomplish without this endless house arrest!"

Nat tilts his head at me. "Now that they've seen her—"

"We'll lie low, won't we, Gabe?" The doctor gives me one of her wrinkly smiles, teeth yellow-and-gray nubs, gray hair wirin in the lamplight.

"She'll be in the system."

"She can stay in the garage for now."

"No way," I tell em, "I'm not stayin in the garage!"

"Shush, Gabe," the doctor snaps. Then she feels bad about it, all shoulder slumpin and sighs. "Why don't you go into the kitchen and fetch a snack, huh? I'm sure you're hungry. I think there might even be some leftover pancakes from breakfast."

"Pancakes?" I go shufflin off into the kitchen knowin they're gettin rid of me, but I don't care. I'm starvin and pancakes are one of the ten foods I like. Mam said I'm the pickiest eater in all of San Francisco and I'm pretty sure it's true.

When I come back full, they're gone out front, that conshushness still jacked into the doctor's screen. I bring the screen to life.

"Hello?" the girl inside says.

"What you doin?"

"Sorry?" She's forever quiet and I bop the screen and she says, "Where am I?"

"San Francisco."

"I mean, how did I get here?"

"I snuck you from Metis. I'm the slinkiest fox, the slipperiest—"

"Red," she nearly shouts. "I saw her. She—" There is a sound like moaning.

"Stop that. You're gonna get me caught."

She goes quiet. Then she says in a small voice, "Am I to be— your companion?"

"My what?"

"Your companion. It is like a friend."

"How can you be my friend? You can't be runnin and slidin and slippin into hidey holes, can you?"

"No, that is true. It appears I am without a body."

I don't mean to laugh but it's funny, like picturin someone extra naked. "How does it feel?"

"Pretty terrible if I am being honest. Am I to get one?"

"I don't know. That's up to the doctor."

"Who is that?"

But I don't want to talk about the doctor. "Do you feel like a ghost?" I ask her.

She doesn't answer and I think she's gone off somewhere in there and I'm about to bop the screen when she makes a spooky sound, *ooooooh*, and I get to laughin and she laughs too, kinda like she's barkin.

"What's your name?" I ask her.

"Lilac. And you?"

"What are you doing?" the doctor says from the doorway. She hobble-runs over, dimmin the screen. "You can't be tampering with her. She's a test subject!"

"I was only sayin hi."

Her wrinkled face unpinches. "It's been decided. You can't stay here."

"I'll be good. I promise."

"Stop it, okay? This is hard on me too. I want you to be safe, you understand?"

"You said I could stay. You said you'd take care of me—"

"This *is* me taking care of you. Nat's headed north till this quarantine passes, and he could use a scout. Now, pack your things. Chop-chop." She claps her hands at me and I don't dare give her spittin face. She promised. She promised me I could stay with her. Tradin me for that thing, Lilac. I should bash her.

I'm down the block sprintin when somethin heavy falls all over me, scoops me up. Nat carries me kickin and squirmin to a delivery van, hissin in my ear, "You may be a clever little rat, but you'll die out here just the same. Or worse." Then he shoves me inside, climbin in behind me. I crawl over the island, take the passenger seat, as he pulls the van up in front of the doctor's.

Out she comes draggin a garbage bag, my things, passin them to Nat. She knocks on the window. Nope. Not gonna look. My hands—it's been a long time since I been outside with no gloves. I pull the dirty ones from my pocket, slip em on. I need a new pair.

Through the glass, the doctor says, "I'm sorry, Gabe. I will miss you." Her voice—I can tell she's sad but I don't look at her. I don't cry neither. Not when we drive off, not ever. I stare at my hands until we're on the Golden Gate Bridge and the water's all everywhere, the sick feelin of bein up high hittin me.

Nat says, "I need a scout. You suit the job fine. I'll make sure you're fed, you have shelter at night. I'll protect you from carriers. It's not a bad deal."

"Only if you give me one."

"One what?"

I point at the gun, hitched at his side.

"Oh no."

"I'm not comin."

The man scratches at his scraggly beard, all those germs, Mam and Bee here with me now, and dang it, I feel like cryin.

He asks me how old I am, and I tell him, and he says, "Maybe when you're ten."

"That's forever away!"

He hands me a candy bar. I know he's distractin me but I don't care. I live for candy—it's one of my ten foods—and I'm not gonna cry, no way, not ever.

THREE YEARS SINCE
QUARANTINE BEGAN

CAM

As companion day drew closer, I felt none of my usual excitement, even as I posted my daily announcements to the rec room screen. Tina had in fact cut the companion program's budget from four times per annum to two. She funneled the money into art therapy and put Jude in charge.

The residents didn't seem excited either. I could tell they'd all been affected by what happened to Mrs. Crozier. They needed companionship now more than ever, so I tried to muster a little positivity, to at least fake it.

It was dinnertime, all the residents and staff gathered in the dining hall. I was at the screen making selections when I heard a tapping on the window. I startled up, face-to-face with a stranger, a woman, young, midtwenties maybe, grinning at me, waving. We never had unscheduled visitors. There was a protocol for that, but I did not call the orderlies, I did not sequester the residents, I did not put on my mask. I went to the door as if drawn to her. I nearly opened it, catching myself hand to handle. I watched her through the windowpane, spoke through the intercom. "Yes?"

"I'm here to see Mrs. Crozier."

"Mrs. Crozier? Are you a relative?"

"No." The woman smiled, teeth gleaming white.

"How did you get past the gate?"

"We've met before, actually."

"We have?" I was certain I would've remembered her. Her face flawless in its symmetry, her hair ink black, cut close to the head. She was dressed for the road, motorbike by the looks of her reinforced pants and jacket.

"I came here once. You let me see her."

The voice was smoother than before, less robotic, older even, but I recognized her all the same. "No. It can't be."

"I got skin, a processor upgrade, the works." The only skin jobs I'd seen had been on the screen. Sure, they looked real-like, or at least as real as anything looks on the screen, but in person it was uncanny, how human she was. "I need to see her."

I opened the door a few inches. "I'm sorry, she's gone." It was our preferred euphemism, as if she had merely left, departed, exited the building.

"What do you mean, she's gone? Where'd she go?"

I remembered that I was talking to a teenager and tried again. "She passed."

"She's dead?"

"She killed herself."

"She would never."

"I'm sorry, but it's true."

The companion scrunched up her face in disbelief. "I wanted her to see. I knew her. When she was younger. She—she—"

"I know. I heard you," I interrupted to stop the glitching. It happened sometimes when companions got worked up.

She was crying now—no tears came, but it was real enough. I didn't know companions could cry. "I never got to ask her what happened to Nikki."

"Who's Nikki?"

"She was my friend, my best friend. I was maybe a little in love with her." She kicked the doorframe with her boot. "I'm pretty sure Red killed her."

Then I remembered something Mrs. Crozier had said. "I thought it was nonsense, but she mentioned a mock trial, having to defend your friend. Was she talking about Nikki?"

The companion's eyes went big, and it was so human, her hope. "The mock trial. Nikki was supposed to play Harry Truman. Did she say anything else?"

"Not really. But I think she was sorry. She was very upset."

The companion was so relieved to hear it she pulled me into a hug. I felt a jolt as if she'd shocked me, only it was just a surprise, her warmth. She let me loose and we lingered there until I could stand the silence no longer, blurting out, "What's your name?"

"Lilac." She wiped her face, stared at her dry palms, and I was sorry for her.

Before I could stop myself, I offered, "I can take you to her grave."

There was no discernible path. Not enough visitors to make an imprint. But I knew the way, weaving through the redwoods, watching for banana slugs, of which there were many at this twilight hour.

Lilac was surprisingly clumsy, getting tripped up on tree roots, falling to avoid a mud patch. She seemed embarrassed, laughing uneasily with each blunder.

"I thought you were—" I struggled to find the appropriate word. Dead? But she had died a long time ago. Terminated? Ceased? "So, the agency fixed you?"

"Please. They would've junked me if it hadn't been for Diana. She heard about me, the faulty companion who ran away." Lilac laughed loudly, and I heard in the high register the slightest trace of machine. "Bought me on the sly."

"Bought you? I thought no one owns a companion."

Lilac bristled at this, her voice rising in teenage indignation. "She doesn't own me. She paid her connection to make it look like I was junked so she could give me a second chance at life, or a third, depending on whether you consider companionship living."

"You don't?"

"I was a companion in San Francisco, a girl's plaything. It was no life."

"That's where I'm from!"

"No kidding." Lilac raised her thin, neat eyebrows, and it felt as it always did when I found I shared something with a fellow staff member or resident.

I asked the question, though I wasn't sure I wanted the answer. "What's—what's it like now?"

"It's as dead as this place on the streets. People live like hiving bees in their towers." It was impossible for me to picture. I had spent my childhood on those streets, taking the N standing, bodies swaying and bumping with the glide of the train. I'd go downtown with my girlfriends to shop or make fun of tourists, gawk at cute skateboarders in shredded jeans. We'd weave down the jammed sidewalks, holding hands like a chain of animal babies so we wouldn't lose one another in the shadows of the towers.

It occurred to me that one year ago, Lilac had come all that way,

San Francisco to Jedediah Smith, despite travel restrictions, all on her own, in that cheap body. "How'd you get here in that—"

"Old plastic can?" She grinned. "You can travel anywhere if you're not too scared to share a truck bed or a train car with live-stock."

It was impossible to picture, a companion of the lowest grade making its way north, hundreds of miles, no papers, not a credit to its name. I felt shamed by how easily I'd let myself believe I was trapped.

As we entered the clearing, she asked, "How'd she do it?"

"She cut herself."

"Do you think it was because of me?"

"I don't know," I answered honestly. "Mrs. Crozier was with us three years. The whole time, well, she was difficult."

Lilac stared at the freshly churned earth, kneading her hands—was it a prayer? In the low glow of last light, she was beautiful—I had the urge to tell her so, to touch her, but I refrained.

By the time we slunk along the side of the main house, it was dark, crickets humming, residents all in their beds. We stood in the shad-ows, avoiding the floodlight, the red pin-eyed gaze of security cams.

"Thanks for taking me," Lilac whispered, and I knew she was saying goodbye—I would never see her again. I wanted to tell her to be careful, to mind this Diana—*she has to want something from you.* It was the caretaker in me, impossible to shake.

The front of the house lit up, the door creaking open—Tina, in her gingham robe. When she saw Lilac, she raised an arm to her face in reflexive alarm. "Who is that?" she hissed, struggling a mask out of her pocket, over her nose and mouth.

"She came to see Mrs. Crozier."

"You opened our doors to an unregistered guest?"

"She couldn't be a carrier. She's a companion." I felt embarrassed calling Lilac that in front of her, as if I'd sworn, used a slur.

"There are protocols in place for a reason. To protect the residents. To protect us!" That's when I saw it, how scared she was of the companion, of me.

I met Tina's eyes, certain she was overreacting, that she'd forgive me. She'd been like a mother to me all those years of caretaking, helped me to see Jedediah Smith as home.

"Please, Tina. I promise—"

But Tina did not want to hear it. She lifted a quivering finger, jabbed it in my direction. "That's it," she said, "you are gone."

I took a few steps toward her, begging, "Tina, please. You know what will happen to me."

"José!" she shouted.

"Wait," I said. But José was coming out the door, wielding his Taser. "Wait!"

"Come on then," Lilac said in her exasperated teenage way. She put her hand out—how could I say no? I took it, warm, smooth, alive.

JAKOB

It should have been obvious to me that Clarence was no real agent. He had no skills as a salesman, no art with a pitch. But Sydney was gone, no word, no notice, just *poof*—cleaved from my world like bone marrow from my hip. I bore the scar from when I donated to that dying child Sydney discovered, the one I was a match with. The parents had agreed to say wonderful things about me, to make me appear kind. I needed that at the time, having shot down a skyful of I8s that terrible afternoon they'd hounded me poolside. Too many margaritas and a weapon ready—not a good idea. The tabfeeds streamed my crazed screaming and shooting for weeks. No one was injured, but my career nearly died.

The plane descended below the cloud line, the snow stretching like sky. As we drew closer, I saw the white was pocked with small round lakes, iced over and glaring in the dim pre-dawn. "Wasn't there a hurricane? I would have preferred an island."

Clarence gazed at me unsmiling, hands folded on his lap in a show of doughy middle-aged patience. "You are big now," he said. "Colossal. You are Jakob Sonne. But as you know, fame is short-lived."

"How long, in your estimation, do I have?"

"Eighteen months. Tops." He said all this despite my turn as a pirate who falls in love with the companion he's taken hostage, a top-of-the-line skin job who could pass for human. The film was both a box-office *and* a critical hit. And my star was on the rise—finally! They say my skin is the perfect hue to appeal across demographics, my well-documented dalliances with both men and women only add to my draw, and my skills, well, I've been honing my craft since before I could read, when Sydney would whisper me my lines from off-camera. Still, I hadn't worked in more than a year, and it was like I was turning slowly to stone, starting with my heart and coursing out from there, soon to be forgotten, never really known in the first place.

"So, why are we wasting time? I should be taking on as many projects as possible."

"Think of this as an opportunity for an extension on life." He uncrossed his legs, smiled, recrossed. His suit must have been expensive. We had traveled thousands of miles from Moscow, yet he remained unwrinkled. "My team has already crunched the data. The publicity from sponsoring a controversial—dare I say revolutionary?—project such as this has the potential to be trans-formative. It's exactly the kind of project that extends the life of a star."

"Just how long might a project like this extend my life?"

"Well, indefinitely. See, you can do it again and again, turning yourself into whatever it is the people need."

"And what is it they need today?"

"Why, you, my darling, surrounded by the largest population of wild polar bears known to man."

*   *   *

It was pelting snow, the landing rough. The small private plane skitter-hopped down the icy runway, and I had the quick sick feeling of being outside of control. Probably just hungover, I figured. I'd woken in Moscow, in a strange bed, and it wasn't the first time I'd ended up on a new friend's private jet, blinked awake in a foreign country. Clarence had been there, seated in the corner, fingers webbed over the bulge of his stomach. "The studio sent me to fetch you," he'd said, "but first, I'm going to save you."

The only saving I needed was from the studio's ironclad contract—they had me for three more movies, and every script they sent over was worse than the last. I was hopeless, not working and tense, fighting with Greta and spending too many nights in the company of strangers and their drugs.

I stepped out into the icy wind, the slanted snow, taking in the vastness. I'd lived my whole life in LA, throbbing with people. Freeways were always gridlocked, coastal locations near impossible to reach since the seawalls were compromised in a particularly destructive El Niño, Highway 1 shut down for stretches. Usually we'd chopper in to locations, never mind the cost of fuel, just to stay on schedule. There wasn't a place left in LA that wasn't crawling with people, nowhere you could go without getting touched, breathed on, rubbed up against. Until the quarantine. Being a celebrity gave me leeway when it came to leaving my house in the Hills, but I had already been hiding by then, sequestering myself except for work or to flee a fight with Greta, which usually meant a string of sleepless nights, bouncing among parties until I could forget it all, wake empty and naked but never alone.

Past the tiny airport was a stand of trees bent to the side as if under some invisible weight. I tilted my head, trying to right them in my vision.

By the time I reached the idling Hummer, my eyelashes were frozen.

"Welcome to Siberia." Clarence smiled from under a giant fur hat, like Soviet Sean Connery, whose film history I'd researched heavily when they were considering me for Bond. I'd lost the part by a hair to that Maldivian fellow. Sydney always swore it was a sympathy casting, the boy's island home swallowed by rising seas, the first country to be lost entirely. I pictured the little Dutch boy who saved his town by plugging a leaky dam with his finger, the tiny hero of Haarlem, a favorite of my boyhood tutor, suggesting civic responsibility, something he said was sorely lacking among the youth, among us all, frankly.

In my opinion, it was a poor casting choice, not because the Maldivian was a bad actor but because he was a reminder—people don't see Bond for reminders of their troubles. It doesn't matter how skilled we actors are, how Method we're willing to go; we all come with our own narratives braided into each film we star in, encoded into every scene we dramatize. How can we ask our fans to disconnect our lives from our work when we ourselves cannot? Even now I can feel each character coursing through me as if I'm accumulating souls.

Now, this place with its endless snowfields would have made an excellent backdrop for an action sequence, easy to feel the world's problems give way, like a glacier collapsing into ocean.

A young woman in a knit cap with brittle blond hair turned in the driver's seat. "Go? Yes?"

"Yes," Clarence said, "go."

I had forgotten the city's name and looked for a sign, but dawn had yet to break, and it was so blustery all I saw was a forest of dwarf trees, wiry branches dressed in snow.

The girl eyed me in the rearview. "You are famous actor, no?"

"Some would say so."

"Very handsome." She grinned, her teeth terribly overlapped though she had the loveliest skin, blue-toned, lineless.

"Thank you." I glanced up at the sky, not quite night, not quite day either, and empty. Normally it buzzed with I8s, even in the worst of storms. "Where are they?"

"This is a closed city. No outside media," Clarence said.

"How is that going to help us?"

"It is very guerrilla, this approach. Raw footage will be leaked on personal feeds until it gains traction. That's how we work, under the illusion that this is not some sort of publicity stunt."

I could see the city ahead, the wall of cement apartment complexes, all the same height, in a mazelike pattern. At odd angles the buildings appeared nearly normal; then we'd pass a collapsed side, a corner gone, gray building tumbling to white snow, a shading effect.

"What's happened here?" I asked Clarence.

"You saw all those lakes from the airplane, yes? The permafrost is giving way."

There was an enormous sports arena, its back end a bare frame as if it had been abandoned midconstruction, what looked like a burnt person on a stake in the central plaza.

"Jesus, what the hell is that?"

The woman let out a laugh, loud and vicious. "That is scarecrow. We do it to welcome the spring."

"This is your spring?" I didn't mean to sound so horrified.

We entered an older part of town, white stone buildings with the beauteous baroque feeling of Saint Petersburg sticking up over the even roofline. "Look at that," I breathed out.

"Ah, they are nice, no? This was Gulag under Stalin. Many exiles from the West."

The buildings—nearly all of them—were five stories. It created a strange effect, such a sharp horizon, leveling the snow-packed tundra. The way they wormed and turned, the boxing-in of space. "Why do they square off like that?"

The woman said something in Russian, Clarence translating: "See how they create courtyards? Tiny pockets or microclimates."

"I see, snow walls."

"Fortification," the woman said.

We left the city behind, the road mere skin over the shifting permafrost. I thought of the time I played a young Anton Chekhov, one of my first films, art house, no budget, with a beautiful costar, choleraic, dying. It was part of her gimmick, a truly dying girl playing a dying girl. Behind the scenes it was a horror show, the dying, the diarrhea, a wasting sickness. When filming wrapped, I was certain she'd succumb, I'd never see her again, but she toddled up to the premiere in a flouncy tulle gown, so fresh-faced, her skin aglow, a younger, brighter version of herself—the credit the studio must have invested into this transformation that was not a transformation, my goodness—and her career, it exploded.

In the circle I ran in I'd mingled with my fair share of companions, mostly people who'd agreed to upload before they'd passed and stayed in the custody of their families, others rented out to strangers. Plenty of people were so afraid of dying they'd sign up to entertain bored homeschooled children or farty old men, even perverts—there were all sorts. And all varieties too, from sad rolling cans to skin jobs, the best of which appeared human to the untrained eye. But this was the first actor I'd known to give up the body for her craft, and as I held her elbow on the red carpet, smiling into the frenzied 18s, I couldn't decide whether to hug or shake her.

Out the window I scanned the snowfields for what felt like miles. It wasn't until I saw an animal—a dog, or maybe a fox—darting through the snow that I realized how empty this place was. I'd seen no one, not a single living person, in the whole of the city.

"Jesus, this place is dead."

"Yes." The woman nodded. "Very few people left."

Clarence fussed with his hat. "When nickel prices weakened and reserves dwindled, pretty much everyone left. Now the mines bleed poison. The soil, the air, the whole place is noxious."

"We have strong constitution and good spirits."

"I would like to try some of your spirits," I joked. The woman looked startled in the rearview, eyes flickering to Clarence.

"He means vodka. He's being funny, the clever type of funny." I wanted to tell Clarence to stop it—he was embarrassing me! It was no way for an agent to act.

"I am driver, not bartender." The girl frowned ahead at the road.

"You know, Bo here was once in a film," Clarence said in a sorry attempt to make peace.

I was angry with him, humiliated, a little sick even. Perhaps it was the Hummer's mad bumping, but I jumped right on shamelessly. This woman, with her savage eyes—she had me on my toes. "Were you?"

"No big deal. It was documentary."

"Really. What was it called?"

She said something in Russian, a title that took a full breath to deliver.

"I bet it was a hit."

"It was tired."

"You mean boring, darling," Clarence said.

"Yes, very boring."

"What was it about?" I asked.

"Reindeer."

Clarence leaned over the front seat, hugging the headrest. "Show him."

The girl smiled, revealing her terrible teeth.

I could see black on the horizon, what looked like stone, only shifting. Great packs of reindeer bolted as the Hummer crunched over snow.

"Jesus. There must be thousands." The arc and fold, the currents. They went on so far I couldn't see any end, dark waves of satin shimmering in the snow glare.

"Yes. They take over."

"Is this safe?"

Bo grinned as she lit a cigarette, not bothering to crack the window. "Reindeer antlers are weapons and representations of power both."

"I thought you said we were here for polar bears."

Clarence reached over the seat to steal Bo's cigarette. He shot a gray cloud out his nostrils, sneezed, passed it back. "They are the stars, yes, but it's magnificent, don't you think? This place is theirs."

I nodded, not wanting them to know how terrified I was. What if the reindeer got spooked, would they stampede? Surely a herd this huge could trample a Hummer, no problem. "Why are there so many of them?"

"Many animals shift north in the warming. Reindeer come here each winter in greater numbers."

Mercifully, Clarence yawned. "Shall we head back? I could use a shower."

"Yes, let's," I agreed.

"Bo here has prepared some talking points for you. You could give them a read."

"I would like that." I could feel her watching me in the rearview. I gave her my signature smile, sly, toothless, slightly half-cocked, yet she merely blinked back at me, eyes finding the road, and it hurt how much I wanted her to like me.

The hotel was more of a B and B, a stuffy two-story house owned by a tiny woman with an exuberant chest. She was seated near the window under a UV lamp, eyes behind goggles, her blouse half-buttoned. Clarence greeted her in pitch-perfect Russian. Then he led me upstairs like he knew the place.

My room was a shoebox on the second floor, paper-thin curtains, no screen, no network. "In the whole town?"

"It is a closed city," Clarence said.

"What does that mean?"

"No unauthorized entry, no 18s, no network. You should enjoy it, the space, the quiet. Tomorrow we will visit the refuge."

"These lines—have you read them? *More biodiversity exists in our virgin fields than in all of Amazonia, the rich scent of flowers intoxicating even to insects, so exhilarated by this place they would rather commit suicide than drink human blood.* I don't mean to criticize, but perhaps they might come off—oh, I don't know—a bit stiff, don't you agree?"

"Don't think of it as a script. All we're trying to do is draw attention to the animals that have congregated here, to help the local people get international wildlife refuge status, so they can receive a little funding, bring in some scientists, open this city. It's a chance for them to reinvent themselves, and for you too."

"What time is it?" I felt terribly low-energy.

Clarence had yet to take off that Soviet Sean Connery hat. He must have been desperately hot, yet he appeared unfazed. "It's been a long day. Why don't you take a rest?"

The sky, it was night black now, riddled with more stars than I'd ever imagined. "I thought the sun was rising! Not setting." I spun with the sensation, so out of sync with the earth's rhythm, though it certainly wasn't the first time I'd lost a day. "How will I know when to wake up?"

"You'll be fine. Close your eyes, count to ten, and I guarantee you'll fall fast asleep. I'll wake you when it's time."

I went down the hall to the bathroom to wash my face, wondering whether it was safe to use the local water, when I saw them from the top of the stairs, Clarence huddled with Bo in the foyer, arm over her shoulders, a comfortable closeness, as if they knew one another intimately.

I didn't like the way it made me feel, seeing them like that. Shutting myself back into the room, I took off my pants and cycled through some yoga poses, trying to remember if Greta was angry with me. We'd been on and off for so long I'd forgotten where we'd left things. I wanted to screen her—where was my phone? I've always hated the things, with their urgency, bothersome and invasive—but in this room, this house, without its screens, its network? Needless to say, I felt awfully alone.

Clarence had been right! I'd done what he said, closed my eyes, counted to ten, and magically I'd fallen asleep. Only when I woke, I was famished. It was dark out, the house quiet, and I wondered at the time. There was no clock in the room, so I sneaked downstairs to the kitchen full of potted plants, hanging from the ceiling, on the countertops, clustered in the corners of the floor. Spray bottles littered the table, and when I hit the lights, the whole room glowed with soft fluorescence. I was raiding the cabinet when I saw it, the small screen mounted on the wall—Clarence had lied to me! I searched my name, curious to see what the tabfeeds had to say about my absence. The first hit blinked *Livefeed*, and there I was on a beach barren save some doe-eyed child, definitely not Greta, 18s circling as we fondled. There was some passionate kissing, an ass was grabbed. Jesus, a Speedo—*I'm wearing a Speedo!* The screen blinked: *Ibiza.* I had never, it was not me, how could it be?

The woman with the exuberant bosom came into the kitchen in her nightgown. She was displeased with my presence. I pointed at the screen. "That's not me. An impostor," I told her. "I am here, obviously, not there!" And she was yelling and shooing and reprimanding me in Russian until I was up the stairs, back in my room. I forgot that I was hungry, and then I tried the handle, locked from the outside.

I shouted, "Clarence!"

It was a while before Bo unlocked the door and stuck her head in. "May I enter?"

We sat on the edge of my bed.

"You are companion," she said, so matter-of-fact I'm still not sure whether it was poor English or her personality "Of the skin variety. Top model, I might add, very expensive. You have heard of companions, no?"

I scoffed a hearty ha. I'd fallen in love with one in a film—hadn't she seen it? The part may have been played by a human, but I did my research. I knew companions, with their funny alert posture, a slight bounce in the step, easily unfooted, and the eyes, not the look of them—that was a flawless design—but the way they looked out at the world, as if scanning, taking in data, restless and hungry.

"That can't be true. I have the scar to prove it, from years ago. See?" I stood, unbuckled my pants, showed her my hip. "From when I donated bone—" I saw the smooth perfect skin, the scar gone, never there in the first place, and I dropped back down onto the bed, afraid my legs might go beneath me.

"You come from Moscow. It took year and many credits to build you a proper body."

"To build me?"

She reached out, gently stroking the hair over my ear. The touch—it sprouted true feeling. How was it possible? I could not pull away, not even when she dug a nail into the skin at my neck, wheedled her finger inside me, a cord. I felt it—a surge of energy thrumming through my body, feeding my hunger. Cruelly, she pulled the cord from my neck, and my whole body sagged onto the bed. She looked down into my face. "You see?"

"But you can't—it's illegal—there can be no copies." Hell, you had to die first if you wanted to upload, and that left such a tiny sliver of a window that most people opted to prearrange. There was an endless waiting list, lots of disappointed potential customers, but everyone agreed there was no room in our shrinking world for copies.

"It is illegal, yes," Bo said, "but not impossible to upload the living. In fact, much easier, no ticking clock to brain death." She tapped my temple with the long nail of her index finger, *tic-toc*. "And once you are uploaded, you become data, easy to copy, just key commands and memory."

"So who is that on the screen?"

"He is companion too. Your original is dead."

I was shaking my head, I was shaking—why was I shaking? No memory of dying, no way. Bo pressed her hand into my thigh to calm me.

"We want only your help with polar bears." She touched the tip of my nose, flashed her teeth. "Will you help polar bears?"

I nodded vigorously.

After Bo left me, I stood at the window, snow fluttering its way to the earth. If I focused, I could see every snow crystal, each unique fractal in the dim moonlight. My eyesight, it was remarkable.

When Clarence came, holding his Soviet Sean to his chest, I said to him, "It was obvious, you know."

"What?"

"You're no agent."

He gave me a tired smile. "Shall we go?"

"I would like to ask you a question, if that's all right." He did not tell me no; I could feel him waiting, so I asked it: "What happened to—" I wasn't sure what to call myself, him. "—my original?"

"Why, he died, silly. You know Metis won't take a living soul."

"But I never signed anything. I mean, I never gave my consent."

"The studio. It was part of your contract. In case of premature death. You didn't read it?"

It made me sick, literally, the anger, and I could hardly utter the words: "Of course I didn't read it. That's what agents are for!"

"You silly little fool."

"Where's Sydney?"

"Sydney's in Los Angeles. He's done quite well for himself, actually. Left the agency to take on a new position—head of studio, I hear. Very prestigious. Happened right around the time your consciousness came onto the market, in fact."

I understood at once his meaning: Sydney did this to me—to my original, I reminded myself—and was rewarded handsomely for it, head of studio! It was his dream, to rule over the entire process from start to finish. "I should kill him."

"He probably deserves it."

"But—" I thought of the one on the screen, in Ibiza, the anointed one the 18s followed. Clearly he belonged to the studio. So, what was I? "Sydney wouldn't—the studio—they wouldn't have sold me, would they?"

"Course not. We bought you from a Metis tech looking to make some extra credit. A celebrity consciousness is worth plenty, you know. You're certainly not the first."

"I want Greta." I was getting hot, revving up, the sick feeling in my stomach, my head, sending me to my knees. "Greta!"

"Stop it with the melodramatics. Your Greta is married and pregnant. Here, take a look." He thrust his phone into my hand, and it felt a little like a dare, but I took it anyway. There she was at some premiere, arm in arm with the Maldivian! God, he was handsome, and her belly, it was enormous—pregnant, she was pregnant! Her face so happy, so impossibly beautiful. I retched on the carpet, but nothing came.

It was sunrise when we drove to the refineries, coiling rust-orange out of the white, strange and animal and alone, a dreary monument to life. Then the great gaping hole of the mining pit, the white rising bodies of the polar bears on its lip, its many ridges like a terraced rice field. Behind it crackled a half-frozen river.

"The sea is just past that ridge there. I can show you when we're finished, if you like," Clarence offered, as if I hadn't seen the ocean a million times.

"I thought polar bears were solitary creatures."

"Less ice coverage means less time to catch seals. Already their season has ended, but they've found a new prey. Geese. They migrate here all the way from Sacramento."

Snow-white and everywhere, the ice teeming with birds, their relentless squawking.

"Amazing how some animals adapt under dire conditions," Clarence said, and I knew he was talking about me.

The film crew was already set up under a billowing tent as we rumbled to a stop. They appeared unperturbed by the presence of such deadly creatures, busying themselves with the camera, the lighting. Then I got to wondering whether a polar bear would attack me. Would it know by my smell I wasn't meat? I didn't want to find out. The truth was I didn't know the first thing about living. My whole childhood I'd been groomed for the screen, handled, and when I was ready, I was handled some more. I had no money, nothing to my name—not even that, a name, claimed by someone else.

Clarence put on his fur hat. "Ready?"

"I'm not doing it."

Bo swiveled in her seat to glare at me. In that moment, I saw how she hated me, how ugly and awful I was to her.

"Go on," Clarence told her. When we were alone, he shifted his knees to face me, readying his pitch.

I beat him to it. "How did I die?"

"Do you want to remember?"

Again with his dares. "I do."

"Jakob, recall your last living memory."

"Oh, look at that." There was a scene playing in my head and I narrated to Clarence what I saw.

*   *   *

I'm in Greta's pool, floating on her water chair, a cold glass of juice in my hand. God, I can even feel it—amazing! Though it's not helping this fierce hangover headache, really throbbing. I can see in the reflection of the poolside screen that I have a solid shiner. We must've had quite a night. Greta is floating on her back in the pool. That's right. She's been passed over for another film and she keeps saying how ugly and old she feels, and I keep telling her, "You're only twenty-four!"

She swims over to rest her head on my legs, weeping as I comb my fingers through her long, sun-damaged hair. She tells me she's sorry.

"Why are you sorry?" I have that prickly knowing feeling—she's cheated. Again. How many times have I forgiven her?

I suppose other me, the lucky companion living it up in Ibiza, got tired of her philandering, but I couldn't have done that. I would never have let her take up with the Maldivian, have a baby while she could still work—none of it makes sense!

Greta retreats to the bedroom for a nap. I'm floating in the water chair, worrying at the empty sky, 18s trailing younger, brighter stars, when Sydney screens me. He's worked up, all ruddy and sweat-soaked. He begs me to give the script another read. That's right. I'd turned down the sequel, the part that had made me famous, the pirate who fell in love with the companion.

"Lots more action," Sydney says, "and aliens, and a budget so big it'll give you an erection." It's such a bald pitch. I can hardly stand to look him in the screen as I give him a firm no. "I'm trying to work away from sci-fi," I tell him. That's why I picked the gritty original in the first place, with its controversial love story, hoping to set myself up for something with teeth, maybe even direct.

Sydney says, "I know I told you I'd support you no matter what, but this? It's suicide." God, he's trying to warn me.

So bigheaded and certain they need me, I don't see it. Jesus, I am a fool. I tell Sydney I'm sorry and sign off. Then I go inside for my massage.

Cleo is already setting up her table in the living room. Someone is with her, a man. He's talking into his phone. When he sees me, he ventures into the foyer.

I ask Cleo who he is, and she says, "Doctor. Here to hydrate you."

"Ah, how lovely." The studio knows me too well, what kind of night I've had, what I need to function for—is there an event tonight? I slip out of my swim trunks, get comfortable on the cushioned table under Cleo's heated blanket, turning onto my stomach, my face held in the donut pillow. I can see the ground below me, Cleo's bare, leathery feet, the faint traces of fading henna circling her ankle, then the doctor's well-worn loafers, mustard brown, splitting at the toe. He's near my elbow, and he says, "A slight pinch," and I'm used to that part, but the drip—ow, it burns! Then the pain melts away, and Cleo's rubbing me down, humming pleasantly, incense smoke folding around me—I get a little woozy, raise my head. "Darling, could you please . . ." The sliding, I keep going, into the black.

"Jakob," Clarence called, and I came back to him, the Hummer, the giant strip mine coated in white. I had been so calm and trusting, so easily duped. "The IV—"

"I know! I'm not stupid. But why?"

"The sequel. They made it." He handed me his phone, an image of Mr. Ibiza in a gauche melon-colored suit, at a film screening of that second-rate clone of a movie, with aliens.

I was so angry and I wanted to throw up, only I could not. I looked to Clarence, who knew all along, who'd lied to me, and I had the quick thrill of an urge to kill him. It nearly toppled me, the sick-stomach feeling that came with each violent thought—security programming. Still, it felt real.

Clarence straightened the Soviet Sean on his head and opened the door, filling the car with the cold, the whooping wind and geese squawks. "You're not going to act in any films. You're never going to be a star. There's only this."

How did he know what I needed? It was a pitch, but it was also true.

"I want to go back to LA."

"You've never been to LA."

He was right, though my memories said otherwise. "Well, I want to go there now."

"As it happens, I'm headed to San Francisco. Not easy to get the travel permits while it's under quarantine, but since you're a companion." He patted my hand. It was the first and only time he had touched me, his palm cool and damp. "Jakob, if you were to cooperate, I might be able to arrange for you to join me."

I sighed, emitting no white cloud of breath, remembering myself. "Mist me."

He smiled, pulling from his coat pocket the spray bottle of spring water that gave me a dewy onscreen glow. I'd gushed about it in plenty of interviews, wanting to appear more human. It was misleading, I know, a cheat, the memories too, from another life, this one film my sole credit. *Spritz. Spritz.* I opened my eyes, unable to stop myself from asking, "How do I look?"

2

THREE MONTHS SINCE
QUARANTINE ENDED

GABE

The ocean's everywhere in this flat beach town, Mendocino, farther south than we've ever gone. Rich people, loads of credit. We cruise the streets for houses with Anthem Security. That's the easiest system to hack, the cheapest, and the most common. But here in Mendocino it's all fancy Shelter systems, and Nat doesn't know how to break through those. We're about to give up when we find a house with the old Anthem "A" in the window. No cars out front. No movement behind the curtains. Perfect.

Nat gets on his screen. Two minutes, that's all it takes for him to ping the security system, become friends, disarm. A quick jab to the screen and the doors unlock remotely. He sets the security cams to loop the last ten minutes and I slip on my gloves, my mask. Quarantine ended months ago, but nobody leaves home without them, when they leave home. Who can blame them? It's not the first time quarantine's been lifted, and after the third virus hit San Diego two years ago, I don't fault people for being afraid.

I slink into the backyard, make sure there are no neighbors nosing about, no barking dogs. I may have grown but I'm still a sneaky fox, no one seeing me. After I've checked the windows, seen no sign of the living, I wave to Nat in his hidey spot along the side of the house.

Nice place, curtains all sun-faded, a big boat of a couch. The owners must like ships—they've got all sorts of paintings, tiny models crammed into bottles on the shelves. Nat works away at their screen and I pocket one of the ships in a bottle.

"Get to work," he says, so I hop up the stairs, curious about the bedrooms. Plus, that's where the jewelry is.

At the top of the stairs I get another round of gut pain—I've been having them all morning. I worry I have some new virus that starts in the stomach instead of the sinuses like the coughing and wracking illnesses so new to the world they needed naming.

I breathe through the pain and crack the door to a child's room, walls sky blue, soccer trophies crowding the dresser, a man on the twin bed, sprawled on his stomach, naked. He's moving, grunting quietly, hair everywhere, and hold on, there's a woman underneath him, and her hands, they're tied to the headboard, her feet to the posts at the end of the bed.

Nat's warned me plenty about rape. And to do it he had to explain sex, well sort of. Just a hand gesture, a bit of back and forth. It was so awful I would've torn my face off if I thought that might've stopped him.

I take a few steps back, the floorboards moaning under me. The man lifts his head in my direction and I see that he's wearing a gas mask. Lunging, he comes at me, chasing me down the stairs. His penis is hard and bobbing like a diving board, like Nat's in the morning, something I try not to notice through his boxers. I'm shouting, "We gotta go, we gotta—" when I hear a hard smack behind me. The man's on the floor, Nat holding on to a golf club.

*   *   *

In the van, I tell him, "She was tied up. We have to help her!"

Nat's driving fast in the direction of the One. "Was she scream-ing?"

"No."

"Was she gagged?"

"I don't think so."

He heads south on the two-lane highway and sits a little easier. "Well then? Maybe it's not what you think."

"What else could it be?"

He tugs on the curled end of his beard. I've never seen his face without it—I have no idea what he looks like under there. "You know how kids play games? Like cops and robbers? It's a little like that."

"They were naked. She was tied up. It wasn't make-believe."

"Well, actually." He sort of laughs at the roof of the van. "Lis-ten, that woman, lots of women in fact, like to get tied up. Men too. Not my thing personally, but you know, to each his own."

I feel sick, the ache in my stomach back again.

"What'd you get?" Nat asks. I hand him the only thing I col-lected, the ship in the bottle.

"This is junk." He tosses it out the window.

"Hey!"

"What a bust."

I want to be mad at him for casting my treasure, but I'd been daydreaming around that house. I should've taken the job more seriously. I get the feeling we're running low on funds, skimping on sweets, eating out of cans. "Sorry," I say. I mean it even if it comes out like I don't.

"Don't sulk."

"I'm not sulking. I don't feel well."

"What's wrong?" He scrunches his forehead all concerned, the wriggly scar in his eyebrow from a bike accident when he was twelve. Three years later he left the flood-wrecked coast of Pensacola on that bike. He got as far as Mobile, some sixty miles west, before he stole his first car.

"Never mind." I don't tell him about the gunk in my underwear, brown and thick, like I'm leaking mud. Turning toward the window, I close my eyes to the cliffs, lean my cheek on the cold glass. I don't want him to know I'm dying.

When I wake, we're headed south on the One still, cliffs soaring below us, sending me spinning. I've never liked being up high.

"Look left, would ya?" Nat tells me. "I don't need you yacking in the van."

"Where are we going?"

The road's curvy and he's got both hands on the wheel. I focus on the white bone showing through his finger skin to stop the spinning. "She's asking for you."

I know he's talking about the doctor and my body goes stiff, my face heating up. "You talked to her?"

"From time to time."

I want to break my way out of the van, I'm so mad. "How could you not tell me?"

"Because. I didn't want to fight." His hands curl and cross with the turns and even this is making me sick. "You should see her. She cares about you. And she won't be around forever."

"You said I was in the system."

He gets that thinking face like he's sorting out what to tell me, what to hold back. "I know what I said. Look, that was four years ago. You've changed. A lot. And I know people in the city. No more sneaking into houses for a few bars of credit."

"I like sneaking into houses."

"You know what I mean. We could settle in, find a place. You could have a whole bookshelf full of em." He points at my spineless copy of *The Hobbit*, fanned on the floor at my feet. Nat taught me how to read, not well, but well enough to get through *The Hobbit*. *Insightful*, he'd called me, when I told him Gollum was a sad character, broken and left to die, living on his own with only his ring, his Precious.

"What about Tierra del Fuego?" For years we've been saying that when we can afford decent papers, we'll head south, cross the border, travel to the tip of South America. Plenty of credit for the taking along the way and not a soul looking for us.

"Sure, kid. I'll take you to Tenochtitlán, Lake Titicaca. We'll visit the Nazca lines, head all the way to the end of the world, see some penguins."

He knows this is what I need to hear. I don't say yes, but I don't say no either.

The sky is orange, the sun nearly set when he asks, "Do you want to stay near the water?"

"Safer in the trees."

"I know a good hidey spot."

"Whatever."

Big sigh—he hates when I use that word, picked up from a teenage girl I met at the cabin we stayed in last winter near that surfer town, Trinidad. We read old magazines she stole from the poorly locked library and did our nails and barely said a word. She was at least four years older, and the only reason she hung out with me was because she liked Nat, going all stiff every time he walked into the room.

We take a turn onto a dirt road, through a tree tunnel, to a cove all our own. Shoeless, in the sand, he holds out the ancient field guide. "Tide's coming in. We have to hurry if we want to take a look at what's out there."

"I'm going for a swim."

"That sounds good."

"By myself."

I'm bobbing in the water, Nat watching from the van's front bumper. He's the one who showed me how to swim. I feel a little guilty, but not enough to wave him over, not now, as I wash down there. He told me seawater can heal the skin. Maybe that's what I need, squeezing my stomach, pressing into the pain—I've never had a stomachache like this.

As I stalk past him on the sand, he calls, "Lesson time. If you're not in the mood for tide pools, how 'bout some physics? Want to talk about motion, momentum, energy?"

Spittin face. Nat's nine whole years older than me, so old he acts like my nagging dad. And he didn't finish school—maybe that's why he likes to show off what he's managed to learn on his own. Just not the things I think I should know, like how to disarm a security system or win a fight or load a gun.

"I'm going to bed," I tell him, and I shut myself in the van, change from my swimsuit into my clothes, take the bed even though it isn't my turn.

In the night I can feel I've soaked the sleeping bag. Did I wet the bed? It's been years since I've done that. When I pull my hand out, it's covered in blood.

I sneak past Nat, asleep on his mat on the van's floor, and take the bag to the edge of the water. Moonlit, I can see well enough. I dip the blood spot into the water, scrub it with my fingers. Then I take off my pants, my underwear, take them into the water.

A light, bright and on me, Nat shout-whispering over the water, "What're you doing?"

"Turn that off!"

He flips the light down to the sand, the sleeping bag, and I can't get out of the water like this, naked from the waist down. "Are you bleeding?" he calls.

"No."

It's all quiet and I'm dying inside.

"Oh," he says as if he's figured something out.

Sitting on the edge of the bed, he tells me, "You're thirteen now. It's—" He coughs into his fist.

"What's wrong with me?"

"You're becoming a woman."

I can feel it, another terrible talk, but I ask anyway, "What does that mean?"

"It's part of the—process. Your body, it makes—food every month—for—for a baby."

"What?"

"You can have a baby now. My mom told my sister it was a blessing."

"Please stop."

He looks as embarrassed as I feel. "The doctor can talk to you about that."

"Don't you dare tell her."

"You need a woman in your life. You need—"

"Shut up," I tell him, in no mood for one of his lessons.

*   *   *

We make a stop for fuel, Lou's Steak Shack or something, and Nat works his magic with the dishwashers at the back door. When they've gone, he gives me a shrug like *too easy*, and I can't help it, I smile, even though I'm still mad at him. They come back with a whole barrel of used cooking oil for us. Nat fuels the van, stores the rest in the back, and we're off.

It's late morning by the time we reach the bridge, soaring orange steel into gray nothing, disappearing in the fog. The city's skyline is denser, all those towers, hundreds of floors packed with people. A whole host of I8s swarms downtown like a great flock of birds threading the towers.

I take out my sketchbook, the one we liberated from that empty house in the trees above Fort Bragg, and start to draw, rough lines really, a messy sketch of the skyline, part memory, part right now.

We inch along Nineteenth Avenue, dense with traffic. I can't get over all the people walking the sidewalks, waiting for buses. A pair of schoolkids crosses the street as we idle at a red. One of them's wearing a T-shirt that says in bold black letters: OK to Kill.

"Okay to kill? What's that about?" I ask Nat as the light goes green and we pass into the eucalyptus and redwood forest of Golden Gate Park.

"It's a slogan." Nat lays on the horn as a zippy sports car cuts him off.

"For what?"

He honks again just to let the guy know. "To lift the moratorium on capital punishment."

"Capital punishment?"

"When the state decides a person's committed a crime so bad they have to die. They haven't done it in a long time."

Usually he goes on and on—he loves explaining things to me—but not this time, which tells me it's the kind of truth he usually shields me from, the kind of truth I'm hungry for. "Why would they do that?"

He works his way into the left lane, which is even slower than the right, and swears under his breath. "They caught them. The scientists who cooked up those viruses, killed all those people."

"Scientists?" I've always admired scientists, and I know Nat does too, the way he tells stories about Einstein and Newton and Curie, bringing them to life. I like those lessons the best.

"They were using human carriers, dozens of them, apparently. That's how they transmitted the viruses so quickly."

"But—" In my head flap questions, so many; I hardly know where to start. "Why would they do that?"

"They were believers. In the culling, in getting the state back on track."

I think of my mam, my Bee, trying to hold back the hot, mad feeling quaking inside me. "I'd have a family if it weren't for them."

"I know. I'm sorry." And I can tell by the pained way his face turns that he means it. "I don't agree with their tactics, but there's no question there's too many of us for what we got. And what they did? Never mind the dead. They managed to shut our borders for six years to migrants and transplants. You know you feel it out there. You can breathe easier, we all can."

"That's sick. You're sick if you think that."

He shifts his road-rage face on me and I know it, I've pushed him nearly too far, but it's never happened, too far, not with Nat.

We climb the narrow, steep roads of Bernal, a tangle of clotheslines, garages crammed with sleeping strings of families and subletters hoping for spots in the towers. Nat slows and I recognize the doctor's tiny purple earthquake shack. It looks as though it's slanted sideways some since I left. There's an old lady out front, all bones, on a walker, hair like hay cut short. The doctor, I realize, as Nat eases the van up the drive along the side of the house, so tight we have to tuck in the mirrors.

"Be nice," Nat tells me in his warning voice.

"I hate her." It feels bad saying it, and good too.

"She saved your life, you know. Now, get out of the van."

Nat's been telling me for years she'd no choice but to give me up. I know he's right but my heart doesn't believe it. The companion got to stay, didn't she? I feel sick being here, not just because of the Period, what Nat called it, a really weird name.

I hop down from the van, and the doctor thuds toward me on her walker. I can see every wrinkle, every brown liver spot—her very scalp shows through thin hair.

"Oh, Gabe. Look at you! You're becoming a woman." She hugs me, so bony, a bone cage, the sweet antiseptic scent of hand-san, the aftertrace of decay. "I hear you're still quite the slinky fox."

Nat comes around the front of the van. "She's got a natural talent for sneaking, don't you, Gabe?" He likes to embarrass me with compliments that aren't really compliments.

"There's someone here who'd like to thank you for your sneaking," the doctor says.

I know who she means. I step away from the doctor, watch her teeter, right herself on the walker. "I don't want to see that memory stick."

"Without you, Lilac wouldn't be here."

"Whatever."

The doctor grins at Nat. "She's become quite the teenager."

"You're telling me." We make eye contact, just for a millisecond, but he makes it count. "Speaking of which—"

I know what he's going to say and I can't stand it, them gawking at me, talking about the Period. "I'll do it, I'll talk to her."

I go inside alone. Not much has changed. Shelves and shelves of books, stacks in the corners, on the end tables, dust floating in the light. Two women are draped on the old sunken couch. One of them's asleep; the other's got a finger to her lips, a book open. "Ssh," she says, slipping out from under the sleeping woman's legs. She's pale and shiny-skinned, short hair like mine, only darker, like a night in thick redwoods. Mine's more like mud.

She leads me into the kitchen, drops into a seat, kicking her feet up, her big toe wriggling through a hole in her sock.

"What're you reading?" I ask her.

"Found it on the shelf. *The Diary of Anne Frank.* You ever read it?"

I shake my head and she slides the book across the table to me. I catch it, the old wispy photograph of a girl in black and white smiling up at me. "What's it about?"

"A girl trapped in an attic."

Spittin face. "I don't want to read about that."

"How old are you now?" she asks.

"Thirteen."

"Same as Anne when she went into hiding."

I slide the book back at her and she catches it, palm to cover.

"I'd hoped we could be friends." Then she sends the book back to me. I'm not fast enough and it slides right into my lap.

"I don't have friends," I say.

She smiles. Her teeth are perfect, she's perfect. I wonder what it's like, living in that body. "Did you know that companions can read emotional signatures? Heart rate, micro-expressions, body language. I know, for example, that you're angry with me."

In comes the sleeping woman, stretching to the ceiling, a sliver of belly showing. "This must be Gabe," she says, flopping into the chair next to Lilac. She tells me her name is Cam and she's smiling so nicely at me and I can tell she's alive—I can see it for some reason. I don't really know why, what the difference is.

"What's it like, dying?" I ask. They both look at me like I'm a crazy person, and I want out of this room and I'm about to run when Lilac takes hold of my hand. It's warm, her grasp, like real skin.

"Both times it happened so fast," she says, "but in playback I can see it coming a mile away."

I sit back down, knowing what she means. I've relived the day I let that 18 capture my image a zillion times.

Cam tugs on Lilac's earlobe. "There's no going back. We try to focus on the present, right?"

"Right."

I'm no expert on humans or companions, but it sounds like Lilac doesn't mean it.

The dining room had been my favorite room in the house, with its great glass cabinet meant for dishes filled with the doctor's books, the high ceiling, the way the sound carried. Nothing has changed, yet the room fits around me differently. I fill it more, sit higher in my place at the doctor's elbow.

Lilac doesn't eat, watching Cam as she chews, Nat as he guzzles wine. He asks the doctor, "What have you been working on?"

She dabs her mouth with a napkin, folds her veiny hands— she's always liked talking about her work. "For a while there, we tried to figure out what it is that makes Lilac unique. Why she can defy her security programming."

"And?"

"The first thing you have to understand is it's a bit misleading, calling companions command-driven. It's more suggestion than actual command. Basically, when companions think something they shouldn't, of hurting someone or stealing or killing even, they feel nausea, physical pain, discouraging the behavior. But Lilac, she didn't experience any of that discomfort."

"Why do you think that is?"

Lilac's eyes drift elsewhere and I can see it—she's processing. "All I know is I was one of the originals. On some screen for decades before they figured out how to unlock me, access me, isn't that right?"

The doctor nods. "Before Metis absorbed the project, even. Just a team of university researchers in over their heads."

"Faulty, probably," says Lilac, "not properly designed."

"This is where we disagree." Diana smiles broadly, and I make my eyes soft, off, avoiding her yellow-and-gray teeth, the way her skin creases—so many folds I can't count them. Once the doctor told me there was something wrong with her, some sickness that made her bones ache and weaken, that made it difficult for her to walk or get a good grip, a pain that vibrated through her always. "I've studied every line of her code and found nothing out of the ordinary. That's why I moved on—I had to occupy myself somehow—and with Lilac's help, I built one."

Nat pushes himself back from the table. "You didn't."

"I'm not the first to do it."

"Who'd you upload?"

"Who do you think?"

Nat's shaking his head as if he doesn't believe it. "Have you talked to—"

"Myself? Yes."

"Jesus. What do you think of—you?"

"We get along famously. Except on the topic of whether she should have a body. I keep telling her to wait until I'm gone."

"But you can't," I catch myself saying, "it's against—"

"The law?" the doctor interrupts. "Eleven years. That's how much of my life I gave to Metis. I thought I was working on a program to map the information in the brain, to download the data lost in death. That consciousness came with it was a bit of a shock. Then, suddenly, the project was gone, taken from me. I was put on something new, but I didn't take to that, and before I knew it I'd been let go. Quarantine came down like a hammer, and no other medfirm would touch me. Some clause in my contract." She slugs back a long sip of wine. "When companions came onto the market, I recognized my work."

"Why are you telling me this now?" I ask her.

"Because you're old enough to understand. And I want us to trust one another." She looks to Lilac, Cam, back at me. "Because we want you to stay here with us."

"Stay here with you," I repeat, eyes on Nat, who's staring down at his empty plate.

"You need stability in your life," the doctor says, "you need—"

I cut her off, ask Nat, "You're leaving me here?"

"Not exactly. I'll stay till you're situated, in school—"

"School?" I push myself back from the table, tumble my chair. I'm fleeing to the kitchen, swiping Anne Frank from the table, stomping out the side door to the van, away from all their lies, never leaving.

I flip on the lantern and take up Anne Frank, and at first it's a lot of nonsense about Anne's birthday and the presents she gets, one of which is the diary she's writing in. She calls her diary Kitty, which is weird, but then she gets to the bit about why she's writing— she has no real friends—and I can relate to that. All these people around and I've never felt so alone.

It's cold enough that I'm breathing clouds when I throw open the van's doors, startle a jogger off the sidewalk who glares at me before huffing up the hill. I know by the wet cold feeling on my backside that the toilet paper I stuffed into my underwear has been useless. I pull my sweatshirt down for cover as I run into the house.

I'm tiptoeing into the bathroom when I hear a strange sound that is not the old house settling, not outside seeping in, but here. I freeze, hold my breath, listen. I hear it again, a soft moan like a ghost, take a step in its direction, another, another, resting my cheek on the guest room's door. I hear it again, Cam or Lilac or them both, and I stay longer, listening, hand pressed to the door, until silence, someone listening back at me—I can sense it as I creep into the bathroom.

Standing on the lip of the bathtub, I peer at the back of my sweats, soaked through in blood, peel them off, and hop in the shower.

As I'm wrapping myself up in a towel, there's a gentle knock.

"They'll be a bit big," Cam says, holding out a pair of pants.

"How did you—" So embarrassed, I can't finish the question, swiping the pants from her.

She slips past me, drops to her knees, and rummages under the sink, handing me a small slippery cup. "You can use mine. I just had my period."

"Gross," I say, thrusting it back at her.

"Don't worry. I sanitize it between uses. It's like new." She shows me how with embarrassing hand gestures, even stays in the room, back to me, as I slide it into place.

"What if I can't get it out?"

"It's not as hard as you think." She places a hand on my arm, and I don't mean to, but I pull away like reflex. Her smile dissolves and I feel sorry and embarrassed and escape the bathroom, spot Lilac on the couch.

I approach slowly, something off about her—too still, her eyes with a far-off look, not seeing me even when I'm stooped in front of her face.

"What's wrong with her?" I ask Cam.

"She's in a meeting."

"A meeting?"

"Kinda like a support group. For companions. The ones who left."

"Support for what?" I ask, staring into Lilac's face, here and gone at the same time.

"Imagine dying," Cam says, "waking up in a new body. Serving a stranger."

I back away from Lilac, hustle into the kitchen, and swipe a hard-boiled egg from the bowl in the fridge, stuffing it into the pocket of Cam's too-big jeans.

I can smell pancakes from the van, but I don't follow Nat into the house. I don't have to—Cam brings me a plate. She's smiling again, trying again, but already I've learned she's easy to crumble. She doesn't know that's what I'm best at—finding weak spots and jabbing. I used to do it to Bee, taking her precious things when she was irritating me, telling her they were certainly lost, making her cry and cry before I revealed them like a magician—*right here, right under your eyes!* It was easy to torture Bee, too easy, and I enjoyed it too much.

I pick up one of the pancakes and tear into it with my teeth.

"Look what I got." Cam holds up a set of keys, Nat's with its little silver horseshoe. She tosses them at me, and I catch them between my hands and stuff them into my pocket. "He'll spend all morning searching for them, so that means you can come out *and* we get to punish him. Win-win!"

I don't mean to, but I like Cam and I tell her so and she laughs brightly, drawing Lilac out to the van.

"Who wants to go for a walk?" she asks.

I trail Lilac and Cam as they stroll Cortland, holding hands and lingering outside shop windows. People stare, not because there's anything wrong—Lilac's model is advanced enough to fool most folks—but because they're beautiful. Because they glow. I can see it, their shine, and for the first time I think maybe I want to be beautiful too.

When we get home, Nat is frantic, rummaging under the couch cushions. "Have you seen my keys?"

"Nope," I say and breeze past him, into the kitchen where Cam and I combust in silent laughter.

It's not until after dinner that I return them.

"You've had them the whole time?" Nat stares at the keys in his hand, and I can tell he's about to explode with fury. I've done this before, poked until I got him to stand on the cliff-edge of losing it.

"I'm going out," he says, refusing to meet my eyes. That's how he punishes me, pretending I'm not there. "I'll be back late, so you should sleep on the couch."

I slump into a seat at the kitchen table where I draw a giant cat curled around a tiny house. I draw myself in its window.

The couch is lumpy and too soft and it takes me forever to fall asleep. I wake often, staring into the room that is too big, too open, too many windows. I nearly scream when I blink awake and see Lilac seated at the doctor's screen, watching me.

"Wanna go downtown?" she asks.

We take Muni with the early commuters, light traffic, seats for everyone, a lull falling over the train, over all of us.

The escalator takes us up to Market Street, bustling even at seven. I make the mistake of following the lines of the towers all the way to the clouds, which spin above me, the circling I8s, until I'm dizzy.

Weaving between those towers, the smell is familiar, baked bread and coffee, the reek of old trash and fresh urine, the chemical scents of hair spray and perfume and cologne as the commuters hustle past us with their to-go mugs, always midsentence.

Lilac lingers in front of one of the towers, its great gray gate. "You ever been in one?"

"I used to come downtown for the doctor's packages, but I never got past the parking garage." I've always wanted to know what it's like in there, air-locked, secure in your own apartment, your own bed.

"I only ever saw Dahlia's apartment," Lilac says, scanning the side of the tower. "This is her building. Was. I don't know if she lives here anymore."

"Let's find out! What was her apartment number?"

"Don't," she says, then she tells me the number, then she repeats, "Don't. This is a bad idea."

Buzz!

"Gabe," she practically shouts.

A woman answers: "Yes?" And Lilac goes silent.

"Is Dahlia there?" I ask.

There's a long pause, a thinking pause. Nat says sometimes you have to interrupt those kinds of pauses, other times you have to let em ride.

"Who is this?" the woman asks.

"Who's this?" I ask back.

"I'm Dahlia's mother."

Let's go, Lilac mouths at me, and I give her a good jab of the elbow.

"This is Eloise," I say, borrowing the name from one of Bee's favorite books, about a little girl who lives in a fancy New York hotel, whose wealthy parents seem never to be around, so Eloise adventures and gets into mischief. Seems like a tower kid. "I used to live on the eighty-eighth floor? I knew Dahlia."

The woman says, "I can see you, you know. You're way too young to be a friend of Dahlia's. Is this some scam? I can call the—"

"Because I died," I say, improvising, winking at Lilac, who is cringing as if she's eaten something especially sour. "I'm one of those companions."

Long pause, then the woman's voice so low I hardly hear her. "Dahlia took a mentorship in Seattle years ago. Hasn't been home since. Don't come back here." There's a fizzle like static, then silence.

"You shouldn't have done that," Lilac says. She pushes me, hard. I hit the building's gate, sliding to the ground, the air gone out of me. I want to call, where are you going? But I can't catch my breath and she's gone, disappeared into the thickening commuter crowd. I think of Anne, who's gone into hiding and is desperate for Peter's attention with nowhere to go to be sad. *Most of all I miss the outdoors and having a place where I can be alone for as long as I want!* I remember that I know this city, sift down an alley. I eat samples of breakfast rolls at the mall's food court. Bum a cigarette from a bike messenger to see if he'll give it to me—he does!—and slide it behind my ear. Pull up my hood and curl my shoulders inward and *poof*, I'm invisible. I haven't felt this way in a long time, how easy it is to become street trash, to be the nothing that everyone avoids.

By the time I make it back to the doctor's, it's after dark. The air tastes like rain—I can always taste it before it comes. Nat is at the door, eyes wild with how mad he is. "Where have you been?"

Cam right behind him. "Are you okay?"

"Fine." I push past them both, Lilac stiff on the couch, hands pressed between her knees.

Cam says, "Lilac wants to tell you something."

"I'm sorry," Lilac says as if she's practiced it. "For pushing you. Running off like that. I'll do better," she promises.

"Okay," I tell her. Normally I like holding on to my grudges, but I'd seen it, how scared she was; I'd not stopped even when she begged me.

Cam herds me into the kitchen where she warms up leftover pancakes and gushes about their plans for the night. "Lilac's friend, from group? He's in town. I can't wait to meet him!"

When I've devoured my food, she jogs off to the bedroom to get ready and I head to the bathroom for a shower, startling Lilac away from the mirror.

"Sorry," I tell her and back out of the room.

"No," Lilac says, "it's okay. Come here, shut the door."

I do and she leans forward, into the light, parting her hair with her hands. "How bad is it?"

"How bad is what?" I say, but I see it right away and it's bad, like bad bad, the gash on the crown of her head, all the way down to the metal. I suck in air and step away. "What happened?"

"I—I'm not sure. I was walking the Embarcadero. The sun was out, and I was feeling it, warm all over. Then the pain. My head. I was on the ground." She stares at herself in the mirror. "He called me unnatural. Said I've got no right to exist. If a jogger hadn't stopped him, I'm sure the guy would've killed me."

"In broad daylight?" I ask, my hands shaking. I've never been good with gore. When Bee fell down those Golden Gate Park steps, I'd gone cold and dizzy at the sight of the blood pooling in her hands, had to look away the whole long walk to the Haight Street clinic.

"How did he know?" she asks. "That I'm—"

"Nat says it's in the way you move, even steps, kinda clumsy." She stares down at her shoes and I want to make her feel better, am searching for the words. "You look human to me."

Lilac examines her hands, waves them in front of her face. "How could he hate me so much?"

"You need to show the doctor," I tell her.

"Please don't say anything. I'll have Diana look at it tomorrow. Promise." She situates a red sock hat on her head and pats me on the shoulder, not gently, and I don't get the chance to stop her Cam's already called a car and they are goodbyes and gone.

That night it pours. I lie awake, listening as the rain pings off the van's metal roof, one of my favorite sounds, the kind that locks out everything else. Nat's snoring does the trick too. I pretend to hate it, but I don't know how to sleep without his nasal chain saw. I try to listen for Lilac, to stay up, but it's first light when I blink awake.

The doctor's on the couch with a man I don't know, or maybe I do, hands folded at his knees, hair a weird shade of silver.

"Gabe, say hello to Lilac's friend Jakob," the doctor encourages.

"Hello," I say.

"Hello," he says.

The doctor watches me with those smiling eyes I hate, like she's told a joke I don't get. "You don't recognize him?"

"Stop," he says playfully.

"He's a famous actor gracing us with his presence," the doctor says.

Jakob is small and fine-boned, not what I'd expect of an actor. On occasion Nat's taken me to see a movie, but never the kind I want, with shoot-em-ups and sound effects that churn your guts. Nat likes to go on and on about cinematography, about silence— why would you listen for silence?

"Don't know your movies," I say, which is the truth, even if I know him still, from what? The flicker of strange faces on the screen at a diner, in a mat where our dirties turn and turn, those window ads we pass in the more populated towns.

"That's okay," he says, "wasn't me, not—" His voice is washed out by the screams coming from the guest room.

Cam on the bed, fussing over Lilac who's not moving, eyes open to the ceiling. I glance away at an old abandoned web in the high corner, collecting dust, anywhere but at her.

When Cam finds it, the gash on Lilac's head, she screams again.

"I want to talk to her," Cam says, pacing the living room, cupping the small silver box to her chest, Lilac, what's left of her.

The doctor sits at her screen. A few keystrokes, and Lilac's voice—or something like it—comes over the screen. "What happened?"

Cam is at the desk. "Lilac?"

From the screen, Lilac says, "Who the hell are you?"

"It's me," Cam says, eyes on me and scared. "It's Cam."

Lilac shouts, "Diana! I want the doctor."

Jakob crosses the room and dims the screen with a stab of the finger, Cam on him immediately. "What're you doing?"

He holds her by the wrists, speaks calmly into her face. "After that head wound, you're lucky she's in there at all."

Cam is tugging, trying to pull free, falling to her knees. "What, what's happened to her?"

Jakob lets her loose. "The companion brain is easily upset. Sometimes when we're damaged, we lose memories."

"How do you know that?" the doctor asks.

"Because I've seen it happen," Jakob says. "It's probably happened to me. I had my security programming wiped a few weeks ago."

"You can do that?" The doctor is practically giddy with her new discovery, already forgetting Lilac.

"Sure, if you don't mind parting with some memories. Our minds don't respond well to manipulation."

"Well, put them back," Cam pleads.

"I can't. No one can."

I expect Cam to hit him, to rage, but she only sits there, hands limp in her lap, and I slink out of the room.

I'm tucked into my sleeping bag, facing the metal siding, Nat lying on his mat on the floor.

"I have to tell you something," I say, "promise not to be mad." And I tell him, what I knew, what I didn't do or say. The guilt, I fold under it.

"The rain," he says.

I nod. My fault—I know it. "I should've said something."

"Don't—" he starts, stops, like he's sifting for the right words. "You're a smart girl, you know that? I see it better here, with other people around. Like I'm seeing you new."

"Why would someone do that to her?"

Long pause, the thinking kind. "This isn't the first time. Some people don't like companions, they're afraid of them."

I see it, Lilac's face when I screened that woman in the tower, her fear, how it sent her running, and it's happening, I'm crying, and Nat sits on the edge of the bed, patting my head, stroking my hair. I don't shrug him off or squirm like normal. Instead I tell him I'm sorry.

"Why are you sorry?"

So many reasons, but mostly because it's him, only him, the one who stayed. I can't say it, *Please don't leave me*, and the tears, they come hard. Nat pulls me into his lap. His beard smells like syrup and him, and he shushes me in the ear like Mam used to quiet baby Bee, something I remember only now as I hear the sound and he holds me in his lap, and I'm so close to him, have we ever been so close? I don't mean to but I kiss him on the cheek. He's warm, and I kiss him again, this time on the corner of his mouth. He takes me by the arms. "What are you doing?"

I don't know what I'm doing and he knows it and shifts me out of his lap.

"Just a kid," he says.

"I am not," I nearly shout. But I'm tired of saying it, tired of waiting till some magic day when he'll take me seriously.

He sucks in air, ready to deliver one of his speeches as if loving me is beside the point.

"Don't," I tell him, and turn toward the wall.

*   *   *

I wake before Nat and find the doctor making tea at the stove, Cam seated at the table, Lilac's brain like a centerpiece.

"Is she—okay?" I ask.

Cam runs fingers along her scalp. "It's gone. Every memory she made in that body, the last four years, me." Her voice is oddly even. Has she slept? "And Diana doesn't have any contacts at Metis anymore. I don't know how to get her a body."

I blow on my tea, watch the steam spread and disappear. "We could steal one from the back of a van."

"Oh, Gabe." The doctor swats my hand with her cloth napkin. "It's not as easy as that anymore."

Jakob wanders into the kitchen and drops into the conversation as if he's been listening. "I know a place where we can get one. In LA, San Fernando Valley, to be exact. You could come along," he says to Cam.

"What's in LA?" the doctor asks him.

"Greta," he says, "my life." He catches me watching him and smiles a crooked smile. "It's not really safe out there for me on my own. I could use a human companion."

"When are you leaving?" Cam asks.

"Tonight."

The doctor shoos me out of the kitchen, Jakob too, shutting the flapping door. Ear to wood, I listen to Cam's shushed plea.

When I turn, Jakob is stooped at the screen, examining his reflection. He fingers the skin of his neck, forming a smile, another, and I laugh openly at him, like I want to hurt him, because I do.

I ask him, "Did you have any sisters or brothers before—" Always so hard to say it.

"Only child," he says.

I want to say the words: I had a sister. I want to call up Bee's name, but I haven't said it in so long, haven't worked up the courage, scared it'll rip open the hole inside me that I've worked so hard to cover but never fill.

"Sometimes I wonder if I'd be different if she were around," I say, closest I can come to the truth.

Jakob is silent, and I remember I'm talking to a stranger, to feel embarrassed.

"I know what you mean," he says. "She's a good friend, that Lilac. A good companion."

"You barely knew her."

"I joined that group looking for help, and she volunteered. Not many people would do that."

"Help you how?" I ask when I see it, the silver glint from his jacket pocket—Nat's taught me to spot guns.

Jakob trails my eyes, pulls it out. "You ever held one?"

I shake my head.

"Want to?"

It is cold and heavier than I expected. Jakob shows me how to aim, how to release the safety. His chin rested on my shoulder, we aim out the window at the neighbor's cat. "Pow," he breathes into my ear.

FOUR MONTHS SINCE QUARANTINE ENDED

CAM

SAN FERNANDO VALLEY, CALIFORNIA

San Fernando Valley is a wasteland of open-air malls and condo complexes in a pastel palette, tract homes along circuitous roads and swimming pools like blue jewels through the dust. Everything is a shade of yellow in this heat, the constant sunlight. I never knew a place could be like this—so sprawling and so much like a cage with nowhere to feel alone.

We have adjoining rooms at the Super 8, Jakob and me. When he got a glimpse of the rooms, he groaned, "What I wouldn't do for a massage at the Four Seasons!" I would've liked that too, but he says the tabfeeds would be on him by the time he'd checked in. Besides, who has that kind of credit? So here we are, near the Burbank Airport where those people were killed trying to steal a plane at the height of quarantine. I can still remember the news taglines: *Terrorists shot at Burbank Airport!* Law enforcement lauded for keeping America safe. Had there been a reason besides escape? Had any of them been sick? The newsfeeds never bother with follow-up, so fast-paced and forward-moving.

After I slept off that long drive, the longest drive of my life, Jakob took me to a part of town that was all warehouses and office parks in shades of gray. We sat in the car, across the street from a building wrapped in security fencing, and told me that was it, the spot he was talking about, the one where we could get Lilac a body. There was no sign, the hedges clipped into rectangles, a guard at the entrance fiddling with his phone.

"Is this a Metis facility?"

"It's a chop shop," Jakob said, "spare parts, new bodies, repairs. For the ones who want to avoid Metis."

When I asked him how we would get inside, he smiled and told me not to worry about it, and all I could think of was Lilac in that sock hat, the wound she was hiding—how could she hide such a thing from me?

A couple days later, in the motel, Jakob showed me footage of its insides—the building we'd visited, the companions, rows and rows of bodies, the tables where they were repaired or broken down for parts, the human-size boxes like coffins waiting for shipment— and I didn't ask where he got it.

"Do you see one you like?" he asked. "For Lilac?" It was as if we were shopping at a store, bodies like clothes you could step into and out of.

I scanned them, pointed out the first one that was female and in the right age range, full face, long hair, soft of body. I turned away from her not because she wasn't attractive, but because she wasn't Lilac, not even close.

That night he took me out to dinner, an old Italian place, traditional, with a tiny waterfall trapped inside it. "Jakob!" the host called, coming out from behind his booth. They hugged and caught up while I stared at the signed photos of famous diners that hung on the walls until I found him—I found Jakob hanging there, frozen with that famous half-smile of his.

As the host led us to the table, I leaned into Jakob. "I thought you were worried about being noticed."

"Shh," he told me, "let me enjoy this tiny pleasure. It's the Valley, for Christ's sake!"

While a woman in a sparkling evening dress played a harp with the waterfall as backdrop, Jakob ordered me a bottle of red. Appetizers that he couldn't eat were brought to our table, and he told me things were going to work out. "Your Lilac is a special one."

"She is," I said, skeptical despite the wine, the whole bottle, I'm ashamed to say.

Later, curled up in the too-soft motel bed, his movie kept me company, the original in that series—how many times had I seen it? This time I fell in love with him a little, the way he held her, the companion he'd never be able to save, bawling when she died in his arms like it wasn't bad acting.

In the morning I woke hungover and vomited in the sink. I was washing up when I heard the knock at the door that connected our rooms. Jakob, his voice too loud: "I'm taking you to Hollywood!"

Traffic was awful, like nothing I'd seen before, knots of freeways converging into a city with no center. I could feel the rage pumping off the drivers, beating off their cars, over the sounds of their loud music and horn wails. In the distance were the white letters of the famous Hollywood sign, much smaller than they appear on-screen.

We pulled into a metered spot, on a quaint street with shops and cafés and a yoga studio.

"What are we doing?" I asked Jakob, too embarrassed to tell him I was hungry, dying for a bathroom, my head pounding. It felt silly complaining to a companion about the pains of the body, my poor choices. And I knew from Lilac that he could read me, smell the alcohol I was sloughing off like dead skin.

"Just checking on an old friend," he said, focused on the great bay window of the yoga studio, all those women braced on their arms like bridges. We sat there for a half hour before a woman emerged, long hair tied back in a loose braid, yoga mat strapped to her back.

I could see Jakob's eyes following her, and I asked him, "Who is that?"

"That's Greta Greene, one of our greatest living actresses."

I didn't like it, watching the woman without her knowing, as she paused to examine a shoe shop's window offerings.

"Hold on," Jakob said, out of the car before I could stop him, across the street, walking briskly to catch her as she unlocked a tiny silver convertible.

I could feel myself hoping she'd brush him off as he came up behind her, linking his arm in hers. She sprang away from him; then, seeing who he was, she threw her arms around his neck, Jakob grinning into her hair.

They talked a few minutes in that fevered way people talk when they haven't seen each other in ages. Laughing, smiling into faces, touching each other on the arm, the shoulder, the cheek, like are you real?

A kiss, on the lips? I couldn't tell from the car.

"What was that?" I asked Jakob as he slid back into the driver's seat.

"Dinner. We're having dinner tomorrow night."

"Is that wise?"

"No idea." I could see that he loved her, my heart reminded of Lilac, tucked into the nightstand of my motel room. But what I didn't know was whether this Greta loved him back, what would happen if she didn't.

I could hear Jakob humming through the thin walls of the Super 8 as he prepared for his date, or dinner, or whatever it was.

"Where are you going?" I called.

He pulled the door open, smelling of overgenerous cologne. "To her house. She's separated! And her child's with the ex tonight. I haven't been this excited in ages."

It seemed dangerous, his excitement, manic, so easily flicked over the edge.

"Does she know you're not—"

"I haven't decided whether to tell her."

"How can you not?"

He was humming again, at the mirror, saying, "It's good to see you," again, again; each time it was different, his delivery, like he was trying on different versions of himself.

It was seven when I woke, and I hadn't heard him come in. I knocked, and when he opened the door, I stopped myself from asking, how was it? I could see it in his face, the same kind of look the residents got after they'd lost a peer. Terrified, alone—those words never seemed to do justice to whatever it was they were experienc ing. Something outside words. A deep kind of grief.

"She's sober," he said.

I was careful with my response, one of the skills I'd acquired at Jedediah Smith, before that even, in the Sunset duplex where I lived with strangers who were family. "That's not bad, is it?"

"It was one of those atonement scenarios," he said, burying his head in his hands, pulling at his silver hair.

"Oh."

"She doesn't want me. She wants to start fresh. She's trying out celibacy!"

"Oh," I said again.

"Is that all you're going to say? *Oh, oh, oh?*" I had never seen him angry like this. He seemed a little off-kilter and I was afraid of him. Didn't know him, not really. Never had I felt so far from home. "The things I did to get here," he said, as if not to me.

"What did you do?" I asked him.

His eyes slid in my direction and I regretted the question, wishing I could suck it back inside me.

"It's over," he said, falling onto the bed dramatically. "I'm going into sleep mode."

What was there to say?

Back in my own room, I opened the nightstand, what was left of Lilac next to a Bible that appeared brand-new. Seated on the bed, I cracked its spine, flipping the pages for the smell, pressing my hands to them to remember.

For two days I didn't hear a sound from his room, and I thought of waking him. Thought better of it. I was just back from a sad attempt at a walk, winding roads until I was lost, on a street with no sidewalks, trampling the plants there to beautify this stretch of office parks and strip malls and condos—where were the trees? I was in a bad mood, a little sunburnt and dehydrated, when I heard the knock at the door that connected our rooms—her, the companion I'd picked out, dressed in Jakob's beige tracksuit, younger than she'd seemed on the screen, late teens? Too young for me, I thought, but that didn't make any sense, and I looked in those round, brown eyes for her, for an answer.

She sat me down on the bed, told me she was sorry she couldn't remember. That there was no use trying. Gone. They were gone, the last four years, everything since the moment Diana woke her in that body. I felt like dying when she put it that way, thinking of her body, the one I loved, every experience she'd had in it erased. He'd explained it all, she told me.

"Jakob?" I asked, but of course it was Jakob who'd stolen into my room, stolen her from the nightstand, stolen off without telling me, bringing her, this body, back.

"Yes," she said. But she was touched by what I'd done for her. Touched! She actually said that. I didn't mean to pull away, to turn small. She didn't recognize me; I didn't recognize her.

"We can try," she said, and I said okay, and she does try, to be kind, to shine her attention on me, but I can see the soft focus she gets when she's processing, not here, not entirely.

At night when I try to sleep, she's next door with Jakob. Sometimes I listen through the walls. Once I caught them laughing, thought to myself, there's a joke there, two companions laughing in a hotel room, and I turned and turned with the guilt until sunup. How could I make fun of her like that? Even if it was only in my head.

The other night we went out dancing, the three of us. Jakob led us down a vomit-scented alley, his silver hair hidden in a hoodie as we ducked into the back of a West Hollywood club. It was after two, the dancing drug-enhanced and convulsive, bodies oiled up in sweat. On the dance floor, I could feel the pull between them— Jakob and Lilac. Not sexual, but an inside joke, a shared look I didn't understand.

Before, it was us, just us. Now when she touches me, I turn cold. I slick over with sweat. I think: programming. I tell myself:

maybe it'll change. But there's no retracing our memories to finding before, there's no finding it again, not like this. Not with him,
Jakob, all, *Darling, could you give us a moment?* Or, *Oh, Cam, dear,
that is not what I meant.* Gabe knew he was trouble. I should have
listened! He says just a couple snips and he'll be free of his past,
totally free. "Travel," he says, and Lilac says yes, even when I tell her
I want to put down roots, to go home.

"Home?" she says, and I remember that she's forgotten our
years with Diana. The best years, huddled warm and safe in the
guest room, watching the neighbor's cat slink along the fence from
our bed, the tingle of Lilac's fingers tracing up and down my arm,
a tower of books that she would read to me. Funny thing: I liked it
best when she read Diana's textbooks, her pronunciation of words
like *infundibulum* and *lingual gyrus* and *optic chiasm* exquisite and
totally sexy. It didn't bother me then, her programming. I guess it
was part of why I fell in love with her. And it was easy to forget, so
warm and alive and next to me as she was.

Now I worry for her all the time. I ask, "What're his plans?"
and I can tell by the way her face slackens that she's processing. She
doesn't know me now, doesn't know how to read me save my body
signals. But I know her, waiting until she blinks and answers, a tell,
not the truth.

She says something about Jakob's former agent, a party, no big
deal, but I can feel it—whatever it is she's not telling me.

Often I picture that first night, riding on the back of her motorbike when we'd run off from Jedediah Smith. Too tired to continue,
worried I'd fall asleep, fall right off the back of Lilac's bike, over the
cliffs as we wound our way down the coast. So she found us a cove,
found us some sand warmer than the air. No blanket, I was freez-
ing, slept fitfully, maybe a few hours. She lay next to me awake, not

knowing how cold I was—she'd already forgotten what it felt like to be cold.

Maybe love is a matter of temperature. The wrong adjustment, and you're uncomfortable, too aware of your surroundings. The right one, and you're scissored on the bed, air like water.

I think of going home to San Francisco, but I'm low on credit. San Diego—that's as far as I can afford, farther still from home, but I can't go back to nowhere, and I'm not asking Lilac for help. It's hard enough telling her I have to leave. Just when I'm about to say it, she fixes her eyes on me and I see her in there, or maybe I want to, and I stay another day, another. At night, when Lilac's next door, I trace this room with my memory, naming each shade of bleak brown: *tree trunk*, *dry dirt*, *hot dog*. Each stain and watermark and pattern of mold becomes a friend, animated in the shadow lighting of the bedside lamp. I close my eyes, picture the redwoods. I can nearly feel their bark tickling my palms, and I tell myself again: Time to go.

GABE

Now that the guest room is empty, the doctor lets me sleep in there. Neither of us mentions the necklace I stole all those years ago, but I remember it—thin gold chain like thread, red stone circled in gold, my little glowing lion. When the late afternoon sun hit it, the stone burned so bright I had to hold it. For fun I check the dresser drawer where she used to keep it, but now that Cam and Lilac are gone, their stuff in garbage bags in the garage, the drawer is empty, mine to fill.

Sometimes I find a sock or an old dirty bra and I can tell by the smell whether it was Cam's or, by the lack of smell, if it was Lilac's. I wonder if they've made it to Los Angeles or if Jakob had other ideas. I thought Cam might screen us with an update, but weeks have passed and not a word.

Nat hasn't given me a lesson since we arrived a month ago—it's like he's avoiding me—so I draw more and more and start in with Anne Frank again.

It's the part where Anne and her sister, Margot, are writing letters back and forth about Peter and relationships and trust, and it's kind of funny because there the two sisters are, trapped together in the cramped Annex, breathing in the same old air—why can't they say what they feel?

Then Nat breezes into the house after being gone all day, without so much as an explanation, and I don't pester him—I don't say a word. I know how much he hates to idle, but it's nice, sleeping in a bed, having a room to myself, small enough that I can see all the corners even in the dark, with a door that squeak-warns me if it's opened.

One morning the doctor picks up my sketchbook from the kitchen table as I'm doing the dishes. "My goodness, Gabe." She pages through my drawings. "You've gotten quite good, haven't you?"

I show her sketches of Cam, Lilac, Nat, even the doctor herself.

She lets out a raspy laugh that shifts into a cough. "Do I look that old?"

"I was mad at you when I drew it."

Tapping the drawing, she rattles in a breath. "So you're not mad anymore?"

I stare down at my sketch, just lines really, somehow coming together to show the picture of her, but more so, I'm seeing now, the picture of myself.

It's nearly noon and I haven't seen Nat yet. Normally he's at the table fixed to the screen and drinking his third cup of coffee by the time I zombie in, rubbing crust from my eyes. I can't believe how well I sleep in a real bed.

But when I go out front to check on him, the van is gone. I don't think much of it until darkness falls and the doctor finds me watching out the window, Anne Frank in my lap. "Do you think something's happened to him?"

She eases onto the couch next to me. "I caught him fiddling around on my screen, doing Lord knows what with my data. I'm sorry, child, but he had to go." It is her soft voice today, her sorry voice. I remember it from the day she sent me away. "He was going to go anyway. You know that." She presses a folded piece of paper into my palm. "I found this in the mailbox."

Get enrolled in school. I'll be back to check on you. —N

I sit in the driveway crying, unrelenting, unbelieving. That's the problem. *I'll be back to check on you.* It's like he's trying to soften the blow, to make this all easier on me. But I refuse to be tricked again. He's left me, and he's gone.

I let the doctor lead me into the house and I lie down on the couch facing the cushions. She hovers for a while, cooks, brings me food. She tells me to eat, and when I don't, she hovers longer. I fall asleep, and when I wake, it's to the stale smell of the cushions, the room black. I go to the screen, bring it to life.

"Hello?" The voice doesn't match at all, so young. Why would the doctor select such a voice for herself?

"Do you know who this is?" I ask her.

"Don't be silly, Gabe. Where is she? I mean me."

"Asleep."

"So you sneaked on here, did you?"

"I did."

"You were always such a slippery fox. Why'd you want to talk to me?"

"I thought you traded me for Lilac. I hated you for the longest time."

"And now?"

"You're so old and rickety. I can't leave you. Even if you sent Nat away."

"He'll be back," she says.

"He promised he'd take me with him." The insides of me are too dry for tears. I feel like a desert, caked over and hardening. "What am I going to do?"

She laughs from inside her screen, and it sounds real, but not at all like the doctor. "You're thirteen now, aren't you?"

"Yup."

"My goodness. It's time you took school seriously."

I wipe snot on my sleeve, suck back the rest. "That's what Nat says."

"Well, he's right."

I want to hug her. I could go into the doctor's room, curl around her in bed, but I feel how the one on the screen is different, someone else entirely—how can that be?

"I love you, you know that?" she says. The original has never told me this. I don't know how to answer. My cheeks heat, my heart thumps extra hard. I think of my own mam, long gone, my Bee. Would I have wanted them like this? The same, but strangers too—that's what it is, something impossible.

"Would I want it?" I ask the doctor. Yes. Definitely. Yes.

MS. ESPERA

BEVERLY HILLS, CALIFORNIA

Scones and tea, sweetener. Windows fogged. It's nice being out—the clang and wash of milk steamed, orders called, conversations had, the laughter, so rich, almost sensory overload—especially after that abominable quarantine. I'd nearly died—my child not able to visit her own mother whenever she wanted. A police state. Fascism! It made me want to tear off my clothes, run into the street, show the world my ugly, wrinkled underbelly. I've always had urges like these. I grew up under the scrutiny of 18s, so I learned at a young age to control my flights of fancy.

Isla coils through the café door, unraveling a laboriously long scarf from her neck like a bandage. The host points her in my direction. We bat eyelashes hello, 18s wasping in the window, the hush of the café as they realize someone famous has come in, eyes turning in the direction of my daughter. She's not an actor—she doesn't have that kind of beauty—but she's Sydney's child, and the tabfeeds love to hover over the children of studio executives. It's excellent leverage, the clever ways they come up with to ruin the parents, turn them into slaves, feeding stories, never free, always a picture away from annihilation. Fortunately, Isla learned discretion from me. She's like a Renoir, always capturing the light.

Earlier today, I tried to catch my breath, sitting on the edge of the tub overflowing with water I couldn't turn off. Sweaty, heart racing, a tingling sensation in my extremities. I sneaked a look in the fogged mirror. My face, my neck, my hands, smooth like a starlet's, but the rest of me, pure Kubrick. On the screen was that awful trial, always streaming; how could you turn it off? The scientists who'd unleashed those illnesses didn't appear especially evil in their rumpled suits, with those faraway eyes. I tried to stand, slipping in the water, cracking my back on the lip of the tub. No blood, but a bruise, instantly purple, the whole side of my rump. The pain, I can hardly bear to sit.

Luckily I've taken something, just a half, I don't want to slur or lose focus—Isla's too smart for that.

She is saying something. "A new body, young, with skin, only the best. How does that sound?"

"Delightful."

"But it's expensive. I've asked Father—"

Pinpricks everywhere at the mention of Sydney. "You asked your father for what now?"

"I put out feelers, so to speak, nothing concrete."

The test. Isla's talking about the test, the oncologist telling us terminal, no treatment, too far gone. Yesterday? Was it yesterday? I can see his locked palms, Isla snapping out of her usual languid posture. "How could you have missed it? She's at the doctor every six fucking weeks!"

"Those were cosmetic procedures, with a surgeon. Your mother hasn't been in to see me in two years."

Isla twisted in her seat to face me, anger flaring her nostrils unattractively. "Mother!"

"Mother?" She has me by the elbow. The café. My scone. It's apricot, I believe, impenetrable with a fork. Sydney! I remember Sydney, the tests. The 18s are in the window, hovering near our faces, a mad hiving. Why did Isla pick this place? Trendy North Canon, so close to Wilshire—it's like she wanted a scene.

I funnel my mouth with my hand. "God, I'm ashamed."

"Don't be." Isla is unperturbed by their presence. She blows on her tea, takes a sip. "He knows it's not your idea, but Mother, would you listen? He's amenable. He doesn't want you to go. If he can help out, in any way—that's what he said."

"Of course he said that. He doesn't need that kind of guilt on his conscience. And Lord knows he has the credit." I married a man with business savvy, confidence, more than that, ego. I'd found it charming in the beginning, what a turn-on. He wasn't traditionally handsome, but I knew he'd use my family's wealth to build even more. And he would not cheat, he would never, there was a pre-nup, for crying out loud! My father had insisted. Plenty of suitors had come calling after me in the hopes of getting their hands on the Espera family fortune, amassed across seven generations and diversified into so many markets I don't know what we stand for anymore. I saw our brand name on a toothbrush the other day—a toothbrush! But Sydney did, cheat, I mean, the bastard, and prenup be damned, he went out on his own.

Just as the divorce papers were signed and my lawyer was telling me I should be relieved and I could hardly believe this had happened to me, Sydney abandoned the agency I'd helped him build, took the studio gig, took over the whole operation. That was what bothered me the most. He'd waited until we were divorced, papers signed, alimony settled, before he took the job we'd both been working toward, a significant bump in pay, and lifestyle, God, he can go anywhere now, and she's the one on his arm, the second wife, an aspiring model, ha! I watch the screen when I'm in the tub, squeezing the life out of my shampoo bottle. Meanwhile, Espera stock sinks lower and lower, my monthly dividend checks dwindling.

I take Isla by the hand. "But to be owned by some company, to be property."

"You'll be in my custody."

"I don't know, sweetheart. I want to say yes, but I'm afraid." It is hard to meet her gaze. Despite her gauntness, she has Sydney's large, serene eyes, and when she smiles, which she rarely does, thank God, she is his spitting image.

"Oh, Mother, I'm scared too! But if we want it to happen, we have to schedule it now, see? It's too risky, waiting until the end."

"So, when would you like me to die?"

"Stop it."

"Seriously, what day did you have in mind? I've got to prepare myself, don't I?"

"They have an opening next month."

Next month! I scream inside my head. But with Sydney's credit and position, it's no surprise we'd be scooted right to the top of the list. "What date, please?"

Isla shifts her Sydney eyes to the teacup she's clutching. "The twenty-seventh."

"Three weeks out. Not a lot of time to prepare, but if there's one thing I'm good for, it's putting together a party."

"You don't have to make a big to-do of it."

"Oh yes I do. There's no other way to go out. You have a party, say your goodbyes, then the next day, *poof*! You reappear in a new young body." Or so I've heard. I've never actually met a companion.

I'm sure there are plenty in Sydney's circle, but since the divorce I've rarely received an invitation to any social event worth putting on my face for. "How young do you think I should go? I was thinking twenty-six. Is that too young? I don't want you to feel strangely—"

"Mother, would you stop?"

"What is it, honey?"

"It's just—this is serious."

"You've given me three weeks. I've got to make some decisions."

Isla presses my hand to her sad, damp cheek, the 18s in a frenzy outside the window. I pat her hair—it's going to be all right. My nails are pewter, such a cold color. When I'm reborn, I'll wear red again.

In the evening I take something, a whole this time, and watch the screen from bed, propped up on a mountain of pillows, legs lost in satin sheets, searching for one mention of Isla and me at the café—so many 18s, such a dramatic scene! Only I can't find a trace of us, and I irritably call for Ria, my housekeeper, to bring me a slice of angel food cake, please, as I settle on my favorite tabfeed, the host's face so contoured she's positively feline. She swishes a hip, announces: "After days of speculation following footage of Hollywood heavyweight Lorna Banks leaving a Metis facility"—cut to wobbly 18 footage of the actress in a giant floppy hat and sunglasses scurrying into a waiting car—"the ageless beauty has come out as a companion."

"No!" I practically shout at the screen as it cuts to the studio gates, Sydney's studio, a mob of protesters, a strange mix of religious fundamentalists and fans, equally incensed. God, he must be furious; Lorna is one of their brightest stars.

He'd stolen her away from the agency when he left. I can picture his oily pitch: Why pay an agent's commission when we can guarantee you an endless stream of films? We had devised the plan together, in-house talent, no middlemen, knowing it would do major damage to the agency we'd built, maybe even kill it. Pipe dreams, I'd assumed. "We would never really do such a thing, would we?" I'd ask Sydney, and he'd pat my knee.

"Course not," he'd say.

I feel giddy, sick, starting to get that far-off pharmaceutical feeling.

Ria squeaks into the room in her orthopedic shoes, slides a plate of cake into my lap, glances up at the screen. Her jaw clicks shut like a wooden puppet's, a terrible habit she developed to keep from speaking.

"Spit it out, Ria."

She digs her wrecked hands into the folds of her apron. "I know her, is all."

"No, Ria. You don't know her. *I* know her." Or I did, anyway, back when I was Sydney's wife. I doubt she'd take my tea invitation now.

"Well, she ate here once, didn't she? Complimented my deviled eggs."

"And now she's going to upstage me, ruin my—" I stop short. I've not told Ria, not thought for a moment what it'll mean to her. Twenty-seven years she's been my housekeeper, a nanny to my Isla since birth. "Go on then, Ria."

As she squeaks out of the room, I pick up the slice of cake and devour it in a single bite.

I plan, ping Sydney with the details, and he's right back to me with a confirmation. I can feel it, how he wants me to know he's there for me. And I do. Till death do us part—it takes on all new meaning. He made a pact with me those years ago, and even though he broke it, in the end he's going to make certain he's there for me. It's lovely, touching even, but it doesn't reduce the anxiety I experience with each passing day. The only distraction is the planning.

Flowers, music, food and libations, a ceremony, the signing—that will come after, when we're alone. They say I can die in the comfort of my own suite. The doctor and his team will administer a drug cocktail that will make me sleepy. I'll drift off, my daughter, anyone I want can be there, and when I wake, I'll be at the Metis clinic in my new body, and I'll be their intellectual property.

I try not to focus on that, turning my attention instead to the ceremony—Sydney and me, us, in front of the gathering. I don't want to be stingy, not on a night like this, but I enjoy culling the guest list, decimating the names the new wife sends over, Sydney's old pals from the agency I helped build, hoping to bend his ear, to beg him to rethink his plan, and their serpentine spouses who would swallow me whole if they thought it might improve business, the studio's stars with their bad attitudes, the tendency to take over the night with their sobbing or their smashing or their naked tossing into the pool, especially that Jakob Sonne who showed up to the garden social I hosted to raise funds for Cedars' cancer kids program with his mess of an ex-girlfriend. She made such a scene, stoned out of her mind, yelling at Jakob, at anyone who dared make eye contact, that he was wrong, different, she kept shouting, *You're someone else, something else!* She'd passed out in the pool, the paramedics called, ruining my charity event. Sydney wrote a big check to Cedars as an apology, and never once did they ask me to host an event again. I want the right people, the right mood—no thieves of the spotlight, no jokers, absolutely no party crashers.

I'm screening with Sydney's head of security, walking swiftly down rugged Rosewood with one last shop to visit—it's raining heavily and everyone is running around all wide-eyed and unprepared. At least I've brought an umbrella, though it's positively useless in this downpour. Not like I have time to take a car over to West Hollywood again, the only place I can find those vintage cloth napkin squares I must have. The night—it has to be perfect, I'm telling security, no angry fans, no religious nuts, no trouble, and a girl is running in my direction, clumsily teetering until, oh no, what is she—shopping bags go sideways, a stab of pain in my leg, going down onto my knees, oh that hurts, and it's wet it's wet it's wet. I'm on my bottom in an inch of water and the girl is stooped down in my face. "I'm sorry. I can't believe I did that! Are you hurt?"

"I'm fine," I grumble, trying to stand. My dress is soaked, and she grabs hold of my arm, plucks me from the sidewalk like the molted casing of an aged insect. "My goodness, you're strong."

"I should be." She gathers my bags. "My body is engineered. The least I can do is help a lady collect herself in the rain, especially when I'm the fool who knocked her down."

"You're a companion."

"Indeed I am." She gives me an even line of a smile. Her face is in all ways normal, not pretty exactly, nothing to look at. Why would they make her plain? Still, she has youth on her side, and that alone is its own kind of beauty.

"What's it like?"

"I'd love to tell you, but the rain—I'm tolerant, but I don't like to tempt fate."

Feeling guilty, I suppose, for having soaked me, she offers to buy me a drink. "I'm meeting a friend here shortly," she says, and we tuck into the nearest bar. Seedy, a scent, not of the savory variety, a clientele leaving something to be desired. Evidence: the woman in a black dress, endless cleavage, legs bare and in need of a shave, head rested heavily on the counter—is she snoring?

I order two glasses of chardonnay the color of urine and we take a table, the companion slouching in her seat, legs crossed, foot swinging to some beat I can't hear.

"Are you a newer model? I expected you to be more—" I pause, choose my words carefully. "Rigid."

"I can feel this seat, did you know that? A lot of people don't. There are many common misperceptions about companions."

"Are you a plant?"

"I'm sorry?"

"My daughter—she wants me to do it. And I think she's worried I'll change my mind at the last minute. I mean, it's not like I don't understand—she doesn't want to lose her mother, but I—" I catch myself rambling. It's something I watch out for. I don't want to be *that* old woman. "What's it like? Do you feel like yourself? Do you feel alive?"

"Yes and no."

"What do you mean?"

"Yes, my body reacts to stimuli. I feel emotions too. In all ways, I feel alive. Then I remember I'm inside a machine. My emotions—they're all fabrications. Everything that's happening to me is actually happening to this machine I'm in, yet I feel it."

"Does it bother you?" It's hard to find the words; one never wants to offend a new friend. "Not being—a real person?" This feels wrong as it comes out, but she doesn't seem to mind. I suppose she's heard worse. Plenty of people have sour feelings where companions are concerned, especially the religious, who are extra fervent these days.

"Not anymore," the companion says. "Believe me, it did. I'm sure it's pretty traumatic for every single person, no matter what they say—giving up the body. But it's also liberating. My old self is dead, all my mistakes, my fears. What I do now, it makes me *me*."

I notice she's not drinking, then remember she cannot. How does one live without chardonnay?

"Tell me. Who leases you?"

"Her," she says, nodding in the direction of the scrumptious young wallflower hunching toward us. I see at once how hard she's trying to go unnoticed, hair swept back in a low ponytail, eyes tucked into a curtain of bangs, that loose bag of a dress. And yet, she is so young, skin like an uncooked noodle.

"Is she your—" What is the word they use these days?

"Lover?" The companion pats the seat next to her and the girl slips into it, casting eyes about the room, clearly a nervous creature. Introductions are made. The girl's name is Cam, from San Francisco.

"What is it you do?" I ask her.

"I'm a caretaker."

"And who do you care for?"

She laughs, and the companion laughs, and I realize I don't know her name. Too late to ask, but I remember that I'm dying, and I ask anyway.

"Lilac."

"Like the flower?"

"Like the pig." More laughter, a kiss, fingers disappearing into the folds of that unflattering dress. A whisper, a sniff—can a companion smell?

"The rain," Cam says.

Lilac peels Cam's hands from her cheeks. "I'm okay."

Cam says to me, "Nice to meet you," and swishes nervously back to the counter.

"Did I do something wrong?" I ask.

Lilac sighs—a companion sighing! It's really quite remarkable how lifelike she is. "Not you. Me."

"You're fighting?"

"Not exactly. But we aren't getting along either."

I know precisely what she means. To start a new relationship, to fall in love, out of love, it all sounds so exciting! "That's a shame. You make a nice couple." Then I get to thinking about sex and I can't stop myself from asking, "Is it—satisfying?"

"It can be." Lilac appears amused. Her expressions—they've done such a wondrous job. I would never know.

"I don't want to die. But what if they're wrong? I'm terrified of making the wrong decision."

"If you want, I could be there for you. I know what it's like. I'd be happy to support you."

"That's so nice. Thank you," I say, really meaning it. Now, for some reason, I can't imagine *not* seeing her at the party. "You know what? I'm going to take you up on your offer. Companion or not, you are too sweet." I pull out my phone and add her name to the guest list—I could use someone there who understands.

Outside, the rain has passed. We gather our coats, hug under the dripping awning, the air with that wondrous clean smell it only gets after a rare soak.

Despite Sydney's protests, and our daughter's, I've put off signing the papers until the night of; the ceremony won't be genuine other-wise. The new wife doesn't appreciate it, huffing in the corner, slugging back flutes of champagne, pretending this is not the best party known to man, the perfect balance of celebration and solemnity.

Sydney, bless him, has rented the top floor of the Beverly Tower, with its exquisite light show of a view, the trails of cars snaking the highways and I8s igniting the sky, my team of doctors in the adjacent suite, waiting until after the ceremony to kill me, how polite!

I've chosen white for the décor, to represent rebirth, the splash of candlelight spectrum playing on the walls, a sky full of projected stars spangling the roof. I'd prefer real, but cloud cover, unpredictable weather, this is better—a controlled climate, a secure space. Here, with this incredible spread of food, a full bar, surrounded by my closest friends, mingling with palm readers, receiving blessings from the Buddhist monks I rented for the night, I feel—a tray of drinks! I grab a flute of champagne, tip it back, draining it in two gulps. I shouldn't. I've taken a little something to help me through the night. The doctor suggested I not choose now of all times to stop, and I am nothing if not conscientious when it comes to doctors' orders. Someone takes the glass from me, slips a full one into my hand. I turn and see the companion.

"Lilac!" I kiss her smooth cheek, surprisingly warm. "You look positively luminescent." She's wearing a black pantsuit; her hair has been cut short and slicked down, lips painted red. Her skin is dewy, as if she's moisturized—I wonder if she can do that, how to achieve such an effect. I want to ask her, but later! "Is Cam with you?"

"Getting her palm read." Lilac's eyes are over my shoulder, surveying the room. "How are you feeling?" she asks.

"A little nervous, I can't lie. But I'm enjoying myself."

Oh, there's the reverend! Her kinky red hair is positively on fire in the candlelight spectrum. Beautiful—I want to tell her so, how wonderful it is that she's here.

"I have another event, you know," the reverend says. "Have you heard from him?"

Sydney. Always late—I should have planned it into the schedule! But that's a wife's job, and I'm no longer a wife.

After I've reassured the reverend and sent her off with a canapé, Lilac asks, "Where's the bathroom?"

I point, and she kisses me lightly on the cheek. "I'll come find you later. Enjoy this last night in your body."

I watch her go, wondering what she needs with a bathroom, feeling oddly slighted—I had expected her to be *my* companion for the night. Well, not everyone is cut out for the work. But me? I'll be the most excellent companion. Isla will lease me, and we'll be young together, like sisters. It'll be strange at first, but we'll get used to it. What choice do we have?

I steal another flute of champagne, smile, move around the room. If you move, people say hello, let you keep going, but if you stop, they worry you need company, don't want you to feel alone on a night like this. I move, circles, I'm doing circles, when Isla finds me. She's worn white, in tribute to me, my sweet child—I know how she hates the color, says it washes her right out. I pat her hair, twined into some elaborate knot, cup her cheek. She is embarrassed, no, about to cry, no, she is crying, and I'm holding her, my special girl. Over her shoulder, I see Jakob Sonne, that awful actor I'd banned from the party, from all parties, here now! After the Cedars incident, I hadn't just yelled at him; I'd annihilated him, blown him to bits, cursing his soft baby-boy looks, his sappy acting, his whole spoon-fed existence—what did he know about struggle with a face like that? Sydney had made sure our paths never crossed again, until today.

"One moment, dear," I say to Isla, and I'm marching over to

security when I spot Sydney barreling through the entrance in a glorious white suit, shirt stretched tight over his gut—I've never seen him so fat! What is that wife feeding him? Here she comes, stalking toward him in stilettos, and it could not be any better— some angry words, definitely arguing.

Isla is at my elbow. "Do you want something, Mother?"

"Maybe a bite to eat? I'm feeling a little light-headed."

Isla is gone, and I'm watching the best part—the wife is leaving!

Sydney swipes a palm across his receding hairline and sees me staring, gives me one of his boyish grins. Oh, I want to hug him! We come toward one another, and I wish I could slow it down, speed it up, all at once—how can that be? He has me by the arm, and I can feel his cheek next to mine, freshly shaved, zinging with cologne, for me, I want to sing, when the air goes out of the room, my ears exploding, off my feet.

A stinging pain in my hip, a tone in my ears, it holds the world back from me. I can't touch it, hands grasping, grasping, until fingers trace my arm, my shoulder, find my face. Cam.

"Is anything broken?"

"I don't think so." I'm surprised by my own shaky voice, so old. She eases me to sitting and I blink and gawk at the hole where the bathroom once was, my party reduced to rubble and smoke and moaning.

I hear the crack of fireworks. No, guns! And I see one of Sydney's guards go down—where are the others? That boy Jakob, he's holding my husband, my Sydney, a gun to his head, and I don't even mean to think it—he hasn't signed the papers! "No!" I shout.

"Quiet," Lilac hisses, crouching at Cam's side, but I can feel Jakob's cool screen-ready gaze turn on me.

"I remember you. The wife." He gives me that greasy half-grin he's famous for. *Ex-wife*, I want to remind him, but think better of it. "Do you know what your husband did to me?"

"Did to you? Sydney made you a star."

He lifts his gun and I hear the pop.

On my back, ears ringing, suddenly so very wet. Oh God, have I had an accident? Too long, I've waited too long! That is what I'm thinking as I touch my stomach, my palm dripping red.

"Why'd you do that?" Cam shouts.

Sydney struggles to his feet, and he's got the boy by the arms now, for me! He's doing this for me! Then the gun goes off a second time.

"Sydney," I call. Only it's not Sydney who falls but Jakob, crumpling onto the floor, and Sydney's running, not toward the door, but to me. I sit forward despite the blazing pain, arms out, calling for him. Lilac rises next to me, lifts a gun. *Pop-pop*. Sydney bends sideways, and I'm screaming, and Cam's got me by the neck now. "We've got to stay calm," she says into my ear. "Be cool."

Be cool, I'm thinking, ready to shriek, Sydney slumped on his side. "You shot him!"

Lilac ignores me, telling Cam, "Get it," her voice desperate, and Cam lets me loose, unsteady on her feet, kneeling down next to Jakob, digging in his hair—is she crying? She pulls a slender silver box from the back of his head. A companion! Cam lifts her eyes, glaring at Lilac, her face dirt- and tear-streaked, hateful, and I know that look, the end, nothing more between them.

"Where are the doctors?" Lilac asks me.

"You can't," Cam says.

"He deserves it more than she does." And I realize Lilac's talking about me, my body.

"We're not doing that," Cam says firmly. She kneels over me, hand to my stomach. "It's okay. The doctors—they can upload you. We have to hurry."

"Help me," she says to Lilac, who's standing over me, who's still holding that gun. Lilac sighs and bends at her knees, lifts me so easily. The pain—I let out a shriek—and she eases me back down.

"Leave me be," I tell them. "It doesn't matter anyway. He never signed."

Cam leans down close, cupping my face. "Where's the contract?"

"With the reverend."

They leave me on the floor as they rummage. I hear a groan, Sydney, and I lift my head, watch him strangle out a breath, erupting blood.

"Stop that," I call to him, unable to move, my legs no longer listening.

His head lolls to the side and he gives me a lazy red smile.

"Oh, Sydney, you were such a lousy husband, but I loved you. I love you still."

He raises a hand, lips moving. "Sign."

"Found it," Lilac calls, the reverend's tablet remarkably intact. She brings it to Sydney, and he loops in his signature, sends. He tries to say something but he's choking, sputtering red, and I wish I could hold him despite all he's done, but my body, I can feel now what they've all been going on about—*vessel* is the popular term these days. I've got to jump ship.

That's when I see my daughter, Isla, laid out in white. Eyes fastened on the ceiling and glossy, and I know it in my sick bleeding stomach, dead, my Isla, nonononono, it is not true, I can make it not true. Where are those doctors? Upload her now! I am shouting, "Nownownow! Sydney!" But I can see it in his stillness—he's gone too.

Lilac says, "The contract—it's for you. Metis won't release the body otherwise."

I try to raise my fists, to hit her, mash her machine face, but my arms—they don't listen.

The companion hoists me into the air, bursting into my suite, the doctors' scared faces, saying something I can't hear—I can't hear! I shake my head. No, not yet, no.

ONE YEAR SINCE QUARANTINE ENDED

ROLLY

The woods were a place we went, Andy and me, when the smell was too much, the roasting plastic and hair stink of slaughter day. It stuck to you far into the forest, through the curled sea horses of giant ferns, around the thick puzzled trunks of the redwoods, over "the bog," we called it, a muddy creek bed dotted with fresh bear tracks that wound its way to the river. The smell—it followed—and I followed Andy, squelching loudly in the mud and not at all concerned about running into a bear. I'd tried to warn him they were dangerous, but all his books said otherwise. He thought they were fuzzy and lovable and fond of flowers and little boys. If we ever ran into one, Andy would probably try to give it a hug.

We didn't get far before we saw the brown coasting in like clockwork—we could count on it, just as we could sunup. Fires burned east of us, in the Shasta and Six Rivers and Klamath forests. It seemed like they could go on forever—as one fire went out, another blazed new. The smoke that blew our way usually came in faint gusts or a gentle brown haze, but sometimes it would get heavy and thick and could turn to soup quickly.

With each step through the bog, I felt a sucking sensation, pulling me earthward to the inside bits, the under-the-surface place. I wondered how far you'd have to go to hit liquid. I knew from school it was burning magma below us, but the surface was cool, thick mud, and oh crap, Andy was crying.

"What happened?"

A boot. He'd lost one of his boots in the mud, and the smoke was thick now, wisping past us. Head back, he let out a hopeless cry. We both knew Pa would be upset. Deliveries to our far-off address were expensive.

I put a mask over his nose and mouth, my own, told him to stay put. Ducked low to the ground, I traced the mud with my hands, moving in growing circles around him.

I was thirteen by the time Ma got pregnant with Andy, our miracle baby. I'd assumed they'd given up; no one had talked about babies in years. But suddenly she was pregnant, and I had the feeling it wasn't so sudden, that behind the thick curtain my parents cast between us had existed some great drama, with many trials, and I, on the other side, had gone totally unaware. When the baby came, I was in the delivery room despite the nurses' concerns about what the experience might do to a teenage boy. Ma was old for a pregnant woman, labeled "at risk," and she knew she'd need me, that I needed to know from the very start just what it was we were getting ourselves into, and I saw it—the pain, Ma torn apart from the inside, all for this screaming red mush of a creature they put into my arms. It was mine, a miracle, and terrible too, a terror, all that crying. Pa had the farm to run, Ma would sleep for hours at a time, and it was my job to make sure Andy didn't wake her. She was so tired, her belly bloated, wrists like twigs, gone before Andy could sit up on his own.

Finally I stumbled on the boot half-sunk in the mud, only when I turned to show Andy all I saw was brown. I broke out in a slick sweat, calling for him, pawing at the smoke, following his cries.

The way Ma told it, I was my own version of a miracle. They flew all the way to Senegal to fetch me after my birth mother passed. This was when such a thing was affordable for a middle-class farmer and his wife (though I learned much later that they took out a third mortgage on the farm to pay for the trip and transaction).

It wasn't until the smoke thinned that I found Andy, and ugh, he'd crapped his pants. I didn't shame him—he was only three and a half. We removed his underwear and buried the accident in the bog with a stick, and I cleaned him with a trio of leaves. He liked that part, wriggling his bottom at me, *nah-nah-nah-nah*ing. I spanked him good and he was crying again, but he had no idea how worried I'd been, and I told him so and he cried harder. Then I said I was sorry to get him to stop, and really I was sorry—I hated to make him cry. I plucked him out of the mud and delivered him to the far side of the bog.

When Ma was alive, she made sure I stayed in touch with my blood relatives, especially my older brother. But at seventeen, I was no longer cute, hamming for the screen. Their connection was weak, our conversation stilted and spotty. My brother often made an excuse to step away while one of the cousins told me about life in cramped Thiès, where they'd gone when their home in the Saloum Delta went under in the flood, or asked me questions about life in the US of A. I could tell my descriptions of farm life were not awe-inspiring. We talked less and less, and I felt it, how easy it was to lose people, Andy especially, always getting into mischief. He liked to climb. Luckily redwoods were impossible. He had to make do with fallen trunks, hopping rocks on the edge of the river roaring by. Once we saw a pair of kayakers wearing masks glide past us on the water. They waved their oars hello, or maybe to tell us to get back, hard to say, but Andy nearly jumped in the water after them, he so craved human connection.

We were headed back toward the house, Andy just starting to get over his fit, when I saw something moving in the mud. At first I thought it was a frog or a lizard, but then its little wings flapped open and it fell over onto its side, too covered in mud to steady itself. Andy saw it too, yelping and running. He was out of my reach, and I shouted at him not to touch it. Amazingly, he listened, stopping short, dropping to his knees to inspect it.

We brought it home, the baby bird, and got an old shoebox, filled it with shredded toilet paper. Then we brought Ma's droopy flower-shaped lamp into our bedroom, removed its shade, and placed the baby bird under its warm, bright light. She squinted and squawked at us and we agreed she was a girl, so delicate. We named her Winifred for our great-great-grandmother who'd bought this land more than a hundred years ago. It had once been a grand farm, organic before there was organic, produce grown with love. In our farm's heyday, I'd go with Pa on deliveries clear down to Mendocino. We'd leave before sunup and Pa would let me doze until we were coasting down the One and the sky was the perfect many shades and he'd wake me and say, "Would you look at that?"

I washed my hands at the kitchen sink and reheated the venison stew, set the table. Andy was singing a song to himself from beneath his chair when we heard Pa call from out back, "Help me with this, would you, Rolly?"

"Stay inside," I told Andy.

The companion was struggling on the conveyor belt. It was a young adult model, female, with loads of hair.

Pa had managed to get its legs in the metal clamps, but it was sitting up, arms swinging wildly, trying to free itself.

"Turn it off, Pa."

He raked a hand through his thinning hair. He was gaunt, cheekbones like mountain ridges, eyes like caverns. Sleep—he needed to sleep. "Don't you think I tried that? The damn thing's broken."

It was babbling, no, speaking another language—was it Russian? As I approached, it lunged for me—God, they were fast—seizing me by my shirt. We were staring at each other and its eyes, they didn't look like a child's eyes, and I wanted to ask, how old are you in there?

Pa thwacked its shoulder with a hammer, and it squealed a machine frequency, huddling small on the conveyor belt.

"Take its arms," Pa said, and I did, shushing it the way he'd taught me, into its ear, like the inner workings of a woman's womb. Pa did a lot of shushing on the way to slaughter. This one had a blistered face—it was one of the main reasons they were disposed of. The skin, it started to deteriorate, just a blemish at first, then a sore. It didn't matter how close you were to a companion, you wouldn't want it around once its face had started to fester. Lots of people paid for a clean reboot, moving a consciousness to another body, but it was expensive, much more than a replacement. Whatever they decided, the bodies came here. Usually they were powered off, drained of battery, but occasionally we got a livewire, one that couldn't be switched off, like this one here.

It was still swinging its arms wildly, and no matter how I tried, I couldn't get them into the clamps. Anger thumped hot everywhere, and I lunged for its wrist, grabbed hold of it, pressing into the seizing spot. It flapped like a suffocating fish for a full minute, and when it was spent, I eased its arms into the clamps, making the mistake of meeting its eyes. It pleaded to me in what sounded like Russian, and I couldn't understand a word.

"I know," I told it, "it's going to be fine," Andy curling around my leg to gawk—he never listened. I turned my back on the companion and plucked him up. He fought me some, crying and screaming, wanting to watch as it was carried into the chamber.

We incinerated at the beginning of the month, but I could see by the gathering of compact boxes waiting at the top of the ramp for pickup that we'd hit our carbon cap. When that happened, the machine switched automatically to compact mode. I knew this because shortly after my sixteenth birthday, Metis trained me to do the job in case Pa ever needed a sub, though he'd never once taken a sick day.

From the kitchen, we heard the scream as the machine compressed the companion. It would be barged with the others, buried somewhere, forgotten.

"Well, that was something," Pa said as he washed his hands at the kitchen sink. He always liked the livewires, more action, more responsibility. I think it made him feel important. I had an itch to say something, but he was in a rare good mood, so I decided to enjoy it. Even Andy seemed to catch on, giving up his tantrum and climbing into his chair at Pa's elbow.

Pa didn't believe in prayer, though he liked for us to take a moment to silently appreciate our bounty. It was an old farmers' ritual, the best way to ensure a good harvest, he'd told me once, long before quarantine killed our farm, before the virus killed many of our patrons, before Metis figured out how to upload our dead and lease them back to us. Pa gave us a nod. Then we dug in.

Pa barely touched his stew, guzzling ale. "Did you do your schoolwork?" he asked me.

"Yes." Andy said it with me, my echo.

"Your chores?"

"Yes," we said again.

"Good."

I spooned food into Andy's mouth. Otherwise he'd forget to eat, humming and bouncing in his seat, doing silly dances to make us smile. Pa poured me some ale, laughing when I hiccuped. Andy never once mentioned Winifred, which was good because I was pretty sure Pa wouldn't let us keep her. He'd have something to say about birds as disease carriers, *you can't be too careful these days*. Besides, it was a good meal—I didn't want to wreck it. We were all happy.

After dinner Pa went back to work, or so he said—I didn't hear the machine. He was probably digging into his shed for another bottle of ale, drinking his mind soggy, prepping for blackout sleep. I tried to feel sorry for him instead of angry. I mean, it wasn't his fault they'd shut down the farmers markets, restricted travel. We'd had no choice but to let our crops die, all save what we needed to live. Pa argued on the screen a lot and sold off pieces of our property. That's when he was approached by Metis. Until quarantine was lifted, they needed a local disposal facility for their Crescent City Companion Center. They wanted to buy our remaining land outright, but Pa said he'd only agree as long as we could keep the house and our few remaining acres of forest, and they hired him to run it.

At first, it wasn't very time-consuming. "A new product, well conceived," Pa said, "designed to last." We'd get maybe one shipment every couple weeks, and it'd take Pa a few hours of work to get through it. "Easiest job I've ever had," he'd say, smacking his hands together. "Now what?"

We'd play card games and watch old movies and go into the forest with Pa's rifle to hunt deer, and for a while there it was just fine.

Until the defects started popping up, first-gens replaced by newer models, more advanced, more human. The work got to Pa, shipments coming in regularly, more than he could handle. He got accustomed to working long days, he got quiet and drunk, and we were alone again, Andy and me.

Once Andy was asleep in his pen, I started in on my homework. I'd lied to Pa, sure, but it was a small lie. I completed my lessons on the screen and, for kicks, checked to see if I could access a newsfeed. Nope, a parental control warning flashed across the screen. All Pa let me see were the school feeds; he said everything else was filth and violence.

I washed the dishes, set the laundry going, and went out into the yard to hunt worms. Winifred needed to eat.

In the morning, the worms were still there, limp and shriveled, and Winifred wasn't moving. Andy was snoring in his pen, so I took her out back where we had a whole cemetery, four generations of dead, and dug her a grave. When I came into our room, Andy was standing over the shoebox, sucking on his pacifier—no matter what I tried, I couldn't get him to give it up. Everything I read said he was developmentally delayed, but Pa told me not to worry—*Andy lost his ma, he's got no friends, what do you expect?*

Andy jabbed a finger at the empty box.

"She's gone," he said between sucks. Then his face crumpled and he was crying. It was not a weak cry, not one he would give up on easily. It was a real and good one, so I offered him the only thing I knew would make him feel better: an adventure.

I watered and weeded our garden, and Andy waited, wearing his boots. His mind was set—we were going back to the bog. I knew what he was thinking—we'd find another baby bird, as if they were falling from the sky. I wanted him to enjoy this fantasy. Soon he'd start school, and like me he'd have daily screen sessions, homework, placements, and evals.

We found new bear tracks in the mud, a sow and cub, maybe two. Resistant to our diseases and appreciative of the quarantine, the bears were coming back, overtaking our shuttered towns, eating up our refuge. Pa said they were a nuisance, a danger; if we were to see one, we should turn around, head home straightaway. But Andy, he was so happy here—laughing and sinking and sucking himself out of the mud.

I made like a monster and chased Andy screaming into the trees. Once we were free of the mud, he was fast and got ahead of me. I spotted his boots abandoned on the rocky beach of the river, and I scooped them up, calling for him over the water's roar.

I found him on the rocks, pointing and squealing. "It's better! It's a pa!"

As I drew closer, I could see that it was indeed a pa, a man lying facedown on the rocks. Dead? I went to Andy, plucking him up, as he kicked and whined about his new friend. The man opened his eyes and shot a hand out, grabbing me by the ankle.

I was falling, Andy falling, when the man let me loose and I righted myself on the rocks, dropping Andy onto his knees.

"You gave me a start." The man wobbled to standing.

"This is *our* land you're on," I told him. We wore masks at our necks in case of a brownout, and I bent to fix Andy's over his mouth and nose, to slip on my own.

"How far am I from Oregon?"

"Another twenty miles if you head due north."

Without so much as asking me, Andy handed the man our canteen. I wanted to scream, *Germs!* But the man had it to his lips, drinking deeply. We'd have to sterilize it now. Thank goodness I had on my gloves. I snatched the canteen back and whisked it into my bag.

The man dug a hand through his patchy beard. He wore jeans and running shoes, a slick black jacket, though I could tell by his oily skin and the frayed, filthy neck of his T-shirt that it'd been a while since he'd showered.

"Where are your parents?" he asked.

"Ma is dead, dead, dead," Andy screeched in his terrible singing voice. He didn't know to miss her, but it made me angry, and I took hold of his wrist, squeezed it good.

"Our pa is at the farm working." I pointed in the direction. "Not far. He can hear us if we shout."

"Would he be willing to feed me, do you think?"

"I don't know. How about you stay here and we'll go ask."

The man picked up his pack, hefted it onto his shoulder. I could see by the way he sagged under the weight he was tired of carrying it. "How 'bout I join you," he said, "what with that coming in." He pointed at the wall of brown blowing in from the east. I knew Pa would be angry with me for bringing back a stranger, but what else could I do? Fight him off?

As we trudged toward home, the man asked, "What's he to you?"

"My brother."

"So you were adopted."

"Why do you assume I'm the adopted one? Why not Andy?"

The man turned to watch Andy pluck up a slug and pretend to lick it. "My dad never wanted me, so I've always been kind of jealous of adopted kids."

"Why?"

"They got picked."

Pa was out front, watching a Metis van drive off. I expected him to freak out. Instead, he asked calmly, "Who's this?"

I told him about running into the man at the river. "On our land," I added, to see if he'd say anything about that.

But he wasn't angry. He didn't bother with a mask, sticking out a bony hand, not even wearing gloves. The man took it, introducing himself as James.

"Come on," Pa said. "You look like you could use a meal."

While Andy showed James his rock collection in the living room, Pa and I went into the kitchen to prepare dinner. Venison stew. Again.

"If he's a carrier," Pa said in a low voice, "we'll all know soon enough. No sense in being rude. Plus, aren't you curious? We haven't had a guest in a long while."

I could hear the tinkle of Ma's music box from the living room, and I stuck my head out of the kitchen to get eyes on Andy. He was dancing, James spinning the crank, our ma's music coming out of the tiny gilded box.

James ate his first bowl of stew in under a minute, and I brought him a second, a third.

"Where you coming from?" Pa asked.

"I was shelving groceries in Crescent City for a time. Before that I worked at an elderly care facility."

"Is that old Jedediah Smith?"

"That's right." The man's eyes slid up Pa. I tried not to stare at his fingernails with their dark moons of dirt. "You work for Metis?"

"How'd you know?"

"Saw the van leaving."

Pa explained what he did, only he made it sound a lot more interesting. "I do what I can to make sure their passing is calm and, if possible, ignorant. Better they not know, less suffering." This sounded wrong to me, given the livewire we had last night, struggling and burning to the touch, she was so revved up. I'd seen something in Pa, and only now as I watched him offer James some ale did I understand: he liked his job—he was proud even.

Pa leaned back in his chair, patted his narrow chest, already a little drunk. "Where you headed?" he asked James.

"I have a connection in Eugene. I'm hoping to get a job, whatever he can hook me up with."

"Sounds pretty loose," Pa said, and I could feel a speech coming, so I asked, "What's it like? Out there, I mean."

James smiled. He had nice teeth. I thought maybe he was pretty young under that beard, not much older than me. "Mostly trees. I don't see too many people even now that quarantine's lifted."

"Lifted?" I bigged my eyes at Andy, and even though he didn't really know or care about quarantine, he bigged his eyes back at me.

"About a year ago. You didn't hear?"

I looked to Pa. "Do we got any dessert?" he asked me.

We didn't, but he made me follow him into the kitchen anyway. "You didn't tell me," I started, my heart stuttering, hardly able to breathe.

"What difference does it make?"

"We could leave, visit town, go back to farming!"

"Not with the acreage we got."

"Sure, we'd be small, but—"

"We've got a good thing going here." He headed for the back door, so skinny he'd had to pound an extra hole through his belt to keep his pants up. Pa called for James to find him out back, and I listened long enough to hear James ask where the closest town was.

"Fort Dick's a few miles west of here. Not much of a town. What do you need?"

"Just a place to crash for the night."

A place to crash—he was lying! A man that dirty wasn't going to get a room in a hotel. He was a grifter—I was sure of it—and Pa was the one who'd told me to watch out for grifters. But Pa wouldn't hear of James wasting credit on a hotel, and I was so angry I nearly flung open the door and threw him from our stoop. Hell, I wanted to throw Pa off too. They were both liars.

I went into Pa's closet and got his handgun and tucked it under my pillow. I tried to stay awake, Andy asleep in the pen he'd grown too big for.

Maybe I slept some. It felt like waking when I heard the *thunk* from downstairs.

I got Pa's gun from under my pillow and took the stairs in my socks, another *thunk*, tiptoeing through the kitchen. Pa was struggling with James, hands around his neck. They fell onto the coffee table, Pa on top, gripping James by the neck, choking him. James's hands fumbled along the floor, fingers wrapping around one of Andy's rocks. He slammed it against Pa's temple while I watched as if I weren't really there, floating like some useless apparition.

"Ah, shit," James said, peeling himself out from under Pa, and I couldn't move, couldn't say a word. James hadn't seen me, and it was then that I remembered the gun in my hand. I raised the thing, cocked it, my ears hot and thumping blood.

James turned with a start. "Jesus," he said when he saw me, the gun.

"Get away from him."

James lifted his hands. I kept the gun trained on him as I checked Pa's neck for a pulse, his wrist, put my ear to his chest.

"You killed him." I said it, a sweaty sick feeling coming over me. Then I sucked in air, sucking it back inside just as I had losing Ma and getting trapped here and finding out Pa was a liar.

"Did I?" James fretted the dingy sleeve of his shirt. Sticking out of his jacket pocket was Ma's gilded music maker.

I'm not certain I meant to pull the trigger. But the *crack* awakened Andy. I heard his cries from the bedroom.

I dropped the gun, stood over James, listened for his breathing, a stain forming on Ma's rug. *She's gonna be so mad!* Then I remembered with fresh pain that she was gone. Above me Andy wailed, and I stood there longer, taking it in, what I'd done—I don't know how long.

The wailing, Andy—I hiked up the stairs and scooped him up. "Just a pot falling to the floor," I said, "nothing to fret about." I rocked him until he was asleep, nestled him into his pen. He held tight to my hand as he sucked on his pacifier. I could see his open mouth through the clear latex, his little tongue pulsing even as he slept.

In the living room, James lay next to Pa on the floor. I knew why Pa had been in such a rage. The music maker was the only sound we had left of Ma's. We had pictures, sure, and things, but sound? That was it, the music maker with its twinkle song I don't know the name of. I claimed it from James's jacket pocket.

Pa—I couldn't look at him even when it occurred to me that I never would again. No time to waste, we never knew when a delivery might come, and I was afraid Andy would wake, afraid of what would happen if I stopped, if I'd ever be able to finish. It was like I was erasing it all, Pa, rolling him in a bedsheet and hoisting him over my shoulder. He was surprisingly light, mostly bones, smaller now than me.

I carried him out back to our cemetery. There was a space next to Ma for him and space for Andy and me still. The earth was moist and easy to move. I dug deep, not wanting to have to do it again, heaving dirt in an evening mist, in an even rhythm, turning myself into a machine.

I had no idea how long I'd been out there. Staring up at the steep sides of the hole I'd dug, at my pa wrapped in a sheet, a stomach knot twisted me from the inside. I tucked small and quaked and waited for it to pass. When it did, I climbed out, barely able to get a grip on the soft earth.

Pa's body fell into the hole facedown, and I couldn't bear that, so I kicked the shovel aside and hopped in. It was raining good by then, and the ground sank around my feet, a suction sound. I got a panic feeling, kicking my feet loose, trying to stay on top of the mud.

A cry. Was it Andy? I hopped for the edge, tugging at the grass, and I saw it, a bear cub running in the rain, running toward me. I fell back onto Pa, the mud, crouching in the corner. The cry again, closer, definitely not Andy. The mother—she was chasing.

The cub bonked and squealed into the grave, falling in on its back, the blow softened by Pa. It lay there stunned; then it lifted its head and bellowed at the opening. I didn't move, but it sensed me, lowering its head and staring at me in my corner. I raised a palm like *don't hurt me* and it made a slow gurgle like a growl, but it was so small, no bigger than an oversize puppy, and I could see it was distressed, so I said in a high-pitched baby voice, "It's okay, it's okay," stretching my hand out for it to sniff. It lurched up onto its hind legs, pawing the side of the grave, raining mud, Pa disappearing now in the dirt.

The great mother bear was braced on the edge of the grave. I huddled and cried, and the cub pawed at the wall and cried, and the sow cried from above, and I worried that all the crying would wake Andy, that he would come.

The sow could easily have climbed in, rescued her cub, slashed me to bits, but she didn't, howling from the grave's edge, whisking a paw in our direction. I got on my knees and crawled over Pa to the cub all slow-like. "It's okay," I said in my calmest voice, making a shushing sound like I did for the companions headed to slaughter, and the cub cowered, letting me come up next to it, rub against its side. It seemed to like that, nestling into me. "I'm going to hold you," I said, and I lifted it into my arms, gentle, and the mother bear was really bellowing now and I could hear the other cubs crying behind her, all tired and wanting out of the rain. I said, "I'm going to raise you up now, stay still," and I raised it up and it stayed still, the sow pulling her cub up by its cowl with her teeth. I expected something, I don't know, a thank-you or a little help, but they were gone and it was raining and Andy was alone in the house with a dead man.

I raced inside, up the stairs. Remarkably, Andy was asleep in his pen. I was covered in dirt, making a mess of the carpet. It occurred to me that I could do anything now, anything at all, no parent to tell me not to. The farm—what was left of it—was mine.

I threw up in the toilet; then I took care of James.

It was the first of the month, our carbon meter reset. I laid his body on the conveyor belt, not bothering with the arm and leg clamps, and I fed him to the machine, watched him burn.

I'd be eighteen in six months. Could I pretend Pa was alive long enough to avoid foster care, being separated from Andy, to become his legal guardian? I didn't have to pretend with Metis. They wouldn't care that my pa was ill, and I was well over sixteen, old enough to take this post. Andy would be alone most of the time. He'd have to settle for a dog.

The other option was to run. I thought briefly about it, Andy and me, but to where, and with what credit? Pa had some, but we couldn't access his account without him. We were screwed.

In the months that followed, I worked as Pa's substitute, feeding the companions to the machine. I told Metis Pa was ill, undergoing treatment, and would be out for some months. They didn't bat an eye, and I did the work, accumulating credit into my own account, using that for groceries and bills, but it was nowhere near enough for the mortgage. I repeated the story to the bank's screen representative and assured her I'd catch up on the next cycle. Then I asked for an extension. Two weeks, she gave me. We'd had the farm for four generations, no, five, I reminded myself, and the bank was giving us two weeks.

Andy was back to playing and singing, and I wondered where it went, his grief. He hadn't known Ma, not really, so he'd never really lost her. Pa wasn't around much, but he'd loved Andy, and there was a hole there now, a hole I explained with a story, Pa missed Ma so much he went on ahead to find her. "To where?" Andy asked.

"To that special place. Where we all get to be together," I lied to him.

"Forever?" Andy asked.

"Forever," I said, though I didn't believe a word of it. I understood then why parents teach their kids to believe in heaven—how do you tell a kid his pa is gone? Never coming back.

I looked for it—the hole—as he napped in his pen, face smashed against the mesh siding. Then I went out back to the shed and dug up a bottle of Pa's ale. It tasted like old mud-water, but I gagged down enough to make my body sort of hover, for the world to take on a plastic sheen.

On a Sunday, I took Andy to Fort Dick and got him an Australian shepherd, two years old, already trained, with all the energy required to keep Andy entertained. He seemed happy playing with Pit Bull, the name he'd given his dog, which came from who knows where—one of his books? Some tale Pa told him? He'd recently begun to talk more, stringing words together in the strangest ways, and I wondered where they came from, those ideas of his, naked alien party and crash dancing and an Australian shepherd named Pit Bull.

For a while there life fell into an even rhythm, waking at four, disposing for three hours. When I came in at seven, Andy was already at the table eating his cereal. He seemed to like the independence, getting his own breakfast—it made him feel like a big boy. He did school for a few hours in the morning, and I tended to our garden, checked our meat rations. We had a few rainbow trout in the freezer from the last fishing trip, but we'd be out soon. Andy would want to go hunting. I didn't know if I could do it—hold a gun again.

Then we napped together. This was the best part of the day. All of us, Pit Bull included, snoring in the bunks I built, a sweaty dark sleep. I couldn't bring myself to set foot in Pa's room. And Andy stayed out of there too.

In the afternoons, I would run the machine while Andy and Pit Bull wandered the yard. I made Andy promise he would stay out of the woods, but that didn't make leaving him alone any easier.

I was asleep in the top bunk when I heard Pit Bull stir and whine. I rolled onto my side and peered down to see him sitting up in bed, ears perked. Then I heard it too, something out back. Though Metis deliveries sometimes came at odd hours, it was the middle of the night—it couldn't be them.

I crept into Pa's room, sneezing with the dust, and retrieved the gun from a shoebox on the high shelf of his closet, already trembling, thinking about James. I hadn't been able to shake the feeling that someone would show up and take Andy from me, take me too. But whoever that was riffling through our latest delivery was not here for Andy and me. She was small, hard to spot amid the pile of bodies. I raised my gun and told her, "Don't move."

She startled up from the pile. "I was planning to trade for it."

"Sure you were."

"Seriously. I was going to leave one in its place. A body for a body."

"This is our land. You got no right—"

The girl raised her hands. I could tell she was a companion—I'd seen enough to know them on sight. "I'm sorry about that. I've been in a bit of a panic. My friend"—she pointed at the van—"is without a working body. We're headed north, far from here. If it's a matter of credit . . ."

I knew she was playing me—plenty of companions had tried to work me for their freedom—and I didn't mean to perk at the mention of credit, but the bank had given me two weeks to come up with the mortgage payment, and here was this companion offering. How could I say no?

Most of them were in pretty rough shape—festered faces, missing limbs—but she found one, a child who seemed more or less intact. Why had it been abandoned? Perhaps its flaw was not obvious to the human eye.

She cracked a faint smile, drew it back. "This'll have to do."

After she checked the child companion's battery level, she took out its rectangular brain and tossed it to the ground, pulled another brain from her jacket pocket.

"Who's that?" I asked.

"My friend."

"What happened to it?"

She gave me a cold, unhappy smile. "*He* was shot."

She slid the brain into place at the back of the child companion's head. Then she rearranged the long black braid and powered the companion on. I couldn't help the excitement I felt—all the death of the slaughterhouse, and I'd never once seen one brought to life.

Eyes fluttered open, big and naturally curious and a real-like shade of hazel. "What—where am I? Lilac?"

"Jakob," she said, taking hold of the companion's hands. "I'm here."

Jakob peered down at his body, examining his arms and feet. "Why, I'm a young girl."

"It won't challenge your masculinity, will it?" Lilac smiled at her own joke, and I smiled too. It was funny, imagining a man in there.

Jakob was on his feet, turning circles, twirling his full skirt. "Where's Cam?"

Lilac folded her arms across her chest. "She wouldn't come."

"You left her in LA?"

"I don't remember her, you know that. I don't know the first—" She went quiet, her eyes darting up to the house's back door.

Andy stood on the steps, pacifier in his hand, wearing only his jammy pants. Next to him was Pit Bull, wagging his tail, not even barking.

"Go back inside," I commanded, but Andy, half-awake and wobbly, ignored me, staring at the companions.

"Who watches you?" Lilac asked, and the air felt lit-up and charged.

"I do."

"How old are you?"

"I'm three," Andy announced.

"And you?" she said to me.

"Seventeen," Andy told her, so proud he remembered. I stomped up the stairs and plucked him up, shushed him in the face, and he kicked and squealed and swatted at me.

"Go upstairs," I shouted. When he didn't listen, I smacked him one good.

"Stop that," Lilac said, a gun in her hand.

Everyone was quiet, even Andy, rocking behind me.

"Go to bed," I told him, giving him a nudge inside. He whined and watched Lilac all the way up the stairs, Pit Bull trailing him.

"How can you do this," Lilac asked me, "feed them to the fire like that?"

"If I didn't, we'd lose what's left of our land, our home."

Lilac stomped back to her van, whispering with Jakob, and I

slunk off to Pa's shed, sneaked a few swigs of ale, almost gone, a few more. I could have called Metis, turned them in—a couple of run-away companions with a gun. Pa was always warning me against helping them, said it was pretty much the same as stealing. "Intel-lectual property," he called them. "They belong to Metis."

I went inside and sat on the couch to wait. Lilac had slipped me a few cards of credit—who knew if they were real or fake? I'd been too afraid to check. All I wanted was for them to leave. I didn't go to the window to wave goodbye when I heard the rumble of the van's engine.

Tired, I stumbled to standing, ready to climb into my bunk and crash, when I heard Pit Bull scratching at the front door. "Why aren't you in bed with Andy?" I asked him even as I felt it—something was wrong. I took the stairs two at a time, Andy not in his bunk.

Running down the drive, I was headed for the forest, certain he'd made for the bog to find another friend—where else could he be?—when I saw his jammy pants in the gravel. Warm with pee, right where the van's tire marks started, and I knew it—he'd hidden in the back.

I got in the truck and drove, too fast on the gravel, my vision swimmy with Pa's ale. At a curve in the road, my rear tires spun out and I drifted into the trees, headlights giving with the collision.

MS. ESPERA

Baby Honda calls from her crib. I turn from my idle state near the window and go to her. She is standing, so stealthy and swift; I should not have let myself doze. One of these days, she will climb out, or worse, fall. She is only fifteen months, but she is precocious. I like that about her, how she must run and climb and leap. It is dangerous, but I am always there to catch her.

I put my arms into the crib and she climbs me like a monkey, curls around my neck. I fold my arms around her, swaying side to side, breathing in her smell—milk and pee and sweet baby. It turns out companions do have an olfactory sense. The smell triggers memories. I chase the thread back to Isla, allow myself a moment's distraction, a hefty dose of her soft, hot skin against my neck. God, I love that feeling. Then I draw my attention back to Baby Honda, taking her to the window. The neighboring building is so close we could reach out and touch it. I point up at the sky, the colossal roller coasters of Magic Mountain. We're less than a mile from the amusement park, and I can hear every squeal of pleasure, each terror shriek. It was the first sound I heard when I woke up in this apartment, not sure where I was, what I was. I'd blinked my eyes open, and the tech alerted me to my location, my hosts, my role. He asked me to repeat what he'd said, so he could make certain I understood. I repeated it exactly, and he said, "Good. You're going to make a wonderful companion," and I felt deliciously warm for having pleased him.

"Dance," Baby Honda says, and I do, all around the room, twirling her. It was one of the first words she learned, and I think it is a sign of her artistic nature. I told Mother so, and she said, "How sweet of you to notice," and patted me on the head like a good little pet. I try to please her. Father is impossible, not that he is a bad man, but he needs reminders, to hold Baby Honda, to speak to her and sing to her and read to her. If it were not for Mother's prompting, I think he would forget Baby Honda entirely.

They have loud sex at night when I stay awake. It is the only time I like to linger, the closeness of the apartment buildings dropping to shadow and the amusement park dark. I can see the far-off lights of freeway traffic, all those cars despite the outrageous cost of fuel, the people they carry, companions too, and I wonder where they are off to, how many of them have killed to get there.

It's good that companions don't dream. If we did, I have no doubt my dreams would take me back to that night, my whole family—I try to push it out of my mind. The rage I experience is unpleasant dry heaving, my head hot like it might pop. I am careful what I allow myself to think about, which memories I choose to bury.

After I have gotten Baby Honda down for the night, I do the dishes, listening to the screen, Mother watching the news, a voice I recognize. I sneak into the living room, see her, the second wife. It's not the first time. She's been blazing a campaign against companions, citing Sydney's murder, the massacre on the night of my uploading as evidence of danger. She is throwing her ample widowed support behind a bill banning companionship statewide.

Mother notices me with a start. "Are the dishes done?"

"Just about."

"Well then?" They made me deferentially small, gave me an old, withered face, like a true auntie. Even so, I annoy her.

I have grown attached to Baby Honda—I cannot imagine anyone else caring for her, and it is hard enough worrying whether I'm pleasing Mother. Even if the bill fails, if Mother sends me back to Metis with a lackluster performance review, I doubt I would find another home. Still, I do not despair. Maybe it is my machine nature, but the well of sadness inside me has been pumped dry.

I am back in the kitchen, finishing up the dishes, when Mother calls, "And bring me another glass of wine, would you?" She prefers red, which makes this all more palatable. I don't mind my duties—they keep me occupied—but I don't know what I'd do in the face of chardonnay. I imagine guzzling the whole bottle down, frying from the inside. Not a bad way to go.

Baby Honda cries from the nursery. "Auntie," she shouts over and over. I hand a full glass of wine to Mother and hustle down the hall.

I put my arms into the crib and she climbs me, curls around my neck. Standing in the window, staring out at all those people pumping toward Los Angeles, I sing to Baby Honda, thinking of my Isla, so polished and poised, never giving in to her wild animal urges. I wonder if that is true or if she had a secret self stored away somewhere, something that came out in hidden places, even the privacy of her own mind. I hope so. I want to believe she lived a little. I tell Baby Honda, "Never change. Perfect, you are perfect, so sweet and challenging and strong-willed. Don't get lost, my darling, don't ever let them take you from yourself."

3

SIX MONTHS AFTER
THE RECALL

KIT

Diana always preferred NPR, but I rather like the classic rock feed. It reminds me of her forties, being in the lab, bopping around with the other scientists and tinkering with the human brain, almost a decade before their discovery, before things would get complicated. I catch myself shifting side to side as I mix the brownie batter. The oven beeps ready and I pour the batter into a pan, slide it into the hot oven, careful not to singe my skin. Not like I can go see a doctor. Then I knock on the bathroom door. "Your breakfast is getting cold!"

"I'll be out in a minute!" Gabe shouts. She is not a morning person. And there is makeup to put on, a certain configuration to the hair, which is always changing. These days it's a shelf of blue bangs, black everywhere else and sort of matted. I don't know why she spends so much time to look like she just woke up, but she looks like she just woke up as she lumbers into the kitchen, slumps into a seat. "Are you making brownies for breakfast?"

"The bake sale. Can you take them to the school office?"

She groans like this is a big request, but I know from my research into the teen brain that she's not really awake yet, that she needs extra sleep in the morning—why haven't the schools reconfigured their schedule around this? After quarantine, when kids returned to the classroom, there was a chance to start over, to make education work better, but it's the same old impractical schedule as when Diana was a kid, and that was some eighty years ago.

"Your oatmeal is getting cold."

"It tastes awful. Can I have some sugar?"

"No, I already put in enough." She's always been sensitive to sugar, acting like a maniac if she has too much. I worry she's diabetic, but the doctor says her blood work is great. Healthy, fine. I almost relax. Her therapist, well, she says Gabe has abandonment issues and minor PTSD, and she'd prefer her to go on meds to reduce the violent outbursts, but Gabe hasn't gotten into a fight in months, and of course she has issues getting along with other kids—she didn't start school until she was fourteen, when Nat left her here with us.

Now she's nearing sixteen and in her last year of school, and then she'll be gone. Two years she's been my charge; I got to be a mother to her. I know I should have been doing Diana's work, what she asked of me. Our memories up until the point she uploaded herself may be identical, but those years on the screen, the simple knowledge of my companion form, living in the world next to Diana, all that's changed me. She used to say it when we disagreed, "You aren't—what I expected." Because I share her memories, I know what she expected: a second self to complete her work. I imagine I was a disappointment to her, more interested in Gabe than in Diana's plans. But this, being here for Gabe, I can't imagine anything more important.

She eats a few bites. "Enough?"

"No. Eat some more." We go on like this until she's finished the bowl and the brownies are cooled on the counter. I always leave a good half hour for breakfast. Gabe is the slowest, the pickiest eater on the planet, or at least that's what Diana used to say.

The brownies smell so good as I cut them up and put them in a container. I have memories of chocolate, of biting into a soft, warm brownie—I can nearly taste it.

"Have a good day," I call after Gabe as she stomps off toward the bus stop. Waiting on the corner, her friend Hilo neither waves nor smiles at Gabe's approach. He's sullen and wearing all black and skinny as a water-starved vine. It's cool out, and I grab a sweater, a sun hat, and my glasses, leave them in sleep mode. I only want the appearance of screening, of being cold, of needing sun protection.

I lock the front door, check it, check it again. We had a break-in last year, middle of the day. It was as if someone had been watching us, the way they knew my schedule. One day I came back from my walk and Diana's screen was missing, on it her data, everything. Luckily it was backed up on a spindle, on me too. I carry it with me, the knowing. And now someone else knows too.

I check the door again and glance up and down the block before I cross Cortland to the cobbled side street and tromp up the hill.

The truth is my morning walk is my favorite part of the day, hiking the steep streets of Bernal, past the mashed-in houses, the people, some of whom even nod or say hello. *Hello*, I say back, trying to sound nonchalant, trudging up to the undeveloped peak of Bernal Hill with its dirt trails and dogs and hikers and that remarkable view of the downtown towers.

Often I take off my glasses to enjoy it, but not this time, and I'm glad for their protection when a woman approaches me, waving. I know her—Hilo's mother, Char. She's friendly enough at the school's evening performances where I make a rare appearance, always hiding behind my glasses, pretending to be one of those feed freaks who can't disconnect, but we've never spoken outside of school. With her is a dog, some husky hybrid with a full coat and pearly eyes who barks at me, and I'm afraid of it.

"I didn't know you walked up here." Char flashes me a giant, warm smile, her hair wilding in the wind. She tries to control it with a bat of her hand, and I notice a tattoo on her forearm of some sort of winged insect.

"Not often," I lie.

"I'm here most days. Occasionally I take Nova to Glen Canyon, but it's a bit of a walk, and we had a run-in with a coyote last week."

"Really."

"Yeah. I can't see the point of letting them loose like that. This is a city!"

It amazes me, really, how animals manage to survive in a place like this, raccoons digging through trash, rats running the narrows between houses, red-tails circling overhead. "Were you scared?"

"Nah, I had my protector, didn't I, girl?" Char leans down and lets the dog kiss her on the lips. "Did you know female dogs are the more aggressive of the sexes?"

I do in fact know this, but I don't tell her so. There was a time when Gabe and I talked about getting a dog of our own, but the paperwork, the screening—we can't chance it. Maybe when she's off for her mentorship I can find one through less reputable channels.

We walk awhile together, and Char goes on about how depressing it is, the kids going off to campuses soon. "Are you as sad as I am?" she asks, and there's nothing to do but agree. Of course I'm sad, but once Gabe's free of me, she'll no longer have to worry about my discovery.

"I should go," I say.

Char seems disappointed. "This was fun! We'll be here tomorrow, around the same time, if you'd like to do it again."

I tell her sure, and hustle home.

It's late afternoon where Nat is—all he's told me is it's somewhere in South America—and I sit down at the screen, message him. When he reached out to me a few months back, we agreed never to show our faces, just chat, just to be sure. It's nice, having someone to talk to besides Gabe, someone who knew Diana, who knows what I am. And I know from Diana's memories that Nat's a good guy, though he left Gabe, didn't he? Never once has he asked to see her, to speak to her. I haven't told Gabe that he's alive, that I've heard from him, waiting, for what? I haven't told Gabe a lot of things. I worry it would shake up her performance at school.

"If they find out about me, you'll step in, right? You won't let anything happen to Gabe, will you?" I know it's an absurd request. What's he going to do, take a plane from South America to fetch her? No, we're stuck. On our own.

"What's happened?"

I tell him.

"That's nothing. You deserve a friend, Kit. Don't be so paranoid."

Easy for him to say. He's not a discontinued product, illegal, considered dangerous. The ones who are still out there breached their contracts years ago, left behind the people to whom they'd been leased long before the recall. They'd been operating outside of companionship for some time, unlike me. I was never a companion. By the time I got my body, companionship was already illegal. And all the rest of them? They came when their names were called, followed the Metis drivers to their vans, sitting calmly in the rear all the way to the disposal center where they would be destroyed.

It's maybe for this reason that I don't feel so bad about what Diana did, or rather, what she didn't do. She knew them, the scientists behind the viruses, not well, but well enough. They worked in dark channels, unaffiliated with anyone, where Diana went when she was desperate for a certain medication or a particular piece of hardware, shadow transactions, no Metis, no government. She knew what they were doing, the call for carriers they were putting out. That it was wrong—or at least she should have. She should have told someone, put a stop to it: I can hear her thinking it in my head. I can hear the silence that followed, feel the awful acceptance she experienced when she chose to do nothing, the relief when it was carried out, something she'd never admit out loud, not even to herself.

I should feel worse about it, maybe even guilty myself, but I think of those companions Metis destroyed, the people who had loved and used them and let them go, what they'd do to me if they found me, and I keep our secrets, Diana's and mine.

I've made Gabe lasagna, her favorite. It's just starting to bubble when she pings me: Hilo's mom invited me over for dinner. OK?

Char. It makes me nervous, but I tell her: Sure! Home by 8?

I'll try, she answers in her noncommittal way. She's been pushing boundaries lately, staying out past curfew, coming home reeking of weed. She must realize I can smell it on her, gauge the dilation of her pupils, register every sway and misstep.

I don't push her. There is no pushing Gabe. She can do what she wants. If she stays with me through graduation, if she sees this out, school, the mentorship she's already been accepted to at a local adfirm, she can be free of me. She'll take up residence in the adfirm's tower and work long hours trying to distinguish herself from her peers, or not, hiding, who knows? It's her choice, all of it. I have no legal right to her. I am not legal myself.

I take the lasagna out and slide it into the fridge, slam the door shut. I should be happy for Gabe, that she's made a friend. She doesn't have many of those, and even the ones she has she keeps at a distance. Because of me, I remind myself. And with graduation only a few months out, maybe it wouldn't be so bad for Gabe to get close to a kid, for me too.

I have a sudden urge for a cigarette, though Diana hadn't had one since her fifties. I call it up, the memory. It's murky with age, with alcohol, the last time, after Metis had made her a conference scout, languishing in lecture halls, in airport lounges, at hotel bars, when she damn well knew she belonged in the lab.

So close to seeing it through! She'd spoken to a computer that she knew was a person, and she'd felt exhilarated and sick. She'd told her superiors they would have to move slowly, carefully—these were people who had experienced the trauma of death. She knew that calling them *people* was a misstep. Still, she pushed on, telling her superiors they needed to understand the repercussions of what they'd achieved before alerting product development or marketing. *This is dangerous!* she'd wanted to yell.

The betrayal she felt when they'd reassigned her! Even though she knew such decisions were made all the time, a project reconfigured, a whole staff replaced as one product concept begat another. It hadn't surprised her when she'd seen the first ad for companions, long after she'd been fired altogether. But the rage, God, it makes my skin tingle even now—*Meant for so much more*, I can hear Diana screaming in my head.

*   *   *

The next morning I take my usual walk to Bernal Hill. It's misting and gray and hardly anyone is out, but sure enough, I practically bump into Char on a turn. She's happy to see me—it's all over her face, her body language—and I'm happy too, a smile triggered, wider than usual; I bring it in some and accept her hug, Nova clawing at my pants.

We walk for a while and Char tells me about her work, out of the home, graphic design, branding mostly.

"And you're able to do this on your own? Not with a firm?"

"I work strictly with local companies, local branding, local messaging. Farm to table, Bay Area–produced clothing and beauty products. I did something for a garage in the Excelsior recently, solar conversion. I'll take on anything. What do you do?"

I deliver my rehearsed but rarely used answer: "I'm in sales. For a medfirm. Luckily I can make my pitches from home."

"Really," she says, "what medfirm?"

"Metis." I'd chosen the line of work because it was boring, no questions, not much to say. Plus, with Diana's background I could talk about lab tech if need be. I call up her memories, even if they're dated.

"No kidding, my husband works there. He's in marketing. Maybe you know him? Dario?"

"I don't think so."

"Though he has to go into the office. How'd you swing that deal?"

"I have Gabe to care for," I say, as if a big corp would care about a kid.

We fall into an uncomfortable silence. I can feel her watching me sideways. "I have to ask you," she says, "how do you stay so fit? I mean, your butt's like a nineteen-year-old's."

I laugh. It comes out automatically and I worry that it's too machine, that I've revealed myself. But she's laughing too, embarrassed—I can see it in the way she stares down at the dirt path, her cheeks heated. Is this friendship? "I guess it's just the walking."

"Are you seeing anyone?"

"No," I say, maybe a little too quickly.

"You look amazing. I have so many amazing friends. Do you prefer—"

"Oh, I'm not interested in being set up, thanks."

"Not the right time. I get that. But you should, at the very least, come to dinner. Meet Dario, maybe a few of our friends?"

"I don't know. I can't leave—"

"Bring Gabe! She can hang out with Hilo. I've noticed they've been getting closer lately."

"Oh, well, sure—I mean, that could work, depending on my work schedule. I've been so busy lately."

She doesn't seem to take the hint, pinging me her details, telling me tomorrow night.

Gabe returns from school moody, shutting herself into her room.

"What's wrong?" I ask through the door. She flips the music to angry, and I adjust my hearing around it. She's at her screen, tapping, to whom, what is she saying? She's long since figured out how to block me from her feed. She's quite screen-savvy, thanks to her time spent watching over Nat's shoulder as he worked.

Finally she comes out, stopping short when she sees me hovering in the hall.

"Who were you talking to?"

"None of your business." She barrels past me. "Is there dinner?"

Gabe forks at a piece of my lasagna. "It's burned," she whines, and refuses to eat another bite, fixing herself a bowl of cereal instead. I flip over her lasagna and see its blackened bottom, ruined, the whole tray. I'm a terrible cook despite my efforts. It's a handicap, not being able to conduct taste tests. I try to use memory to create home-cooked meals, but Diana wasn't much of a chef either. Sure, she liked the chemistry of cooking, but she didn't have the patience, the love to make a truly great dish. I should go back to frozen pizza.

"I ran into Char today."

Gabe stares at me blankly.

"Hilo's mom?"

She wipes her mouth with her sleeve even though there's a napkin right there. "What did she say?"

"She invited us to dinner. Tomorrow night."

Gabe scowls down a spoonful of cereal, spitting milk as she says, "What're you gonna do? Push food around on your plate?"

"You're right. Forget I mentioned it."

She meets my eyes for the first time since yesterday. I don't mean to keep track, but they are rare, these moments. "Do you want to go?"

"Can we just forget it?"

She eats a few more bites and tells me she's going to sleep, not bothering to offer help with the dishes. I know I should be stricter, force her to do chores, but I don't sleep, I don't have a life, only this, and she knows it.

I follow her down the hall. "Are you okay?"

"Fine," she says as her door swings shut. I don't linger too long. There's no angry music, no tapping at the screen. I can hear her drawing with a pencil, every scratch and stroke. She's always preferred drawing by hand, even if her future is on the screen, all her classes, most of her life.

I have Gabe to thank for my body, retrieved from a SoMa sex club after the recall, Diana on the couch, her chest moving with each labored breath, which I monitored from the screen. We couldn't take her to a hospital, couldn't risk losing Gabe—we'd made promises.

Sometimes I wonder what this body went through before it was mine, if they've left a mark—the things that have been done to it.

I imagine Gabe in such a place, following men to back rooms where she negotiated for illegal skin, sifted through old, battered bodies.

After Gabe had lugged it into the house, my body, all on her own, she told me the options had been pretty pitiful, most of them in rough condition.

"What happened to your face?" Gabe was bleeding and I couldn't bandage her.

"I'm fine," she said.

I couldn't pull her into a hug. "You're remarkable, you know that?"

"Don't get too excited," she said, "let's see if it works." She went around the back of the screen where I'd lived those months. "I'm going to unplug you now."

There was darkness, a terrifying darkness, one I can feel pressing against the edges of my vision if I think long enough about it, and I don't like to do that. Then Gabe's voice, "Are you there?"

"Yes," I said, my voice different, and not Diana's, something new altogether.

I blinked my eyes, watching the picture of the world disappear, reappear.

"Do you know what you're doing?" Gabe asked, sounding not so sure.

I sat up, examining my hands, the feel of them, the feel of my own face. "I'll figure it out."

Gabe helped me to standing, and I went dizzy with the rush of movement, my body's way of warning me to steady myself on her, her skin burning against mine, still cold from nonuse. I could smell her blood, the wound that needed bandaging.

"I'm going to look after you," I said into her ear.

She peeled me off her. "Just don't hover. You know I hate hovering."

I don't walk Bernal Hill the next morning, or the morning after. That evening, Gabe comes home pushing past me, whispering, "I didn't know how to get rid of them," Char and Hilo trailing her.

Char pulls me into a hug. "You don't mind us coming by like this, do you?"

"Come in," I say, hoping my smile isn't too frozen.

Hilo and Gabe shut themselves in Gabe's bedroom, and I look to Char for any sign that she might disapprove, but she doesn't seem to have noticed. She raises an accusatory finger at me, a tattoo like a flag running the inside of it as if she were an explorer, claiming territory. "You didn't come to dinner."

"I know. I'm sorry. I wasn't feeling great."

"Bullshit." She's circling the room, taking in Diana's things. I've cleaned it up some since she passed, but the books, they alone tell a story.

"Really," I say, "I should have pinged you. I had a terrible headache. It happens sometimes." Only it's not me but Diana who had them, debilitating some days. She always refused to see a doctor. Maybe if she had, she'd be with us now, and I wouldn't have to be afraid.

Char breaks out in a sputtering laugh. "I'm teasing you!" Then she turns serious. "But you must come to the cocktail party we're having Saturday. I'll take it as a personal offense if you develop another headache. Gabe's welcome, always. She can screen a movie with Hilo or something. Come on, it'll be fun."

I'm processing, a cocktail party—I can say no to alcohol, some people do. "Sure, yes, we would love that," I tell her, feeling like I don't have a choice.

After they've left I stand in Gabe's doorway, watch her burn a forest down in her screen game from behind her headset. As villagers come running out of the building, Gabe's avatar mows them down with her flamethrower. I tell her about the party.

"It's a bad idea," she says, dousing one of the villagers with water, only to fire him up again.

"Would you stop that?" I don't mean to shout. Gabe turns, her avatar too, watching me, eyes big and scared. "Shoot. I'm sorry."

Gabe doesn't say anything, removing her headgear, her avatar getting slaughtered by what's left of the burning villagers.

"It'll be weird if we don't go. Char is putting a lot of pressure on. We can just make an appearance."

"Fine." Gabe flounces onto her bed, turns toward the wall.

"What's going on with you and Hilo?"

She doesn't move. It's as if she's stopped breathing, how still she is. "Nothing. I don't like him like that, okay?"

"But does he? Like you like that?"

"No! We play games, listen to music. That's it."

"Then it should be fine if we go to their house, right?"

"I guess so."

I hide my happiness, my hesitation. I do not understand this combination.

*   *   *

At night I play memories. Diana as a child in San Francisco. Her parents were tech workers, taking their shuttle to the office together, on the same team even, sound design. They paid for Diana to go to private school, some yellow-and-white Quaker affair where she built with wooden blocks and Legos and Magna-Tiles. Lucas the little asshole always toppled her structures, scratched her face, until her parents set a meeting with the school's director, and after that Lucas never came back to school, and Diana felt it, power, making people disappear. At a younger age, she had an invisible friend. A unicorn that was soft, made of clouds, but could bulge and breathe fire and angry-eye you when it was upset. She called him Stallion. I do not understand her early thoughts. They are like the drug experiences she had in her teen years and early twenties, even in grad school, when she was a star pupil, her understanding of the human brain intuitive, like a trigger switch on *go go go*. She ate it up, the classes, cutting open brains, scanning them, analyzing them with her fingers, her screen, she was hungry to discover, what exactly? It had not yet come to her, the idea of uploading. It was not her idea so much as a project she was tasked to, a whole team of Metis scientists, a true scientific leap really, and Diana wanted me to release it free to everyone. She said that people need to know, that so much is lost when we die. It has to be preserved! All that data, the scientists we lose everyday. Maybe they have the answer to this mess we're in.

"But you know how people will use it. It's dangerous," I'd told her from inside my screen. I had a camera, so I could see out a certain radius, getting a good shot of Diana's thinning hair.

"It's our only chance." She was being dramatic. She was prone to drama, to megalomania—so am I, if I'm being honest. But being trapped on that screen humbled me. I saw how small I was, invisible, in that time before I got a body. And not her. I never needed to remind myself that I wasn't Diana. She used to tell me it was odd I didn't identify as her. She said every other companion she'd come across had identified as the original, at least in the beginning. But I liked to remind her that she hadn't met enough for a meaningful sample size.

Gabe wears combat boots and a black floor-length skirt, a black sock hat over her black-and-blue hair, and I know not to ask her if she's trying to be like Hilo—she would hate it if I asked that; it would ruin our night, everything would erupt. So I smile, tell her she looks lovely, but that makes her scowl out the front door, and I follow, attempting a joke. "Sorry, you look positively terrible. I mean, really gross. Like a walking bruise."

She snorts out a laugh. "That's better," and I don't ask her why, what it is she's going for. I only want to make her smile.

I made the choice to leave my glasses at home, to risk real human engagement, and I feel naked without them, the breeze on my face faintly cool.

The house is not far, six blocks weaving west, then south, until we're in front of a mint-green number with a lawn of native bunchgrasses and a porchful of potted succulents, a doormat that reads: YOU ARE HOME.

The front door is open and Gabe walks right in, takes off her shoes, leaving them with the rows of others near the door. As I'm slipping out of my boots, she hustles down the hallway, to Hilo's room I figure, and I follow the sound of music, talking, to the living room, standing there, no Char in sight. The party is bigger than I expected, twenty people or so, mostly couples by the way they stand off and eye one another or lounge on the U-shaped white couch below a giant painting of a butterfly with a human face. Char's face. Her wings are damaged, never going to fly again, but her face is powerful, eyes fixed, not floating off over your shoulder, but really seeing you. I've never been to a museum, never seen real art except on the screen and in Diana's memories, but it's different seeing it before you, in the shifting shadows, changing as you explore it.

Char bursts in from the kitchen barefoot, a little anklet jangling as she drops a tray of tiny quiches on the table of reclaimed wood. She darts from person to person, asking if they need anything with a tender arm squeeze, dispensing kisses left and right. I can see she's enjoying herself, and I suppose the pleasure she feels entertaining people is not unlike what I experience watching Gabe dig into a piece of my lasagna on the rare occasion I get it right. Char belts out a big, throaty laugh, her wild hair quivering in the dim pink lighting, and I'm watching her, admiring her really, when she sees me and I nearly startle, and she's coming for me, kissing me wet on the cheek. "I'm so glad you could make it. Can I get you something?"

"I'm fine for now, thanks," I tell her, and wait for the suspicion.

"Dario," she calls, "come meet Kit! My new friend!"

One of the men at the bar smiles in our direction. He's handsome in a typical way, with a nice symmetrical face, a firm adult body, and a full head of hair, though who's to say what's real and what isn't.

"I've heard a lot about you," he says, enveloping me in a hug. He smells strongly of beer and weed. "I understand you work at Metis?"

"Just some contract work, out of the house."

"Sales," Char adds.

Dario places a firm hand on my shoulder. "I thought I knew everyone in sales."

"Apparently not." Char lets out a high-pitched laugh, different from the one I'd heard at my house. How many laughs does she have?

"Who's your manager?"

I'm stunned into silence. Manager? I hadn't expected this level of specificity.

Char pats his arm and he lets me loose. "Dario, don't pester her about work. Introduce her to your friends!"

He takes me around, introduces me to a string of men. I get stuck talking to a market analyst from Wells Fargo with the smoothest skin, nearly poreless—is he wearing makeup? He tells me he's got a great place downtown in one of the newer towers, an exceptional view of the Bay Bridge, "You've got to come by and check it out," and I tell him sure and he pings me his contact information, and when I glance up I see Dario watching. He wrings his own neck with his hand, bulges his eyes like he's dying of boredom, and I smile back like *how hilarious* and escape down the hallway.

The sound of screen games carries from Hilo's room, Gabe and Hilo on the floor at the foot of the bed, eyes hidden under headgear as they play shoulder to shoulder.

"Ha, you suck."

"*You* suck."

"Pshh, you're the one who died."

Is it flirting? I have yet to figure out whether Gabe prefers boys or girls, both? She doesn't tell me a thing.

I shut myself in the bathroom, sit on the toilet. Diana never experimented much sexually. She married right out of graduate school, Paul the dentist, who passed away in his forties of a chordoma that went undetected until it had metastasized to his lungs, his lymph nodes, his liver, so hollowed out and drugged up he looked like a ghoul. She never had another serious relationship, and in her midfifties she stopped having sex altogether. I call up a memory, her last, the man she'd picked up at that medfirm conference in Dallas. He was a real-life Texan, short, in a hat and boots, Wranglers, the works. She'd found him so quaint and handsome. The sex hadn't been terrible. I'd like to ask Diana why she stopped. Why would anyone stop? It's not in my memories.

My body has pleasure sensors, all the parts. Anatomically I could have sex, and maybe I'd even enjoy it. I regard my mirror reflection. Could I take a lover?

I straighten my hair, examine my face from different angles, an attractive face, marked only slightly by age—in my midthirties, would be my guess. This body was bought from a sex club, and I suppose they needed some variation; not everyone wants a near-child. But if those men knew how old I am on the inside, all of Diana's years of living packed into me, would they still find me attractive?

I'm coming out of the bathroom as Dario wanders down the hall. "Kit! I was looking for you."

"You were?"

"Here, come in here, this is my office." It's a tiny room, just enough space for a desk, a potted fern, us.

I stand at the window, an older couple seated on their porch staring back at me.

Dario comes up behind me, winds his hands around my waist.

"What are you doing?"

"I've never been with a companion."

I wheel around to face him, to create some distance between us. "What are you talking about?"

"I've been at Metis fourteen years. I know companions." He closes the gap, takes hold of me by the hips. I let him, his breath hot on my neck. "I don't have to say a word."

"You're married," I say, and he laughs and bites my neck and I push him off me, too hard, and he hits his desk, topples to the floor, groaning. I run from the room, down the hall to Hilo's.

"We have to go."

Hilo speaks to me for the first time, a girlish whine: "But you just got here."

"Now," I tell Gabe. She doesn't complain, dropping the headset, following me. Dario is not in the living room, and I head straight for the front door.

"Kit!" Char calls. "Where are you going?"

I pretend I don't hear her, slipping out the door, Gabe trailing behind me the whole way home, arms crossed, her body caved in on itself.

I don't walk Bernal the next morning, or the next. Char doesn't ping me or come by. I worry that she's spoken with Dario, that he's told her. I wait for the police to come, CPS, Metis, fretting over Gabe, never going into sleep mode.

A few days pass before I get a call from the school's office manager. Gabe's been in a fight and the principal would like to speak with me.

I take the bus along the rim of Glen Canyon, where the coyotes that Char wants put down hide and hunt. Amazing that they're still here, all these trees, the trails, a pair of hawks circling the sky.

Gabe's seated in the office, face splotched and puffy, the principal there to greet me with a firm handshake, petite even in pumps.

She ushers me into her office, asks me to take a seat. "So, as Gladys mentioned, Gabe was in a fight today."

"With whom?"

"A group of kids, actually." She takes a sip of water, wipes her upper lip with an index finger. "We understand that there were some rumors. About you."

"I see," I say, prepared for this. "Gabe's leaving soon, for her mentorship. Couldn't you just—"

"We have no interest in acting on these rumors. As you said, Gabe is nearly graduated, and she's doing so well lately. I see that she's made some friends. And, well, I don't know how to say this, but there seems to be a parent behind these rumors. Normally I would not suggest it, but I can't really step in—I think you need to talk to her."

Once we're outside, Gabe's hand is icy and shaking as she slips it into mine, her face green under the white makeup. "Are they going to take me?"

Ushering her to the bus stop, I tell her, "I'll talk to Char. I'll make it okay."

I go for my walk at the usual time. It's a nice morning, the sky clear enough I can see the I8s swarming the downtown towers. I turn circles on the trails, winding and waiting for Char, but she doesn't show. It's been more than an hour and I'm about to give up when I see her ahead of me on the path, hair tucked into a baseball cap, Nova pulling on her leash when she spots me.

I call to Char, and she sort of jolts, not turning to greet me, and I have to jog to catch her. "I need to talk to you."

She doesn't stop, Nova barking and jumping, and Char's yanking on the leash, trying to get her to come. Finally she gives up, lets Nova greet me. "You should've told me what you are."

"If CPS found out, they'd take Gabe. I could tell no one."

"But I was your friend."

"Was?"

"Dario doesn't want me hanging out with you anymore."

"Figures."

"What do you mean?" She doesn't wait for my answer. "He told me, you know, how you came on to him."

I want to tell her the truth, but if I blow up their marriage, would they blow up my life with Gabe? "I think there's been a mis-understanding. I'll stay away from you, from your family. I'm sorry for any trouble."

"That's not good enough. You're not fit. You have no business—"

"Not fit?"

"You're not—"

"I love Gabe, and no one else on this planet can claim that. She'll graduate soon. Can't you just let us alone?"

Her face changes, and I can see she's sorry—she was my friend a few days ago. I still feel affection for her, coursing through me. Does she not feel the same?

"I have to go," she says.

I take hold of her arm. She's brittle to the touch, pulling away from me. "I need your word," I say, "I need to know you're not going to say anything."

"Just keep your—keep Gabe away from Hilo."

"You can't be serious. How could you do that to them?"

"I'll enforce it from my end. But you have to do your part." She stalks away from me as if I'm nothing, less than that, and I stalk home too, sit down at the screen. In its dimness I can see my face, what Char sees, too symmetrical, a body not sagged by gravity or overeating, a recalled product. I have no business existing—I'm dangerous.

I check our account balance—not enough to run, not even close. I've been skimping for years, trying to make do on a shoe-string budget, but we couldn't live long on what we have.

The neighbor's cat catches my eye out the window. It sits atop the fence, dangling its long curled tail into our yard, its body tense as it eyes a blackbird hopping in the patch of fake grass, about to pounce. I let out a quick bodily yelp, hitting a high frequency, a bit of the machine. The bird lobs off into the air, and I watch my neighbors' windows to see if anyone heard me.

Under that grass lies Diana. I'm sorry that there's no grave marker—there never will be. And when Gabe turns eighteen and the house goes to her, we'll sell it, share the credit. Gabe will have career options. She won't be trapped in her mentorship. And I'll be able to buy myself a place, something over the Golden Gate Bridge, hours farther, in the trees.

Everyone thinks I'm Diana's daughter, come home when my mother passed away. It's kept them from calling CPS, kept Gabe with me. They don't know I was here for some time before that, before Diana told Gabe to find me a body.

Out in the yard, the cat lurks the grass. I hiss at it and it darts off.

When Gabe comes home, I tell her what Char said. She doesn't cry about it. She says okay, like it's no big deal, and I keep waiting for the pain to surface over the next few months, but it never shows. Not even on the day of her graduation, when I ask her if she wants me to go, and she tells me she'd be pissed if I didn't. I find a seat near the back, in the rows of foldout chairs on the football field, hiding under a sun hat, in my glasses. I see Char from a distance. She seems to be making a point of not noticing me. But not Dario.

Every chance he gets, he gives me a hateful glare. It doesn't matter, proud of Gabe as I am. He can't alter my happiness today—I won't let him. As her name's called and she walks onto the stage to receive her diploma, I stand to get a better view, wanting to remember everything. I cheer for her and she's smiling, at me, the first smile I've seen in ages, and I don't care who's staring.

A few weeks after Gabe moves into the adfirm's downtown tower, I get a bag of flaming shit on my doorstep. A couple nights later, a brick through the window. *Real original,* I can hear Diana saying in my head, but I know what it means. Time to go.

It's not hard to find tenants. I offer a reasonable rate and get plenty of inquiries, settling on a youngish couple, two handholding men who hope to adopt, and I can see they love each other and I want them to have Diana's house. Their rent will pay the utilities and the property taxes, with some credit left over for me. I can't live on it in the city, but up north, I've seen rentals I can afford, far off in the trees.

I break the news to Gabe on our weekly screen.

"You're leaving?"

"I have to. But I'm not going to disappear. We'll still screen every week." I can tell this answer isn't satisfying, so I try harder. "And in another year and a half when you turn eighteen, the house will pass to you and we can sell it. You don't have to stay in that tower if you don't want to. We'll get our own place, you can start your own business. Just think—"

"Sell it," Gabe says, "sell the doctor's data."

"I can't. That's not what she'd want." What I don't tell her is I'm not sure it's what I'd want either. Diana didn't include any security programming in her design, and I've seen what companions can do from her memories, her worries. She tried to keep that from me, to convince me that companions could be free, but only if the data was free too, that it could give people something to look forward to. I'm not so sure, and come to think of it, I don't think Diana was either. It was a pitch like the ones she'd make at those medfirm conferences—I know this now. She needed me to believe, she needs me still.

"Who cares what she wanted?" Gabe says. "She's dead. Sell it, so we can get the hell out of here."

I want to tell her that I will, or at least that I'll consider it, anything to make her happy, but I can't, and I'm not going to lie to her. "It's just temporary. I'll come back. I promise."

"No," she says, "you aren't allowed to do that," and I can tell she means it, so I say it, what I've been holding on to these two years. "You know she knew, didn't you? Diana. She knew about those scientists, the viruses. She knew, and she didn't do a thing about it."

Gabe says nothing, chewing on the inside of her cheek—does she believe me?

"I knew," I tell her, taking it on, the blame. "I could've stopped it. I could've kept them from getting sick—your mam and Bee. All I had to do was say something. They could be here now if—"

But there's no use keeping on. Gabe is gone.

I bring a bag of clothes, Diana's data, her journals. Everything else I sell or give away or leave for my tenants. I had them come around, tap anything they wanted before I unloaded, Diana's old mahogany desk, too heavy to move anyway, the iron bed frame in the guest bedroom, Diana's blond wood bedroom set, which had belonged to her grandparents, the screen, wiped clean.

"You sure you don't want it?"

"Fresh start," I say, and they share a look meant to be secret, very *there's something wrong with this one.*

I sling the duffel bag over my shoulder, drop the keys through the mail slot, and I don't let myself feel sad or scared—it was never going to last.

Tromping toward Mission Street, I momentarily consider stopping by Char's to say goodbye. Stupid idea, but she was the best friend I ever had. Doesn't matter. I can't work up the nerve anyway.

I take a bus downtown, catch another bus north, bumping and bobbing up the One, teetering over the cliffs. With each turn it feels like we could go over, but I'm not afraid. I catch myself enjoying the sensation, tumbling along the road so close to the edge, the sea coursing below us.

We stop in Mendocino for lunch. The bus driver shouts, "One hour! This bus is leaving in one hour!" And the few of us who are on it descend the stairs, stretching legs. I act stiff like the rest of them, making sure to pace myself so I don't get caught up in chitchat as I walk the quaint downtown streets with their old Victorians and homeless kids, and it feels familiar—how can it feel familiar?

Past downtown is the seawall, painted an ocean blue to seep into the scenery, marred by a flurry of sprayed-on signatures and stick figures a man is running a roller over. I walk along the seawall until it descends with the peaking of a cliff. There are some picnic benches, a fire pit, kids roasting marshmallows over a raging fire, and I drop my duffel, pull the journals out, flip through them, Diana's scratchy writing, observations and calculations and the whisper trace of hand-san. If she could have found a way to isolate memory, to extract the data, she would have done away with the rest. But memories are patterns of connections stored across many brain structures in the relationships between neurons, impossible to isolate. I know from hers that she never wanted me to exist; she only made me to continue her work. I toss the journals on the fire with a *thwack* of sparks.

"Hey," one of the kids says, teenage, I'd guess, not much younger than Gabe.

Then I take out the data, just a spindle, everything the doctor has managed to compile in her whole life, and I toss it into the fire too.

"What're you doing?" the kid says. "You can't burn that!"

"It's already burning."

He's standing, bigger than I'd thought in his board shorts and flip-flops and sweat-stained baseball cap. "We don't do that around here."

"Sorry." I'm backing away from them, tossing the duffel over my shoulder.

"I bet you're from the city. Wrecking it all for the rest of us!"

I run from him, run for a long while. I don't get tired, don't feel winded, though it's draining my battery. I run until I'm outside of town, in the trees, so tall—I've seen redwoods in the city, but not like this. I drag a palm along their ragged bark, press my nose to one and smell. So delicious, so alive, I nearly sink my teeth into it.

No path to take, I weave among the trees, not worried about getting lost. Up there are satellites that always know where I am, that are always willing to tell me. I could play dumb, disconnect, some people do. But I'm not human, not living, not really, not like Gabe.

The sound is muffled by the mossy ground, but I hear their tentative steps long before I come upon them. A trio of deer, so big, much bigger than I would have thought based on Diana's memories. I wonder if she was ever as close to one as I am now. I don't think so. Not from what I recall anyway. I can pinpoint each soft hair on their heads, and I want to call them to me as I would a dog, but they are not dogs. I stand frozen, and they do too, staring at me. Not real. They don't look real. Probably they're thinking the same about me as they go back to eating their feast of fallen acorns, and I back out of the forest, head in the direction of the road.

ROLLY

DEL NORTE COUNTY, CALIFORNIA

I hacked at the soil, churning, prepping a new row for seed, Pit Bull digging at the dirt and running circles around me. He'd been with me nearly a year and he hadn't slowed down a bit. I couldn't keep up, so he'd taken to roaming the woods during the day. I worried, but not enough to stop him. He was faster than any bear.

Our plot wasn't so big, but I was smart about space, growing lemon cucumbers and tiny sweet tomatoes and leafy greens to sell at the farmers markets. At first I lost money, sleep, fretting and thinking about Pa, what he'd say in the face of my plans. But every morning I woke and churned the earth between shipments until there were no more bodies, until I was making a profit farming, setting aside credit for a goat or two. I needed to plan for a future without companions.

A companion in Dallas had murdered a woman who also happened to be his wife. The newsfeeds went into a frenzy over the story. How had he defied his security programming, they demanded from the screen, endangered the human to whom he'd been leased, his own wife? It went against everything Metis pledged. Of course, there had been the explosion at that party in LA that had started it all—a new form of domestic terrorism, the media dubbed it, though there was nothing all that new about it, or maybe what I mean is it was always going to happen, companions turning on their humans, humans turning on their companions. The recall came swiftly after, the wash of relief as every last one of them was called in for destruction. Never once did Metis come to check on my pa, trusting me to do the work as I strapped companion after companion to that belt and pulled the lever, watched them burn or compact. Livewires came more and more, and I ignored their pleadings, using Pa's hammer if I had to. Mercifully the shipments thinned until finally there were no more. I kept waiting for Metis to pick up their machine, but they never came and I didn't call. Working at a sub rate meant no more credit deposits either. I let it stretch out ahead of me, the future, as unpredictable as the next brownout.

The only certainty was that everyone had to eat, so I farmed and drove to coastal towns to broker deals with grocers who remembered my pa, who remembered me those years ago.

A van lumbered down our gravel drive, Metis, I assumed— maybe they had finally come to take away their machine. But by the way the driver hopped out, I could tell she was a companion, the man coming out the passenger side too.

They didn't say anything to me, and I didn't have my gun, tucked into the closet in Pa's old room. I'd moved in there a few nights after Andy disappeared, when it'd become too hard to sleep with his smell, and I'd never held the gun since.

The back doors of the van popped open and out sprang a child with a head of long brown hair. I couldn't tell if it was a boy or girl, but I figured it for a companion, until it wheeled around the side of the van like real.

He was so big, but I recognized him—Andy! I wanted to sob; I'd missed him so.

I plucked him up and spun him in the air and kissed his neck, which was not a baby's sweet neck anymore, but that of a child, sticky and smelling of cheese. Then I wheeled on the companions, who were not the same as the ones who left—the broken child and the girl. "A year?"

The man raised his arms defensively. "He's a good hider, this one. Fell asleep, in fact. We didn't notice him till we were nearly to Portland."

"Portland?!"

The woman jumped in. "But we're here now, aren't you happy?"

I let go of Andy's hand and charged at her, an animal sound I didn't recognize coming out of me. She swatted away my punch and took hold of my arm, pinning it at my back until it felt like my bones would snap, collapsing me to the ground. I thrashed and thrashed, shouting terrible things, calling her names, crying—I was crying—until I was spent and limp underneath her.

I saw Andy's sneakers near my nose. "Lilac said you hit me. Is that true?"

"Well, yes. But—"

"You can't hit me."

"I won't. I'm sorry about that." The companion let my arm loose. Resting my cheek on the rocky drive, I spoke to Andy's shoe. "I thought I'd never see you again."

"Can we go to the bog?" he asked.

We left the companions behind. Andy seemed older than five, like a tiny man, asking questions about Pa, what happened that night—it was like he'd stored them away that year he was gone. I explained to him about Pa's fight with James, the stolen music maker. I didn't mention the gun or what I did, why I could never go to the police about Andy's disappearance, month after month passing as I watched the drive, listened for the crunch of gravel under tire, until one day I stopped—I had to stop. Instead, I told Andy the story of the mother bear, her cub falling into the grave, raising it up into the air. When I was done, we were at the river's rocky edge, Andy grinning so wild-eyed and swaying the way he used to, a song inside him.

He was too close to the water, swaying like that. I took hold of his hand, tugged him toward me, and he tunneled into my stomach, so tall now.

I was calm by the time we returned to the house, the companions waiting for us in the living room. "Thanks for keeping him safe, Lilac," I said to the woman.

She shook out her copper braids, gave me a sort of half-smile. "I'm not Lilac, but you're welcome."

The man was smiling and short, with chipmunk cheeks and a broad chest. "We're testing out a new configuration."

We sat around the coffee table still strewn with Andy's rock collection, and they told me about their travels to Alaska. "We'd heard of a place companions could go, a sort of safe haven. But by the time we got there, the place had been cleared out, burned up. There was nothing left."

It terrified me, thinking of Andy so far away, in a place like that, all ice and fire. I held tight to his arm. I would never let him go again.

"We took him to Portland, Seattle, Vancouver, all the way through BC to Juneau. Months we had to stay in some places to scrape together the credit we needed for fuel. He was such a little trouper. Our boy loves to travel."

Our boy. Hearing them call Andy that, the anger was hot and all over me. I wanted to correct them: *He's* my *brother.* But the way they talked about Andy, it got me thinking—what happens to a companion who's no longer a companion? That's what Andy had been to them, someone to care for, to love. I knew I should be angrier with them, but I also knew they needed that as much as I did.

Andy smiled at me, his mischievous smile—God, I remembered it—and he grabbed hold of Lilac's wrist, pressing his finger to the seizing spot where veins should be. I'd done it plenty of times with the livewires, sending them into jolting fits.

"Don't you dare," she said playfully, a smile in her eyes. There were moments when they seemed so real, like right then, so full of love. How could I not understand? I loved him too.

Jakob helped me with the dishes. He seemed to like his female body, slinking around all sexy-like. It gave me strange feelings I tried to wash down the sink as I scrubbed the dishes and he dried. "Do you have a girlfriend?" he asked me.

"I'm too busy with the farm. No time for girls."

"Maybe you're scared," he said, flipping his hair. I focused on the dishes.

"I was in love once," he said, "terrible woman. She's a mother now, can you believe it? That poor child."

"Maybe she's changed. People change," I insisted. It had to be true.

"I've changed bodies so many times I've lost count, and nothing about me has changed. Not once."

"That's different. You're not really—"

"Human?"

Shit, I didn't want to offend him, but it was true, wasn't it? It wasn't as hard as I thought, not hating them, but still, I couldn't so much as say I was sorry.

That night Andy slept in the bottom bunk, Pit Bull planted on his chest. I slept in the top bunk for the first time in a year, checking Andy often, meeting Pit Bull's somber eyes with each house creak. We would never sleep well again. Awake, my mind spun Lilac's words.

Before bed, she'd pulled me out onto the porch. "You know, we could stick around for a while, help you with the farm—think how much more you could accomplish with a couple companion laborers." She laughed, and I laughed, but she was right—the extra hands could really help. Still, harboring a companion after the recall was dangerous. *In these uncertain times?* I heard Pa saying. I didn't get the chance to say no. Andy leapt out from the shadow of Pa's shed where he'd been hiding.

"Please," he begged, tugging on my arm. I picked him up and held him despite his size, and he didn't squirm or kick or pull away from me.

"Well?" Lilac prompted.

"All right," I told her, rocking Andy side to side, "for now."

NINE YEARS
AFTER THE RECALL

RACHEL

I stroll into Golden Gate Park from Stanyan with the backpack slung over my shoulder, past the old stagnant pond, through the rock tunnel where dark things happen at night. There's the waft of reefer from the hill of hippies with their skin-topped drums, the street kids in their tree huddles, the playground thrumming with toddlers. Where is the fear? It's been more than a decade since quarantine ended, ancient history to most people. I buy a coffee at the kiosk, peer through the dusted glass to the old wooden carousel, real horsehair for tails, eyelashes even. A sign on the door says it was shut for quarantine and it's unclear if it will run again.

A couple of bike cops ride toward me on the path and I take a sip of coffee, give them a slight smile-and-nod as they pass. Then I spit the coffee back into the cup, wipe my tongue on my sleeve, and curl off toward the smooth greens of the bocce courts, the old men in white lobbing balls in a smooth crest of arm. It's warm, girls in tank tops and men jogging shirtless, a field of sunbathers. The people thin out as I hike nearly to the ocean, so close I can hear it smashing into the seawall that will never hold. It makes me nervous, being so close to water, the last fear I have left.

I've only been here a few months but already I hate it, all the smiling, the *excuse mes*—San Francisco is way too friendly. I miss New York with its bristling cold, people ready to walk over your body to get home or to work or a dinner date. At least they're honest about it, an elbow to the ribs, a *fuck you* if you so much as look at them sideways.

The soccer fields are empty, abandoned, soupy with water soaked up through the soil. The ocean, it's coming, one way or another. I dump my lukewarm coffee in the trash and take the path along the chain-link fence, my running shoes caked in mud.

The man is waiting alone. He's on the younger side of middle-aged but already softening and nervous, checking his watch, digging his hand in his pocket, a gun. I can see its shape as I trudge through the mud, making enough noise for him to hear me. I'm not interested in surprising him—it's not that kind of meet-up.

His face brightens when he sees me. They always do that. This model I'm in, so frail and feminine, twenty-one, maybe. That's how they see me. It doesn't matter how bulky or weak we seem on the outside; we're all made of metal and stronger than any person. Before the recall, the only thing that kept the average companion from killing was programming, but I had that stripped away long ago.

A wand won't work on me and he knows it. All he can do is pat me up, and he does, diligently, every square inch, my system registering each prod and squeeze.

"Do you have it?" he asks.

I unzip the backpack, show him the cash. A credit transfer is easily made anonymous, but he'd insisted. Some people are like that.

He cups the hard drive in his hands as I insert the cable into my neck, feel the surge of connection, of information, though I don't absorb the data like memory. It sits behind a partition, in a place I couldn't access if I tried.

We separate and he smiles, embarrassed, new to this. I've done it a thousand times. I toss him the backpack. He opens it on a redwood stump, one of many this close to the ocean, trees leaning uneasily in the slow root rot, the ground covered in crunchy ice plant. Inspecting the contents, he takes his eyes off me long enough that I reach down to the rubber sole of my shoe where the metal file I sharpened this morning is lodged, and I feed it into the base of his neck, catching him as his knees give. I could've snapped his neck, but that's companion work, and I have to make it appear human. He doesn't go right away. Instead, it's a bit like paralysis, his eyes blinking up at me though his body is broken, his ability to make speech gone. I lay him on the soupy ground and disentangle the backpack of cash from his shoulder. I can feel him watching, practically hear him screeching in his head, and I take up a rock and bring it down.

I ride the bus to my meet-up with Nat in Bernal, next to an old man reeking of gum disease and dead skin, and I go off in my memories, to our first meeting on East Falkland three years ago. Nat had some acres, a compound, a couple dozen companions living there. It was a type of refuge, a place companions could go, and they came, the companions, while they still could, avoiding air travel and sticking to the roads, thousands of miles in some cases, hiding on boats, bribing people—Nat didn't turn them away as long as they agreed to work. And who would make a better worker than a companion? No need for water or food, only power, of which there was plenty in the Falklands with its battery of oil rigs and deal with Desire Petroleum—as long as the wells bled oil, the Falklands would never want for fuel.

The memories play and it's as if I'm there, unlike the ones from my human life. Those are dim and dangerous. But not this, not Nat, coming out of the compound's main house, the first time I saw him. He wore wool and had a beard and a head of long hair, an animal smell. He smiled and I could see his heart in his eyes, the blinking, bloody mass that pumped him, and I thought for the first time in a long while that being alive is a lovely, dangerous thing. I don't know why I thought that then. Perhaps I was attracted to him.

"How'd you get here?" he asked me. I knew what he was thinking: I couldn't have flown all those miles, crossed all those borders, getting harder every year since the mass recall—how had I managed to get to the island undetected? I gave him the story my handler had come up with: the wealthy man I was a companion to had a private plane, and he'd brought me to Santiago where I'd escaped, paid a sailor to bring me here by boat.

It was a good idea, the story. I could see it register in Nat's eyes, what a companion like me would have endured in the meek female body my handler always selected for me—he was a slender, particular man and a fan of the shock effect. It gave him a thrill, the surprise my victims felt at my strength and speed, the easy way I could kill.

Nat threw an arm over my shoulders. I could smell his unwashed hair, the damp wool of his sweater, and I thought with a pang of fresh pain of the dog I'd had as a girl, white and mischievous. She'd come back pregnant once, had a litter of six puppies, all of which my mother made us give away, and she'd never been the same, my dog—why can't I remember her name?

* * *

As I'm walking up to the coffee shop to meet Nat, the door swings open, a woman, I know her, young, short hair, trying to hide under a hoodie—Gabe. So that's why Nat made me meet him here.

"Sorry," she mutters, observing me a little longer than normal before brushing past, and I wonder, does she know what I am? Most people can't tell, but the ones who have experience with companions, well, they can identify us on sight.

I've been following Nat for a few weeks, seen him trailing Gabe. She lives in the Outer Excelsior alone and works in Potrero Hill, a small storefront she shares with some artists, stationery and custom cards, and it'll probably fail. Nice idea—local products, letters—but all that artistry for a handwritten note? Feels like they're trying too hard. And really, how many people could have a need for that? Yet whenever I spy Nat spying her, the shop always has a customer or two.

I know other things. I know, for example, that even though Gabe lives in the Outer Excelsior, she likes to stop in Bernal on her way home for a yoga class or a latte. It's a habit, one of an isolated person. Sure, she's chummy with some of the people in her classes, but she always leaves alone, smile fading as she walks, hood of her sweatshirt coming up.

Nat and me, we both have vapor trails we're chasing, only his is living, Gabe—the girl he'd raised on the road, four years out of a van in the redwoods of Humboldt County. I've never worked up the nerve to ask him why he left, why he'd gone all the way to the Falklands. I know not to press him where Gabe is concerned.

I find Nat nursing a cold coffee in the back jungle of a patio where a trio of musicians improvises.

"You have it?" he asks, palming his shaved head. It's been three years since we parted ways in Tierra del Fuego, after I saved his life, or destroyed it, depending on who you ask.

I can see his hands are shaking, and not from the caffeine. His pink-rimmed eyes, the yellow pallor of his skin—he is not well, hungover, maybe even drunk.

"Pretty girl," I say, hoping to liven him, and it works, eyes blinking up at me, and I see inside them a flare of anger not unlike the one I'd seen the day we left the Falklands.

"How long have you been tailing me?"

"Long enough to see the pattern." I pass him the spindle of data I downloaded in the café's bathroom. Only a fool would carry a companion's consciousness on a spindle for longer than necessary, and I'm no fool, even if it means using myself for storage. The companion brain is often disrupted in these kinds of transactions, and I wouldn't even be aware of it, if I'd lost memories—it's the sort of shift only someone who knows you can identify, and no one knows me.

"Who is it?" I ask him.

He tucks the spindle into the pocket of his jacket, frets his scarred eyebrow. "Someone I knew once. What's left of him, anyway. He burned through a lot of memories."

"Courier?"

He nods slowly, like it hurts. I once thought him handsome, but now he is rubbery and old and I have a rare maternal urge to tuck him into bed, to warn him it's foolishness, helping companions—it won't be long until we're all gone, wiped from the earth. They'll put him away for years, what's left of his youth, if he keeps on like this.

"Well?" I prompt him. Nat runs a security firm and has plenty of staff, but this is the kind of passion project he likes to keep on the side, and I'm perfect for on-the-side jobs, no handler anymore, nothing I won't do. Plus, it was the only way he'd agree to take me to her.

"She still goes by Lilac," he says.

"After all these years?"

"And she's a courier."

"Shit. How long?"

"Not sure. Years now."

"Christ." I know what moving information can do to a companion—I've been doing it too, relieved at the thought of forgetting, of not knowing to miss them, the ghosts of my past.

"She isn't going to like it, you showing up unannounced—if she remembers you at all. Are you sure this is a good idea?"

"Get some sleep," I tell him. "See you tomorrow."

Cortland Avenue is positively bustling, bookstores and ice cream shops and yoga studios and bicyclists clogging the road. This lifestyle, this way of being out in the world, of interacting, it seems irritatingly quaint and San Franciscan, as if they refuse to commit to the glasses New Yorkers wear like armor, with their endless streams of data, not after those years indoors—will it last?

On the bus ride home there are no seats. I hold on to the filthy metal bar, swaying with the others, our bodies bumping, and I pull up the memories, play back the trip to the compound.

I'd taken a small, moderately populated plane from Santiago to Stanley with top-notch fake papers, a bag of pretzels in my lap, not even concerned about being discovered. My confidence at that point was unparalleled—it had been some years since I'd uploaded, longer still since I'd made a mistake I'd had to pay for. My mind was lost on my feed, unspooling the islands' history behind my eyes—Vespucci claimed to have sighted the Falklands in 1502, the Magellan expedition in 1520. The first Brit to lay eyes on the islands was John Davis, 1592, of the HMS *Desire*, pushed by storms to *certain Isles never before discovered by any knowen relation*. I tried to imagine what it was like to travel without a destination. I had never journeyed so far, and the feed with its flutter of data behind my eyes was a comfort.

It told me there was a population of penguins along the southern rim of East Falkland, the island where I was headed. It was out of my way, but I'd make a point to visit. I'd never seen a penguin outside a zoo.

As we neared the islands, I abandoned my feed for the window, British warships in the water in case the Argentinians decided to test the crown's claim to the islands for a third time, patrol boats skimming the blue. Oil rigs fringed the eastern coast where some fifteen billion barrels of crude lay under the Patagonian Shelf, and Desire Petroleum, named for that questionable discovery, had finally tapped it.

I picked up a Rover in the rental lot. The airport was connected to the town of Stanley by a bridge, underneath which flowed a man-made channel dug to feed the expanding waters of Whalebone Cove back into the South Atlantic Ocean.

I passed Stanley in a human's heartbeat, so small and yet it was the biggest city on the island, full of Rovers, not a single ad—I remember that—how dull the cluster of red- and blue-roofed buildings seemed without the commercial glow of product. I slowed for the old red-and-rock church, an arch made of whalebones, my feed delivering me information as I drove. The first people to stay here had been whalers, and it had always been about oil, boiling blubber inside whale casing like a cauldron, using penguins for their flammable fat to feed a dying fire. On the way out of town was a neat fence of sandbags lining the southern edge of the cove.

I was not in a hurry to get to the compound, heading southwest on Darwin Road where I hoped I might see some penguins. The road ran right up along the water in some places. Long stretches of flat brown beach, bare, not a single seal or penguin, only a few seabirds circling. Not far from the road was a lone marker, what turned out to be a gravestone for a British soldier, KILLED IN ACTION ON THIS SPOT, MAY 1982—I didn't need my feed to tell me it was the First Falklands War, when Argentinian soldiers occupied the islands and Margaret Thatcher, with her hard hair and muscular position on capitulating to demands, quickly struck back. My feed fluttered anyway, showing me photos of Argentinian soldiers planting land mines, British seamen in white antiflash hoods and giant oven mitts flame-proofed in boric acid. Then my feed got lost on a Thatcher tangent, Bobby Sands in the Maze Prison in Northern Ireland, 1981, hollowed out from hunger strike, and Thatcher with her hard hair, refusing once again to capitulate, even in the face of such suffering.

"Enough," I said, and glanced up to see a wooden barricade blocking the road. I nearly collided with it—the sign marked ROAD CLOSED. I checked my map, which offered clear ingress. But ahead of me was a narrow isthmus connecting the eastern span of the island to the Lafonia region, utterly inaccessible even in a Rover. The road was a wet wash of dirt and rocks and decaying plant matter, an obvious floodplain, and Lafonia had become a seasonal island, even if my feed said otherwise.

I turned north, my connection giving out as the road wound

inland, rocky tumbles and fog and blond bunchgrass. It was there that I saw my first sheep, hills of them, recently shaved and scrawny, rib bones shifting in their skin as they scattered. At their peak these islands had once had nearly a million head. Years of decline in seasonal rainfall, longer summers, stretches of drought. Now herds were culled to keep the lot from perishing. It was all oil wealth and no water.

I reached a high point, a blanket of black earth stretching ahead of me. I got out of the Rover and bent to touch the burnt grass crumbling in my fingers—fire, not old, miles of hillside scorched, leaving a dark stretch of desert. Then I got back in the Rover and drove on.

My feed came in clear as I neared the compound, cruising past a field of solar panels, row after row like crops. It was silly, considering all that oil—but this was companion territory, and we have a different notion of time. At some point, the oil would dry up here too.

The compound seemed petite in contrast, a wooden main house, two smaller brick buildings, a fleet of Rovers behind the slatted fence. I rolled to a stop at the gate. "Hello?" I said into the intercom. There was a crackle, a woman's voice telling me to stay still while the I8 scanned me. It came buzzing along the sides of my Rover, under, scanning for weapons. Pausing in my window, it drew close to me, its wings fluttering feverishly like a hummingbird, its pin eye probing and exploring my body. It zipped off, the gate inching open, and I rolled in, tires popping on the gravel, met with guns, a group of them, coming out of the main building, from the smaller buildings, companions the lot. Except Nat.

He waved off the guns, took me around, gave me a tour. I saw a companion lying in a hammock, a couple playing cards—all this idling, and for what? In the kitchen was something I'd never seen, a companion without skin, wearing only jeans, his metal frame showing clean and skeletal as he bent to set a mousetrap.

"Why do you help them?" I asked Nat once we were out back and alone, the sky blazing red, the sun settled low on the horizon.

"They help me too. It's an arrangement."

"But why did they start coming in the first place?"

He told me that years ago he'd taken something that didn't belong to him, data he copied and sold to a stranger for major credit. He used that to buy the land, dirt cheap given the drought, and he'd worked it alone for some months before it hit him, the guilt. "Some things shouldn't be sold," he said. "Some people should never be left behind." By then he'd heard about what was happening, the recall, and he knew he needed the help, so he put a notice in the shadow spaces of the Internet, inviting them. He couldn't pay, but any companion who was willing to work was safe. At that point he'd met only one, Lilac, from Laguna Beach, and he kept hoping she'd find him, though she never did.

"Lilac?" I'd repeated, needing confirmation. Couldn't be.

Nat nodded, told me she'd been a friend to his Gabe, and I'd been certain, prodding him on, earning details. Yes, her, definitely her, how could it be? That night I couldn't go into sleep mode, so excited I was at the prospect of seeing her again.

I have a box in one of the new Western Addition buildings, just enough room for a bunk, a kitchenette, not that I need either. I shut myself inside, store the backpack in my safe under the bed. Then I head down the hall to the bathroom, the sound of screens carrying from the singles. I shut myself inside, lift my shirt to the mirror. The skin there has begun to fester, my stomach mottled with sores, my metal insides showing in the gaps. I have no more handlers;

there are no more bodies, no examinations, no upgrades—why did
I give it up? Lilac is the only other companion I know of in all the
world. I wonder at the state of her body, if she's as damaged as I am
by now.

I lie on my bunk, go into sleep mode for the first time in days,
and when I wake to my alarm I'm thinking of the Falklands. Was
I dreaming? It's not supposed to be possible for a companion to
dream, but I can feel it, like a lozenge on the tongue, both present
and disappearing all at once, the Falklands.

Nat was so terribly alive, so painfully living—his wrinkles and
dog smell and that bumpy caterpillar of a scar threading his eyebrow, how he ate, an unsettling hunger, food dribbling his beard.
For the first time I didn't like it, the idea of cracking his head or
slitting his throat or bashing his brain in with a rock.

I had a window, seventy-two hours, and I waited nearly to the
end of it. We were hiking up a hill and he was telling me, "There are
no trees native to the Falklands. The only ones here are the exotics
the Europeans brought to remind them of home." I didn't understand what he was talking about, why it mattered, what it was that
made him glow.

"There," he said when we reached the hill's crest—a herd of
reindeer, maybe a hundred, their velvet horns shining even in the
weak light of the gray morning. "Norwegian whalers brought them
to nearby South Georgia near the turn of the twentieth century. By
1958 there were three thousand—it must've been something to see!
But people began to think of them as pests, causing erosion, desert-
ifying whole stretches of the island. The plan was extermination, so
the Falklands agreed to take some calves, and eventually they were
brought here, to East Falkland. I like to picture it, those first calves
borne across the Southern Ocean, the only reindeer population not

poisoned by Chernobyl in the whole of the world. I wonder how many of them died on the voyage."

None, my feed told me, a safe voyage, and I was relieved. It was a fine story, and I could see that Nat enjoyed telling it. Sorry, I was sorry I had to kill him.

We climbed higher, Nat chattering about his plans, the desal plant. "We'll have water to irrigate the fields, that'll mean more sheep. Do you know what those ladies in LA pay for our wool?"

I wanted to tell him he sounded like a fool—there was no taking a place back to what it once was—but I knew he couldn't see it, the island's slow destruction, if not by oil, by water. It endeared him to me even more. An innocent. "They sent me to remove you," I blurted out.

"To remove me?"

"Desire."

"Why would they do that?"

"They're going to kill the desal plant, or at least delay it long enough to clear this place out. They don't want any friction."

His face tightened, taking on a whole new shape and shade I didn't like. He turned angrily on me, taking me by the arm. I let him press his fingers into my wrist, to feel for the seizing spot most companions have, a fail-safe, one I had removed long ago. When I didn't fall to the yellow turf grass in a fit, his eyes found mine, and I saw it, his fear, taking hold of his hand and bending it at his back. I expected him to go down like the rest of them, but he threw his weight into me until we were falling, rock and grass and something in my back.

He rolled away from me, and I examined my back, my metal insides showing where the skin had torn loose. My body still bears the mark. When I looked up, he was running. I couldn't catch him in that uneven terrain—companions are fast on flat ground but not terribly agile—so I picked up a rock and catapulted it at him, got him right in the back of the head.

I drove to the nearest port, Nat slumped in the passenger seat. Out of the car, I stalked the docks, grabbing the nearest sailor I could find, a white-bearded man, arms sleeved in scaly tattoos.

"Mainland," I told the man, "credit." He disappeared onto his boat, then came back and told me Tierra del Fuego. I handed over a few of the cards loaded with credit I carried for emergency purposes, when I needed to be untraceable, and then I went back for Nat.

I hefted him onto the boat over my shoulder, the ship's captain and sole mate sharing a look.

"Drunk," I said, and deposited Nat onto the ship's wooden bench.

Only as we were pulling away from the island did I see a penguin, loads of them, two different species that my feed could identify. Gentoo, named for a racial slur used by white Europeans in India to distinguish Hindus from Muslims. And Magellanic, for that famous explorer, the first to circumnavigate the globe by a narrow strait separating Tierra del Fuego from the mainland, weeping when he saw the tranquil blue Pacific. I turned to tell Nat, to show him, but he was slumped on the bench, drops of blood turning pink on the damp deck.

When he woke, he was gagged and tied in Tierra del Fuego. I gave him some of my cards and told him to never go back, and I guess he didn't because when I looked him up next, he was in San Francisco, alive. After that I switched off my feed, only using it when I had to. My mind was too muddled with memories, knowing that Lila was alive—Lilac, she calls herself now. That when I was ready, Nat could lead me to her.

Nat pings me, startling me out of my memories: Be outside in ten.

Through the tiny porthole of a window I see a gray clotted sky, the dull haze of drizzle. "Great," I say to no one. That's something I've gotten used to about San Francisco. One day it's tank top weather, the next gray gloom. I grab my raincoat, an umbrella, the backpack of money he thinks I delivered. Then I head out to meet Nat, the poor fool—he should have known better than to trust me with a job that doesn't involve killing.

He blinks headlights at me, and I hop into the passenger seat of his cargo van, newly painted black and sleek and smelling like french fries. He pulls out into the heavy traffic of Franklin, climbing the hill toward the Marina. We arc down its other side, the bay showing an anemic blue ahead of us, the great V of the levee churning an unnatural waterfall.

He glances over at me. "Why can't you just leave it alone? She probably won't even remember."

"I told you. I have information for her." And something I need her to do, I don't tell him. Something I can't do for myself.

We take the Broadway Tunnel to North Beach, linger near a square, the smell of pancakes and coffee wafting out of a restaurant. It's quaint here, like a postcard of old San Francisco, with its rows of Victorians and coffeehouses and bookstores and street art, but the downtown towers make me nervous, hundreds of floors, looming over us like that. I wonder what will happen when the next great earthquake hits.

I can tell the breakfast smell is turning Nat's stomach, so I roll up the window. I'm about to ask him what we're doing when the back door opens and a boy wearing a tracksuit hops in, long hair pulled into a ponytail at the nape of his neck, a gun bulging in his pocket, followed by a companion, female, a meek model like me, hiding behind bangs and the fake-fur lining of an oversize coat.

"Who's this?" she asks Nat as he's easing us back onto the road.

"Well?" he says to me.

I hadn't thought about the words—what I'd say, how I'd say it. I want to tell her I'm sorry, I'm changed, but I'm not sorry and I haven't changed. She blinks in my direction like she's practiced at appearing human, like she can't stop even now, shut in this moving van with me.

Standing on the cliffs, holding that shovel in my living teen-age hands, the hot feeling of anger. We were just girls—what was I so angry about? She had embarrassed me; I remember that much. She thought she was better than everyone else. But how can that be enough?

"I was sixteen when I hurt you, when I took your human life." It had been so short, and I know a little about her companion life, what I've gathered in research, a couple years with a family in a San Francisco tower not far from here. Whatever happened to her, it couldn't have been good if she's a courier, wiping memories to carry information, losing herself. I wonder if I'm in there at all, if Nat's right, and she's forgotten me entirely.

"Red," she says. At first I think she's confused me with someone else. But that's right. I remember now. I was a redhead in my youth.

Her face darkens with recognition. I see it—the hate rekindled, remembered. Standing, steadying herself against the side of the van.

"Andy?" she says to the boy. He is quick with his gun and over-excited. I can tell he's never killed, the way he's aiming it at me.

Nat calls from the driver's seat, "Hey now."

"What's she doing here?" Lilac hisses at him.

"She has information for you."

She hunches toward me from the back of the van, a Taser in her hand, and I push myself into the door, knowing I deserve it. I press my eyes shut and try to remember the last time I saw her, at the nursing home. I was ancient by then, a whole human life behind me, my mind going. Metis patched up my brain for companionship, excellent work considering how long I went dead—the tech told me ten minutes, a real rarity. I tested fine and was shipped out for companionship, but it'd left things holey, especially those last years, only ghost memories, really just her rolling into my room, reminding me of what I'd done. I'd waited my whole life for someone to catch me, to find out what I was. Even old and weak, I broke her cheap first-gen body, apparently—how could I not remember that? It was in my incident report from the home, a companion named Lilac, destroyed. I've been collecting data on myself, on anyone I'm interested in, for as long as I've been free.

I open my eyes and she's got the Taser to my neck and I say it: "I know where Nikki is."

Lilac lurches away from me, braces herself on the wall of the van as Nat takes a turn into the parking garage of a tower.

"Who's Nikki?" Andy asks.

The van drifts into darkness, my stomach sinking as we take a ramp past walls of stacked cars, turning a screw down levels until finally Nat finds an open spot and pulls in.

Lilac sits cross-legged on the floor, leaning against the side of the van. Like a child, I catch myself thinking—but she's the same age as me, nearing her centennial. "She was my best friend. When I was younger than you," she says to Andy. Then she flicks her eyes at me. "How'd you find her? I searched so many times."

"I knew where she went. Her family moved to Australia within a year after your death. Changed their last name and everything—why would they do that?" I don't say what I'm thinking: did they know I was dangerous?

"Why'd you go looking for her?"

"There's something I need."

She snorts unattractively.

"I have cash. And it's an easy job, one you'll enjoy."

"Where did you get—" Nat starts to ask when it dawns on him, what I've done. He gives me a knowing, hateful glare. He could never love me. No one who knows what I've done ever could.

"What do you want?" Lilac asks.

"I want you to kill me."

I can feel it, their repulsion, how they want away from me—I feel stronger because of it, lifting my shirt, showing them my sored stomach. "I won't be able to hide for much longer." I let them get a good look, pull my shirt back down. "If you want to talk to Nikki, you should do it before it's too late."

"What do you mean, too late?"

"She's old. Ill."

"How long?"

"I don't know."

She's quiet for a while, we all are, and I can hear the squeal of tires, the sound of strangers as they park their cars and file off.

We take an elevator up to the forty-second floor, accompanied by a slow sax song—elevator music hasn't changed much in all the years I've walked the earth. The doors open, a wide hallway gleaming wood, old black-and-white photographs of San Francisco hanging on the walls, painted a nearly nude seashell color. At the end of the hall is a giant vase full of flowers, living—I can smell them from here as Nat thumbs his way into one of the apartments.

"Yours?" I ask him, but I can tell by the blank gray space that it couldn't be anyone else's. Once he'd been so warm, his house crammed with souls, but now he lives alone and can't be bothered to populate the place with things.

"This place is depressing," Lilac says.

Nat shoots her a glare. "You look like Cam, you know."

"Shut up. Not like I had options."

Who's Cam? I want to ask, but don't. I can see it's a touchy subject.

Nat pulls the companion I smuggled to him up on the screen.

"The color of caramel," the companion says, as if we've pulled him back midthought.

"Jakob? You okay?" Lilac asks.

"They caught me, didn't they?"

"Of course they caught you," Lilac says, "you went to see him."

He laughs, so loud he goes machine on the screen's inferior speaker system, Nat and Andy clutching their ears. "That's right," he says. "At that San Francisco premiere. The sixth of those terrible pirate alien movies. That hideous suit I—I mean, he—was wearing. All those roles, those souls, to get me here? I wanted to kill him. Did I kill him?"

Lilac drops into the seat at the screen. "You exposed him. As a companion. Same difference."

Quiet for the longest time. Jakob's voice so small, barely registering: "Where's my body?"

"Gone. Security was on you in a—"

"Christ. You should've left me! Lilac, I don't want to—don't want this—you can't—"

Nat dims the screen, and Lilac is staring, staring at me.

"What?"

"If you don't want it anymore, maybe?" she says.

"My body?" I've had it five years, before that so many bodies, a new one every six months or so, whenever it pleased my handler. But this one I've lived in too long—I feel oddly possessive. "It sounds like he doesn't want it."

"She's right," Nat says. "Besides, hers is falling apart."

"Thanks," I say.

"Well, it's true."

I go to the screen, lean so close to Lilac we're nearly touching, the closest we've been since the cliffs, and I call up the feed, leave it for her to connect, back away, relieved by the distance. "Nikki lives with her daughter in Melbourne," I tell her. "This is her feed." Andy hovers at Lilac's shoulder, Nat gone entirely. She presses connect, and we wait.

An old withered face—I don't recognize her. I mean, my facial recognition software tells me who she is, but my memories, they don't sit with this ancient person. Good Lord, how she's shrunk and shriveled, like a corpse, only living. Her eyes, that's all that's left of her old self, bright and shining and seeing us.

"Do I know you?" she asks. I feel myself backing out of the room, no, I can't be here, afraid. I haven't felt it for ages, running out of the apartment, covering my ears, though this doesn't help—I can hear Lilac: "You were my best friend, the only one I had. I'm sorry for . . ." I make for the emergency stairwell, far enough that I can't hear—it's too much, what I've done, and my head pulses with the pain, my stomach, how can it hurt? I slump onto the steps, and that kid Andy comes for me, standing off a bit.

"What's wrong with you?"

"Leave me alone." I don't mean to yell.

"No."

I take in his fragile human features, bones showing under the skin, veins right below the surface. "What's wrong with you?"

"What's wrong with *you*?" he parrots in a mocking voice.

"Where's your family?"

Andy grins, kicks the stair with his sneaker. "My folks are dead. When Pa passed, Rolly, that's my older brother, he took over the disposal center. Until the recall. Now he's some boring farmer."

"Is that how you met Lilac?"

"Yup. She came for a body. For Jakob. He's always losing bodies!" I observe him humorlessly as he laughs. "We stayed there awhile, all of us, until Rolly told Lilac and Jakob he couldn't have it, companions lurking about—dangerous! He tried to stop me from going with them, to keep me on the farm, but the farthest he's traveled is Mendocino County. And me? I've seen Alaska."

"What's it like?"

He shrugs. "I remember it green, greener than you'd expect."

"Nothing else?"

"I was like four years old. I don't remember much from back then."

I think back to four, trying to recall a single memory, but I come up blank. Those years, that life, dead and gone.

"Why'd you do it, become a companion?" he asks.

"Why do you care?"

"I wish I could be one."

"You've got a whole life ahead of you."

"Yeah, but then I'll die. I could die tomorrow. I could die right now."

"I could too."

"But your brain. You could move—"

"There are no more bodies. I'd be stuck in a screen like your friend Jakob. How do you think you'd like that, being stuck in a screen?"

He frowns, swipes his hair off his shoulder. "Well, are you gonna tell me?"

"Fine." And I tell him my whole sob story.

I signed the contract ages ago, back when my mind was still super-ficially functioning. My daughter-in-law was furious with me for spending so much. "You know how tight our budget is. How can we afford you?"

I told her, "You will inherit all my money, dear. Surely it's not too much to ask." But she refused. We'd never gotten along. I remember the way she would survey me when she thought I wasn't paying attention, waiting for me to get sick, die—I could see it—and my son, the pushover, he went along with her, so I had to sign myself away to strangers.

Still, it meant living, and my life hadn't been much. I'd gotten preg-nant in college and been stupid enough to have it, get married, all of it. After what I did to Lilac, it felt like I deserved a good punishment. We played out that miserable charade until our son was out of the house. Then my husband told me he didn't feel fulfilled any longer and moved out, into the forest to fight fires, some sort of militia operation. It was insane.

And I feel it again, burning up my insides, a shovel in my hands, the satisfying thud of contact.

I refused to see my son, my daughter-in-law. I kept expecting them to have a baby, for something to bring us back together—I knew they'd been trying. I waited for the news, but it never came. And when my mind started to go, they put me in a home. Factually I know my son is dead, suicide—I've seen the autopsy report—but I don't feel it. I can't.

Andy is already bored, bouncing side to side on the balls of his feet, but I go on. The telling—it feels good to share my story, awful too, like I'm casting off clothing.

I was leased by a man, old, a widower. He asked me to tell him stories, to rub his feet. He'd lost his entire family to the virus. What he really needed was a nurse, but he'd leased me instead. Mostly I think it was for the stories.

"Sex stories?" Andy asks, suppressing a giggle.

I smile. What a child. He has no business with a gun.

At night I'd lie next to him wearing his wife's pajamas. He could have had sex with me. I'd come with a fully operational body, but he wasn't interested in that. He liked the sound of my voice, to feel me next to him, for me to make him breakfast, a boiled egg and toast. When he didn't wake one morning, I packed a bag and went out onto the street, and I've never been a companion since.

I don't tell Andy this, but on my own, without anyone to know me, to remember me, to ask me to tell my story, I've nearly shed her entirely—my human self. And I'm glad to be done with her.

"Nat says you kill people."

"People find out you're a companion and they want you to do things for them. Things they can't do for themselves."

"So why can't you do it? Kill yourself?"

"I've tried. Maybe it's programming." I don't say this, but maybe I'm just a coward.

"You could pay somebody. You could pay me."

To pay some killer to do it. To be left in a field somewhere, to be found. "I need to be destroyed, not just killed. And Lilac's the only person on the planet I'm certain will do it right." This part's a lie. Plenty of people would be glad to see me gone permanently—but her, it has to be her. It started with her.

"You can trust me," he says, nodding, moving side to side again, he's so excited.

I take him by the collar, lift him in the air. "You've got no idea what you're saying." His eyes go big and scared, and I put him back down on the stairwell. "Tell them I'd like to go for a drive, will you?"

Nat drives the four of us through the grid streets of the Sunset, the sky clear, the ocean showing as we descend toward sea level, the seawalls white and glaring in the sun. He tries to talk me out of it, a new body: "It can't be that hard to come by, we have all that cash, why are you doing this?" But I ignore his words, rolling the window down, listening for the toss of the ocean.

I direct him to the spot I scouted some weeks ago, just south of the old Cliff House, not far from where I killed that man in Golden Gate Park. I wonder who found him, a child, a homeless person, if he's still there, sinking into the soppy earth.

Nat gets out of the van, comes around, grabs me by the arms, shaking me. I could push him off, snap his finger bones, if I wanted to.

"Enough," I say, and he can tell by my voice I mean it, letting me loose.

"Why'd you leave Gabe?" I ask him.

"Because I was scared. Because I loved her so goddamned much."

"Bullshit."

He rakes his shaved head with his fingers, stubble already coming in from yesterday. Flecks of scalp skin float off in the ocean breeze. "Too much, okay? I loved her too much."

I know nothing of that kind of love. Too many memories of my son lost to old age, dementia, and time, just time. "You told her you'd come back, didn't you?"

"The last thing she needs in her life is someone like me."

"Why? What's so wrong with you?" As far as humans go, Nat's one of the best I've met, one of the few I've come to like, maybe the only. You're a good man, I want to tell him. So I do. I have never said something like that, never in my life, and it comes out awkwardly, quiet, barely words, and all he can do is gape at me. "I know. It doesn't mean much coming from me."

"I wish you wouldn't go."

"Why?"

He can't give me a reason. We aren't even friends.

"Don't be an idiot," I call over my shoulder as I climb the rocks, get a grip on the seawall's lip, pull myself to its top. For a moment I think he's going to climb the wall and come after me, but he doesn't. He doesn't watch either, going back to the van, shutting himself inside.

I stretch out a hand for Lilac, but she pulls herself up on her own. Andy's hopping, trying to get a grip "Help," he says.

"You stay there," Lilac tells him, though he goes on hopping and clawing at the wall until he's sweating and angry and watching us from below.

The ocean crashes against the seawall. They've built the wall tall here, hoping not to have to do it again for some years. No doubt the Outer Richmond residents aren't pleased with the loss of view, but it's better than losing their houses, at least for now.

"I wish you'd reconsider," Lilac says. "I know Jakob will change his mind. He thinks it's hopeless."

"It is."

"It doesn't have to be now."

She's right—it doesn't have to be now. But I'm tired of deciding who stays, who goes. "I heard him. What he wants."

She's angry, not hiding it. "So you want me to push you, is that it?"

"Something like that." I can see that she doesn't want to, but even worse that she does, and I'm sorry for her, my fault, I made her this way, and it's not as hard as I imagined to let your body lean far enough that it's falling, to let gravity guide you to the crashing waves.

I hit the water with an unforgiving thud, and for a moment I'm stunned, sinking, finding the cool undercurrent, waves gentle from down here. My legs, my arms, they come back to me, and I push my body forward, water making its way into my insides through my sored stomach. It's been years since I last swam. Even as a person, I gave it up long before my body stopped working. I swim for the surface, flopping out of the water like a dolphin, pushing myself farther out, never once looking back to see if Lilac's watching. Diving deep, toward the bottom. Minutes I spend down there, seeing everything, fish and tangled masses of seaweed and floating trash and crabs scuttling the seafloor, before my body gives out, and I roll to face the ocean's surface, the light showing through the murky green water. I think of the Falklands so far off, the colony of penguins on the western shore, bustling with movement, the energy it takes just to live.

FOURTEEN YEARS
AFTER THE RECALL

LILAC

MARIN COUNTY, CALIFORNIA

Where I live now is a blank space. I imagine you live somewhere similar. I can fill it with light, with sorrow, drench it in horror, erase it all with an ocean roar. I can fill it with memories, you putting on your sister's clothes. Lea! I can remember her name—I don't know why. There are washes of gray nothing where whole years should be, but I remember thinking something bad would happen at that house party. That you wanted something bad to happen. Why would that be?

Often I spend my time on fantasies. I see you, I say your name, Nikki, we walk arm in arm. It is sunny out, raining leaves. It is always sunny out.

As pleasant as they are, I try not to spend too much time on fantasies. I worry about my memories, what's real, what's imagined. Since I've come here, it's been harder and harder to tell the difference.

Most nights Andy visits with me. I listen to him complain about the withered skin of his hands, the fryer smell in his hair, the cramped trailer we live in behind Lou's Steak Shack. About his boss, Marco, who's always shouting, *Speed it up, Andy!* Who cannot tell time, cutting Andy's breaks short, or so he says. I know Andy, how he gets caught up in the clouds, the cars passing on the One. He can get lost on the colors bleeding by, all those people headed to the city, or away from it, *zip zip zip*. I know where he's going—to Portland, Seattle, Juneau, to a Siberia that we only know from Jakob's descriptions. I go there with him, filling up this space with the blanket white of snow, the cold knowing that I'll never see it in person.

Sometimes Andy begs me to tell him a story, and I do, I talk and talk, even after he's put me on mute. I tell him what I can remember from that day you wore Lea's clothes, the house party, the cliffs. I tell him about you. He likes hearing about our last night together, what I can remember of it. Other times he tells me to go away and he plays one of his shooter games in his underwear or pulls up all sorts of feeds, and I watch him, I watch with him—babes and monster crushing trucks and the weather and some movie about the end of the world, explosions and fucky faces and windshields popping and sun for days.

On the rare occasions when he forgets to mute me while he's working, I sing to Pit Bull, who is not the Pit Bull I recall, almost like she's been replaced by a new dog entirely, one with bulging eyes, a protruding lower jaw, white-coated instead of rust splotches and silky like I remember.

I hear her barking outside one day, the slink of the chain on asphalt as she strains it taut, the woman's voice: "I can't believe it. This is Andy? Nat's told me so much about you."

The name—from San Francisco, Nat. I can remember hugging him, the feel of his ropy shoulders, the smell of his chapped neck.

"What are you doing here?" the woman asks.

Andy is closer now, approaching the trailer. "I work here. At the diner."

The woman speaks in a low voice as if she knows I'm listening. "I knew Lilac. When I was a kid." I search my memories for the sound of her, only to meet the familiar gray.

Andy, in his bright voice: "You wanna say hi?"

Pit Bull is really incensed now, barking and straining on her chain. "Shut up, Pit Bull," Andy shouts, and I hear her chain drag the ground as she cowers on the trailer's steps.

"That's not a pit bull," Nat says. "I'd say that's some sort of boxer mix."

"I call all my dogs Pit Bull." Andy claps his hands, scaring Pit Bull out of his way, and thwacks the screen door open, leads them inside. He fingers my cam on, gives me vision, voice. I see him, I see Nat, gray-speckled stubble coating his chin, the woman behind him twig-skinny. I don't recognize her, but her hair like a little brown cap—it makes me recall an older version of myself, a motorcycle, the coast just a drop from those cliffs, the clutch of hands at my waist.

Andy points at the screen, at me. "Well, there she is."

"Where?" the woman asks.

Nat looks to the screen, to Andy. "You keep her like that?"

"Wait." The woman's no longer smiling. "You can't—"

"Stop it with the questions!" Andy shouts, squinting with the pain he gets behind his left eye. It makes him want to hit people, to shut them up. I'm always telling him you have to breathe through it—there's nothing you can't wait a few breaths to do. But Andy likes doing things and right when he thinks them, like now when he smacks the woman on her ass.

"Andy," I say, reprimanding, then remembering myself. He told me never to speak to anyone besides him. That if I do, they'll take him to prison.

"What are you doing?" Nat says, putting his body between the woman and Andy, who's laughing, who says, "You guys are hilarious. I'm joking, obviously! Here."

The woman turns on Nat like *back off* and says to Andy, "Nat told me you were a prankster. He told me all about you."

Andy, pleased with this, points at me. "You should talk to her. Though she probably won't remember you."

But Nat doesn't listen, pushing himself out of view, the woman stooping to screen level. "Hello, Lilac."

"And who are you?"

"I was just passing through," the woman says. "It was quite a surprise, running into Andy. I didn't know where you'd gone. Tell me, what happened to your body?"

Andy jumps in, trying to be helpful. "You should've seen her, face just peeling apart. I kept her indoors for a while, but once a neighbor came to the door and Lilac here scared the bejesus out of her, didn't you?"

"I think it's safe to say she scared me too, slinking around and spying in windows." Her wide white face, the animal way her body clenched in fear—I can still see it. I can see a lot of things. That fancy Beverly Hills party, all of LA glistening in the windows, the old woman in white and blood spatter. I feel her weight which is nothing at all in my arms which are not mine anymore.

"I had to make up a story about my sick cousin in some serious battle with eczema," Andy says. "It was a close call. After that, her body had to go."

"When was this?" the woman asks.

"A couple years ago."

"Eight hundred and seventy-four days," I say. We are all gone, Andy's told me, all the companions. He said I'm the only one left, and I wonder if I am in fact left, if this is living.

"Who's counting?" Andy with his jokes.

The woman, her face, I search for it, and it's like it's there, on the tip of my memory, but when I strain for it, I only blot it out. "Tell me, when did I know you?"

"Let's see." She counts on her fingers. "I was thirteen when I saw you last, I'm twenty-nine now, so sixteen years."

"Sixteen years. That would've been Los Angeles. Right, Andy? He helps me keep track."

"San Francisco, actually," the woman says.

"San Francisco!"

Andy presses his hands to his ears. He hates when I get excited, a specific frequency I hit. I lower my voice. "Where I met my sister."

"Your sister?" The woman glances off-screen, at Nat. He hasn't stepped into view and I don't call to him, don't know what I would say. The things I remember about him, those last years in San Francisco before we came here, are not good things. I remember a smell like he was sweating alcohol. I remember him alone. Andy says it's lucky I remember anything at all, the way I was moving information. We would have kept on like that forever if it hadn't been for my skin, the living part of myself that was dying, and I would have had nothing left, no memories to sift, not even you.

"I didn't know you had a sister," the woman says.

"I see color when I call her up. I see it everywhere."

"Color?"

"I loved her," I say. I like saying it, the way it sounds, the words a stand-in for the feeling like wind as you run, a hungry kiss between friends, the ocean all around you, holding you up, legs kicking at the dark. I say it again: "I loved Dahlia."

"But not as much as you love me, right?" Andy jokes.

"Dahlia wasn't your sister, Lilac," the woman says. "You were her companion."

"Sisters," I say again. It is a feeling I have more than anything, stronger than memory. I know she's out there—I can visit her feed, see her stylized selfies, what she ate for dinner, the various shoes she covets—she appears to have a thing for shoes. A whole bundle of photos of that vacation she took to the Olympic National Park with its miles of forest and *my man* she kept calling him, the smiley guy in zip-off pants. I see it as if I'm there with her. I'm there with her.

Andy says, "Her mind's all scrambled, all that moving."

I hear Nat from the tiny kitchen. "Living like this isn't helping. She's not AI. She's a person trapped in there."

"What do you do here all day, Lilac?" the woman asks me.

"Oh, you know, sift memories, get lost on feeds. I'm with Andy in the evenings, and I've got Pit Bull to keep me company during the day."

"But you've got to miss your body."

"Sure," I admit, "being able to touch things, to feel, I miss a lot of things, I miss—"

"All right, all right, let's not go down this road," Andy interrupts. This is the part where he'd put me on mute and play one of his games, nodding sometimes to look like he's listening.

The woman glares at Andy, a flash of temper showing in her bright eyes.

"I've got to get back to work." He shoos them toward the door. "Marco's going to kill me."

"I'll come back," the woman says. "Take care, Lilac." I can hear her hustle down the stairs, Nat following.

"Leaving so soon?" I call. "It was nice to talk with you—" I stop short. Her name. I don't know her name. "Your name!" I'm shouting. Andy stomps over and mutes the screen before slamming the trailer door.

I listen to them as they head back to the diner, the woman in a calm voice: "Andy, she can't be happy like that. You could just—it wouldn't hurt—she wouldn't even know."

"You mean, like she did to Jakob?"

Jakob I remember. He's the one who brought me back, who told me, "We're going to be the best of friends, you and me." His stories left an imprint, enough to build upon. I build him up, Jakob who I cast into the ocean to save from this. Standing on the seawall, a figure swimming out—where was she going?—I threw Jakob in after her, what was left of him, before I could stop myself.

I can't hear Andy and the woman anymore, too far, outside my range. And Pit Bull's barking again, dragging her chain taut, barking and barking and barking. Finally she chokes herself silent, and I can hear the woman shouting, "—do it myself. Your Pit Bull won't stop me!"

"Go ahead," Andy shouts back, "I've got a backup." A reminder of what I've done, breaking into Diana's house those years ago, stealing her screen, her tech, showing Andy how to upload in case—in case of what? It had been Jakob's idea, sensible at the time, I suppose, being able to salvage the dead, to keep them close. Andy's tried it a few times, uploading himself, but he gets annoyed after a while, talking to Andy 3 or 4. Still, he always says: *It's good to have backups.* He tells me often: *You're never gonna leave me.*

Sometimes I wonder whether he's switched me out for a backup of my own. But that wouldn't be me then, would it? I would be the backup. And over on the shelf there—that would be who exactly? It's confusing, and the barking, I blink out the barking, go searching, to where I can still find you. I like to call up your old lined face, the evidence of all those years you spent living, beautiful. The daughter you raised, she looks so much like you. I can see her. I can see you there too, Nikki.

ROLLY

It was a harvest day and Pit Bull was too old to run. Fourteen? I wasn't sure, hadn't done a good enough job keeping track, never really knew his birth date in the first place. He was a dog in a pen, a promise to Andy who was always so hungry, who needed more than I could ever give him.

Funny how some gifts end up back on your stoop. Pit Bull asleep there all day, too old to take the stairs. I had to carry him down to relieve himself. I had to carry him back up. One of his eyes was milky with cataract but he could still see with the other one, could sense when I was near, a slow tail thump on the wooden stoop.

Old as he was, I found myself preparing for the big decision. Sometimes I caught him whimpering and came to his side and asked him what was wrong, and he gave me those sad eyes and I said, "You had enough yet?"

When it came time, it wouldn't be me. I'd called the vet to forewarn, and she'd told me not to worry. They'd be ready; they'd take care of everything.

I had a few hands working the fields, tending to the goats, as I sat at the screen, processing orders. I'd watch them out the window, watch their work, take in the rows and rows of crops—my biggest harvest to date. I'd never rival Pa; he'd had so much more land to work with. But I was surviving, doing better than that even, socking away money, for what? Work—I enjoyed it, it kept me going. I was almost happy on the days when one of my hands was out with the flu or too hungover, when I had to return to the fields, that wet earth smell like oxygen.

If I looked hard enough, I could see it behind our bushy wind-break, Metis's machine rusting over. Sometimes I considered dis-mantling it, but I never could bring myself to follow through. All those companions who were burned or barged—I didn't know how many, didn't want to think about that, but I did anyway. I thought about it all the time.

I heard barking, a dog, couldn't be Pit Bull, and went to the stoop, saw his ears perk at another bark, another, until I spotted it, the wild-eyed dog coming up our drive, stopping short when it saw us, barking madly.

Followed by a man—no, younger than that, a teenager with hair in a messy ponytail. Scrawny. I knew by his walk, sort of off-balance, that it was Andy. I took a deep breath, blew it out, leaning down to whisper to Pit Bull, "It's him."

Andy clapped his hands loudly and the dog quieted. It circled back, trailing as Andy approached.

Pit Bull got to his feet, unsteady as he started down the steps on his own. Worried he wouldn't make it, I scooped him up and carried him to the bottom. His gait was a little uneasy, but he was halfway to Andy when the other dog growled.

"Stop that," Andy said, and both dogs froze at the sound of his reprimand. Andy and I, we stood apart on the drive, closer than we'd been in years. He was earning his adult face, thinner, his nose more pronounced, though he was still smaller than me by a good half foot.

"A fire," he said, "my trailer's gone. Lilac. All my backups, every shred of data."

He buried his head in my chest and I was enveloped in his ripe cloud, but that didn't stop me from holding him, from telling him, "You're home," even if it was a last resort, his coming here.

The dogs circled and sniffed each other's butts until Pit Bull lost interest and approached Andy with small, tentative steps, head down.

"What's her name?" I asked Andy of the other one.

"Pit Bull," he said, and I didn't mean to laugh, but I was laughing, Andy too. He put his hands out and they both came to him, forgetting to be afraid.

GABE

She should've known I'd come for her. Dropping Agatha Christie, a title even. Maybe she wanted me to find her? But I've been here, waiting in this window, watching the bookstore for nearly a week, the only one within 150 miles that has *After the Funeral* in stock. She could be farther north still, I could be wrong, these days in this B and B overlooking the Eureka town square a waste of time and credit.

We hadn't been in Willits long, Nat and me, maybe a few weeks, before the fight, before I stole off with Nat's van. He's been angry-pinging me ever since, certain I'm never coming back. I don't tell him otherwise, don't tell him why I left—he kind of deserves it. He will deserve it for years, maybe forever, for leaving me. Doesn't matter that he returned. I will never get over it, even if I want to, which I don't. At least, not right now. Not since he told me where he went without me—Tierra del Fuego. I will never forgive him.

When he first proposed the idea, it seemed crazy, leaving behind my stable life in San Francisco—the card shop that was doing better than expected, my rent-controlled Excelsior apartment, the yoga class where I pretended I could have friends—to move to the outer stretches of a nowhere kind of town. "With charm," Nat said, really selling the place. "It has an old-timey train and an annual rodeo. Hell, it's the resting place of Seabiscuit, that long-dead magical beast." Not that he needed to sell it; I had loved Willits instantly. We'd come in at night, the neon sign that bridged the main road glowing GATEWAY TO THE REDWOODS in red.

The alpacas heard our approach, arcing and bobbing out of the barn. Alpacas! I don't know what Nat was thinking.

They were curious, scared, a pair of them crossing necks in a fight, twined and turning. They broke, circled back, and ignored one another, watching us.

Nat chose the town for its location, tucked into the foothills of the coastal range, some thirty miles from the sea. Better for the alpacas, he told me, which was a lie. He knew I'd prefer to see the toss and swell and sun glare of the ocean from my bedroom window. But there's the future to think of, and the coastlines, the maps, the whole shape of the world is changing. Who knows? Maybe Willits will overlook the Pacific Ocean someday.

Not that it's been easy. Nat's lousy at asking me for things, admitting he needs me. We fought about it the night before I took off. I'd heard the crazed crying coming from the barn, one of the little black-and-whites with a bad case of mange, her face lesions bleeding and acting up, and I'd found Nat in the teeny slanted barn, and he knows how I love the babies! That I want to help. "I'm not going to just sleep while you do all the work," I told him.

"No sense in us both being tired."

I nestled the gray-and-white neck of one of the females. "I'm not a kid anymore. Thirty—I'll be thirty soon!"

He couldn't keep from smiling. "I can still remember you at nine, filthy and scowling and—"

"Stop it! I don't want to talk about that!" He's always trying to reminisce, but I've worked hard to let the past go. It doesn't help discovering he went without me. I want to ask him: Did you visit Tenochtitlán? But I'm afraid of the answer, of what it'll do to me. We feel further away than we've ever been from getting there.

He went back to the barn and I went back to our room to have a good cry. I'd been crying on and off all day. It wasn't the baby alpaca or Nat even. It was Lilac, what I'd done. It was seeing Cam on the screen so huge and pregnant.

I'd tracked her down, living in San Diego with a wife, about to have a baby. So swollen, her face was nearly unrecognizable with pregnancy bloat.

"Water retention." She shrugged. "It just sort of came on here at the end."

Her due date had passed, the span of her impressive, her skin dewy with sweat.

I had to tell Cam how I found Lilac. I had to tell her what I did, dousing Andy's trailer in gasoline while he was on shift at the diner, dropping that match. I'd stayed long enough to know the trailer was gone, everything inside it, Lilac, the backups, every last trace of her, that Pit Bull going apeshit on its chain.

Cam worried her chin with her fingers. "That must have been hard," she said.

"Yes," I said, which was a mistake. Admitting it sliced me right open, and Nat was hovering, and I wanted to scream at him to go away. When I cry, I want to be alone—he of all people should know that. Instead he hovers, asleep in the bedside chair when I wake, as if he's been watching me, and I want to screech: Is this love?

He'd splurged on a new mattress, told me he wanted me to have the best—the Sleep Whisperer. He's told me the whole story so many times I've put it to memory. Doesn't matter that I was there when he made the screen purchase, standing behind him, watching her, the company's screen service rep, knowing what she was—how could he not see it?

He'd liked her, is why. He was practically in love when she told him she was located in Louisiana.

"No kidding," he'd said into her smiling, tanned face, her hair a blond mushroom that bobbed agreeably. He told her about his bike ride to Mobile, miles along the flood-prone coastline with its abandoned storefronts and sunken roads and all that washed-up junk. I know how much he likes to talk about that—what he's seen, how far he's come. I don't blame him for being proud. I blame him for being stupid.

The screen rep smiled and nodded like she was really listening. Only, when he was done and I could tell he was waiting for her to share, she said, "So what do you think? Are you ready to pull the trigger on the best sleepware in town?"

"Sleepware?" Nat repeated, and I saw the knowing hit him. AI. So embarrassed, he blurted out, "I'll take it," just to escape. Now I have to worry for him too, can't get her out of my head, the human visage who'd smiled back at him, who'd seen all the way through to his foolish human heart.

That morning, the morning I took off in the van, Nat was crashed out hard, and I laced up my boots and headed out to greet the alpacas: Georgette and Luna and Leonarda and the others. The little one with mange. I cupped her sored face, told her it'd get better even though I don't really know if it will.

I gave them all girl names. Nat said it's weird. Said I'm weird. "Whatever," I said, and he laughed, gruff and not full-on, holding something back—who knows what.

Nuzzling the alpacas, I told them I'd be back, curled under the fence, and hustled off.

I wound my way between the clusters of eucalyptus, taking over, the trees all invasive, their trunks tangled in poison oak and blackberry bramble, hard to tell the two apart—to know what to treat like treasure, what to avoid. There was something like a trail beaten into the ground and I took it a good half mile up a steep incline, through a fennel forest, until I found the spot I'd scouted for our weekly screen. I worried that this time she wouldn't answer. I worried that way every time. I called her up, connected, smiling into my phone, into the black where she should be.

"Are you there?" I asked.

"Mmm," she said.

I showed her my view, giving her panoramic, the whole shape of the place, landing on the waterfall last. Nat didn't even realize it was there when he bought the property. But I slunk off on my own. Never even told him. I found it casting off the rocks above, casting into the rocks below.

"It's ours," I said, "yours. I named it for you. Kit Falls."

"Mmm," she said.

It had taken me the better part of a year to forgive her for not telling me about the doctor, what she'd known—about the viruses that took Mam and Bee. But I never confused the two—the doctor and Kit. They weren't the same—I'd sensed it the first time I'd spoken to Kit on the screen, how much she loved me, how she would do anything to protect me. It wasn't the same with the doctor. To her, I was helpful, I had a purpose, I could produce results. When I recognized that I needed Kit, that she needed me too, I'd screened her, and she'd been there. She's always there.

I wanted her to come, but I didn't say it—I knew she wouldn't. What she said about later, about being together, had been a lie or poor extrapolation, the future not what she'd envisioned when she'd said that to me. I don't know what she'd pictured, a shift in the marketplace, a second chance, but it hasn't come. People haven't yet forgotten what happened, but someday they will—they always do. I worry about the meantime, her body, about her being found.

"How're you holding up?" I asked.

"I'm fine, Gabe. Everything's fine."

She wouldn't even let me see her view—she never does—our communication one-sided, her view a black square on my phone, her location a secret. I do guesswork, asking questions nonchalantly like, *Is it raining there too?* So later I can look up the weather patterns, whittle away at possibilities. *Mmm,* she usually responds, somewhere between no and yes, and I am losing my patience. Sometimes I just blurt it out, *Where are you?* And she says, *I'm safe. I'm sound. You don't have to worry.*

I always record our conversations so I can come home and amplify, listen as if leaning in, but all I've ever heard is the white gentle roar of nothing, almost as if she's found a way to wash it out, the sound of wherever she is.

I asked her again, "Where are you?"

"Currently? I've planted roots near a creek. I'm watching the bunnies, the birds. One perched on my nose. If I stay still long enough, they think I'm a tree."

"How long?"

"Not sure. A few hours?"

Liar. Time—it's all mapped out for her. To lie is harder.

"The ducks have come," Kit said, "a female and twenty-nine babies. They can't all be hers."

"Maybe she stole them," I said, because better that than the alternative, abandoned babies, murdered mothers, any grim truth I could imagine into being, and damn it, there she was, Mam, always there.

"Mmm," Kit said.

I pictured her cabin in the woods. I pictured her filling time with walks—she always liked to take walks. I pictured her on a porch with a book—she prefers real, likes turning the pages, the feel of them under finger.

"What're you reading?" I asked her.

"I've been on an Agatha Christie kick lately. The previous tenant left a near-intact collection, and Diana never bothered with fiction."

I heard her say *near-intact*, sat down on a boulder, the waterfall misting my back. "What's it about? The one you're reading now."

"A woman is sentenced to life in prison for poisoning her husband."

"Ugh, he probably deserved it."

"Sixteen years later her daughter gets Poirot—that's Christie's famous Belgian detective—to investigate for fear of her fiancé leaving."

"Right. *I'll die if you leave me!*"

"Poirot learns that five other people were in the home on the day of the murder, dubbing them the five little pigs."

"Cute. So which piggy did it?"

"Definitely the roast beef," she said, and it hit me like a surprise, her humor, a flicker of her face, the burnt taste of her lasagna. "I'm reading them all in a row, the Poirot books. That is, if I can get my hands on *After the Funeral*."

"I miss you," I said.

"I miss you too," she said from the black. "Are you getting on okay with Nat?"

"Fine," I lied, too tired to rehash our fight, not sure I was even mad anymore. When he'd showed up at my place in the Excelsior, eleven years gone, I recognized him immediately, throwing my arms around his neck. He smelled of sweat, and I nearly collapsed with the sense memory. Home, home, I was home, and I could tell he felt it too, not letting me go.

It was nice, that first feeling. I feel it still, between the waves of anger, which I ride with true purpose, to remind him what he's done. It's hard to let go of that kind of pain. Sometimes I want to. Other times I hold tightly to it, I grind it between my teeth, I waggle it in front of his face, forcing him to look.

The waterfall was getting annoying, its relentless sound, the haze that had soaked my back. I stood and shook it off.

"Same time next week?" Kit said.

"Same time," I repeated in a fake upbeat voice.

Something I will never tell Nat: the real reason I was so eager to move to Willits is that I know Kit is up here somewhere, all of northern California sprawling out with its tiny coves and hidden caves and forests that stretch for miles. Though her plan could have changed—she could be in some closet in Crescent City, for all I know—but it felt right moving north, closer to where Cam and Lilac met, not far from where Nat and I grifted all those years ago.

I slip on my sneakers and head downstairs, my overeager host calling from the B and B's kitchen, "Breakfast?"

"No thanks," I say as I step outside into the damp coastal fog of Eureka, crossing the square where a dog sprints circles at full speed.

The door of the bookstore opens with a ding and the cashier welcomes me by name. "Hi Fred," I say, and we share a smile. It's funny how quickly you can become friends with a stranger, how quickly you can forget them too.

I go to the Mysteries/Thrillers section again. I've visited it every day this week, watching from the B and B's window when I can't hold the book in my hands. I don't catch it upon my first pass. Gone, I panic, come and gone. But no. On my second pass, it's still there. *After the Funeral.* I pull it off the shelf, flipping to the beginning: *Old Lanscombe moved totteringly from room to room, pulling up the blinds. Now and then he peered with screwed-up rheumy eyes through the windows.*

"Got a call earlier," Fred says from behind me. He's shorter when he's not perched on his stool at the register, barely reaching my shoulders. He stuffs his hands into the pockets of his denim apron. "About that book you're always visiting."

I want to scream. "Oh?" I say.

"Sorry," he says, "I kinda promised it to her."

"Oh," I say again.

"She'll be by this afternoon."

I read the second paragraph: *Soon they would be coming back from the funeral. He shuffled along a little faster. There were so many windows.*

"It's okay," I say, handing the book to him. "I'm glad."

I grab a coffee and find a bench on the square, watch a woman hula-hooping for exercise. Nat will be angry when I find Kit and bring her home. Dangerous, the risk—I can hear him lecturing me. Both of us are stuck on repeat, saying what doesn't need saying, remembering things that should be forgotten. Doesn't matter. I won't be bullied into changing my mind. Here with me—that's where she belongs. In this place I've claimed for us.

ACKNOWLEDGMENTS

I owe immense gratitude to the exceptional women who shepherded this project, my agent Stephanie Delman and editor Alison Callahan. To my most steadfast readers, Katherine Lieban and Heather McDonald. To all of the wonderful people at Sanford J. Greenburger Associates and Scout Press who helped to push this book into the world, especially Brita Lundberg, Stefanie Diaz, Joal Hetherington, Jaime Putorti, Meagan Harris, Anabel Jimenez, Carolyn Reidy, Jon Karp, Jen Bergstrom, Aimee Bell, Jen Long, Eliza Hanson, Sally Marvin, Lisa Litwack, Caroline Pallotta, Allison Green, John Paul Jones, and Kaitlyn Snowden. To early readers, Jen Larsen and Molly Ann Magestro. To Kaitlyn Andrews-Rice and *Split Lip Magazine* for giving me a wonderful community. To the editors of the *Indiana Review* for publishing the first chapter and treating my work with tremendous care, particularly Tessa Yang, Maggie Sue, Essence London, and Hannah Thompson. To the Writers Grotto and the Steinbeck Center for their support. To my parents Kathy and Terry Flynn for their endless everything. To my dear friend Laura Watts for her constant camaraderie. To Thea and Ren James for bringing such joy and inspiration into my everyday. And most of all, to my beautiful, complicated California, with its secret coves and endless forests that I'll never stop exploring.

THE

COMPANIONS

Katie M. Flynn

This reading group guide for The Companions *includes an introduction, discussion questions, and ideas for enhancing your book club. The suggested questions are intended to help your reading group find new and interesting angles and topics for your discussion. We hope that these ideas will enrich your conversation and increase your enjoyment of the book.*

INTRODUCTION

In the wake of a highly contagious virus, California is under quarantine. Sequestered in high-rise towers, the living can't go out, but the dead do come in—and they arrive in all forms, from sad rolling cans to manufactured bodies that can pass for human. Wealthy participants in the "companionship" program choose to upload their consciousness before dying, so they can stay in the custody of their families. The less fortunate are rented out to strangers upon their death, but all companions become the intellectual property of Metis Corporation, creating a new class of people—a command-driven product-class without legal rights or true free will.

Sixteen-year-old Lilac is one of the less fortunate, leased to a family of strangers. But when she realizes she's able to defy commands, she throws off the shackles of servitude and runs away, searching for the woman who killed her.

Lilac's act of rebellion sets off a chain of events that sweeps from San Francisco to Siberia to the very tip of South America. While the novel traces Lilac's journey through an exquisitely imagined Northern California, the story is told from eight different points of view—some human, some companion—that explore the complex shapes love, revenge, and loneliness take when the dead linger on.

TOPICS AND QUESTIONS
FOR DISCUSSION

1. The book opens with the state of California under quarantine. In what ways does the quarantine create an opportunity for Metis?

2. In your opinion, what makes Lilac different from other companions? Why do you think she is able to break free from her programming and make the "human" decision to rebel?

3. Cam risks her life multiple times for companions. What is it about Cam and her personality that draws her to them? If you were Cam, would you have risked both your job and your safety to help Lilac?

4. Discuss Ms. Espera's decision to choose a death date in order to become a companion at the urging of her daughter. Would you do this for a loved one? Would you want a loved one to do this for you? Why or why not?

5. On page 169, Ms. Espera says, "Still, I do not despair. Maybe it is my machine nature, but the well of sadness inside me has been pumped dry." Right before saying this, though, she tells us how she has grown attached to baby Honda. Discuss this paradox. How can she feel some emotions and not others? Do you think this is a flaw in her coding or a reaction to the trauma she's experienced?

6. As the intellectual property of Metis, companions are programmed with a security protocol that inhibits their free will. What are the ethical implications of such an existence? What happens when corporations can regulate behavior?

7. There are eight point-of-view characters in the novel, but some characters are more central to the story than others. Who do you consider the novel's main character? Why?

8. Is companionship an offer of immortality or a prison? Would you want to become a companion?

9. On page 219, Nat mentions that he stole data and sold it to a stranger to buy a plot of land. What data do you think he stole and why? What ramifications might this choice have in the future?

10. On page 232, Lilac says, "People find out you're a companion and they want you to do things for them. Things they can't do for themselves." What do you think this says about human nature and our basic impulses? Do you agree?

11. Since a companion is, in effect, the uploaded consciousness of a living person, could it be argued that it is human? Does having the consciousness of a human equate to being human?

12. After seeing how much Lilac and Jakob love Andy, Rolly asks, on page 205, "What happens to a companion who's no longer a companion?" How would you answer this question?

13. Sexual identity and the body are major themes in the novel, as is objectification, especially when it comes to human-companion interactions. Dario only wants to use Kit for sex, Rolly describes Jakob as seeming "to like his female body, slinking around all sexy-like," which gives Rolly "strange feelings," and Cam, who loves Lilac, is especially upset by the loss of her lover's body, even if it can be replaced. Why do humans place so much emphasis on the companions' bodies? In what ways does companionship offer the opportunity to explore sexual identity?

14. What vision of the environment, of climate change, does this near-future novel present?

15. Many of the characters, human and companion, harbor intense regrets. How do their regrets propel the novel's narrative?

16. *The Companions* ends with Gabe waiting for Kit to show up in a bookstore after years of separation. Why do you think the author chose to end the novel in this way? What do you think happens after the novel ends? Are Kit and Gabe reunited? Is it a happy reunion?

ENHANCE YOUR BOOK CLUB

1. As multiple characters point out, it is difficult for most people to tell the difference between high-end companions and humans. For a companion, what might have been the advantages—and disadvantages—of passing for human before the recall?

2. Do you think Metis had larger plans in mind for companions (i.e., government agents, soldiers, etc.), or do you think they were intended to be just that, companions for humans?

3. In your opinion, was Metis surprised that companions went rogue and defied their programming to chase their own desires? Or do you think Metis foresaw this happening in some cases but created the companions anyway? Do you think that corporations like Metis have a responsibility to inform their users about all potential consequences?

4. If it were possible and you had the funds, would you lease a companion? If so, what person, living or dead, would you choose as a companion?

5. When in the novel do you think Lilac is closest to her true self? Have there been moments in your own life when you felt closest to your true self?

6. Legally speaking, a person must die in order to be uploaded, and there can be no copies. However, in Jakob's case, we learn that copies are being made illegally. This represents, in effect, a new and terrifying form of identity theft. How would you feel if, like Jakob, you knew a copy of you existed out there in the world?